TEN YEARS TO LIFE

Cheryl E. Lee

◆ FriesenPress

Suite 300 - 990 Fort St
Victoria, BC, V8V 3K2
Canada

www.friesenpress.com

Copyright © 2019 by Cheryl E. Lee
First Edition — 2019

All rights reserved.

No part of this publication may be reproduced in any form, or by any means, electronic or mechanical, including photocopying, recording, or any information browsing, storage, or retrieval system, without permission in writing from FriesenPress.

Library of Congress Number: TXu001718347

ISBN
978-1-5255-2570-4 (Hardcover)
978-1-5255-2571-1 (Paperback)
978-1-5255-2572-8 (eBook)

1. FICTION, ROMANCE

Distributed to the trade by The Ingram Book Company

PREFACE

Denise Rush has been in love with Gerald Williams all of her adult life. She supported him through his partying college days, months of unemployment, and years of bad decisions. But when Gerald mistakenly finds himself in the wrong place at the wrong time, it lands him in prison for twenty years.

With parole possible in ten years, Denise vows to remain faithful and wait for him to return to her. But when ten years turns into eleven, and eleven into twelve, Denise begins to realize the impact prison is having on her life and begins to question whether she and Gerald will ever have a realistic future.

His prison years are beginning to look and feel like a lifetime of loneliness for her.

That is until she is reunited with Malcolm Anderson, an old High School Friend. As she and Malcolm rekindle their friendship, and feelings of romance and love between them grows, her loyalty to Gerald fades and the future she once knew was certain, becomes a distant dream.

Will Gerald return before she gives her heart to Malcolm, or will he lose her love forever.

ONE

"Hi, sweetheart, I'm sorry I haven't been able to be there to read to you."

"I didn't know what to do. I was afraid you were never coming back."

"I'll always come back."

"What's gonna happen when I can't remember anything anymore? What will you do?"

"I'll be here. I'll never leave you!"

"I need to ask you something."

"What is it, sweetheart?"

"Do you think that our love can create miracles?"

"Yes, I do. That's what brings you back to me each time."

"Do you think our love could take us away together?"

"I think our love can do anything we want it to."

"I love you."

"I love you, Allie."

"Good night, Noah."

"Good night. I'll be seeing you."

Denise buried her head in her pillow, sobbing as music played and movie credits rolled on the TV screen.

"Why do I do this to myself every week?" she asked herself.

Every Sunday Denise watched *The Notebook* and every Sunday at the end of the movie she cried herself to sleep. In part because it was one of the most beautiful love stories she'd ever witnessed and also because she was unable to share the kind of love Noah and Allie had with the person she loved because he was incarcerated.

Grabbing a tissue from the nightstand to dry her tears, she reached for the remote to turn down the volume. It was midnight and she needed to get some sleep for a busy work day in the morning.

She climbed out of bed to complete her nightly ritual. Checking the doors to make sure they were locked. Placing Creasy, her fearless Papillon, named after the character made famous by Denzel Washington in the movie *Man on Fire*, in his crate for the night. Doing her nightly facial. Turning off the kitchen light and climbing back into bed. Denise stared at the glare of the TV, which she left on for comfort each night, thinking of Gerald.

Rolling over she looked at the ceiling as shadows cast from the TV flashed across the ceiling and let out a deep sigh. What was Gerald doing? She glanced at the phone, wishing she could pick it up and call him, but several hours had passed since lights out at Tree Mountain Federal Penitentiary. Was he having trouble sleeping too?

He was her Noah; she was his Allie. She was sure he was missing her just as she was missing him. She truly believed their love could create miracles and take them anywhere they wanted to go. The only problem was he was incarcerated. Ten years to life for aggravated assault. So their love and their future were on hold for the time being until he was eligible for parole.

§

"Power 105.9, your station for gospel hits of today and classics of yesterday!" blared loudly from the clock radio on the dresser next to the bed.

"Ugh... not already," Denise moaned, rolling over to hit the snooze button for the third time. On the fourth alarm she mustered enough energy to roll out of bed to let Creasy out of his castle and outside while she prepared his gourmet breakfast and sparkling fresh tap water from the finest sink in Bastrop, Texas.

"Creasy," Denise said calling his majesty back in. "Hey, boo boo. Are you hungry this morning?" Creasy was a bit too hyper a dog for Denise, but he provided her the comfort she needed with Gerald being away. "Yes you are hungry aren't you?" she asked, bending over and making faces at him as if he were a baby, lowering the bowl of food to the ground for him to eat. "Here ya go, boo boo."

Denise jumped into the shower. As she was finishing up she heard her cell phone ringing in the bedroom. Hoping it was Gerald she grabbed a towel, ran out and dove across the bed.

"Hello!"

"Denise! Girl, did you see the news last night?" a woman's voice asked. Denise sagged with disappointment.

Sabrina Walker had been her best friend since the eighth grade. Now at twenty-four she was a successful lawyer and partner in the Walker and Wheeler law firm. As long as they'd known each other, Sabrina excelled in everything she did. In high school she was voted most likely to succeed, and succeed was what she did. She was president of the student council, a member of the National Honor Society and a member of the Future Homemakers of America. She was voted homecoming queen, prom queen and class president. She was head of the debate team and editor of the school paper in college. After receiving a master's from Harvard University she settled at Walker and Wheeler where she advanced to partner. She had accomplished in her first year what took most people three to five years. If there was a category for it, the name Sabrina Walker was sure to follow.

"Hi, Sabrina. What was on the news?"

"Not what! Who!"

"Okay, *who* was on the news?" Denise asked with sarcasm.

"Malcolm!"

"Malcolm… Malcolm who?" Her voice showed her irritation.

"Malcolm Anderson. Your senior prom date Malcolm Anderson!"

"Shut up! Little scrawny Malcolm? With the glasses and the chili bowl fade?" Denise asked laughing. "I always wondered what happened to him. What was he doing on TV?"

"Child, wonder no more. He just signed a five-year contract with the Detroit Pistons!"

"What? When? How? He never played basketball in school. He was always in the books."

"Well, he's playing now. He was spotted by one of the coaches at a gym and they were so impressed with his skills, they asked him to come to a practice. The rest, as they say, is history. They're saying he could be the next Jordan but for the Pistons!"

"Wow, who'd a thunk it."

"Not me," Sabrina declared. "You know that boy was a nerd in school. I never could figure out why you went with him to the prom."

3

"I felt sorry for him because people like you kept turning down his advances. Despite what you think you know about him, we had a good time. He was very respectful. A gentleman."

"Whatever." Sabrina said sarcastically. "Anyway, are we still on for tonight?"

"Yes, I may be running a little late though. I'm going out to Tree Mountain today."

"Denise, I don't know why you keep wasting your time on that man. He ain't ever getting out of that prison, girl."

"Yes he is! Don't say that, Sabrina. He's supposed to be getting out this month. It's just a matter of time. I will have my baby in my arms, on my skin and in my mouth—"

"Eeewwww!" Sabrina screeched. "TMI! In case you forgot, it was supposed to be a matter of time six months ago and a matter of time six months before that and a matter of time two years before that. A matter of time in his prison time is like comparing a matter of time in dog years to human life as far as that boy is concerned."

"Whatever. My baby will be here this month, Sabrina. You just wait and see."

"Uh huh and in the meantime, do you need some more batteries for your little substitute friend?"

"Bye, Sabrina," Denise laughed.

"Bye, girl. I'll see you tonight. Be careful on the road."

Denise hung up the phone. "Malcolm Anderson… hmmm."

Gazing out the window to check on Creasy, she flashed back to the night of high school graduation.

§

After graduation hats were thrown in the air and directions were given to the after party, Denise ran into Malcolm in the football stadium parking lot.

"There you are," Malcolm said, hugging her gently.

"Hey you! It's finally over. No more high school. Are you glad?" Denise asked.

"You bet I am. Aren't you?"

"I have to admit, I'm a little nervous about not being able to see all of my friends every day."

"What college did you say you were going to?" Malcolm asked.

"Prairie View," Denise announced proudly.

"Wow! Well, good luck."

"Thanks. What about you?"

"I haven't decided yet. Pop wants me to hang around and help him with the shop." Malcolm's father owned a car repair shop. One of the most popular in the black community.

"Is that what you want to do?"

"Well... I guess, for now. Until I figure out my next move, anyway."

"Well, I wish you the best of luck Malcolm, in everything you do. You're a good guy. I'm sure you'll do well at whatever you choose to do."

"Thanks."

"I better get home and spend some time with my family before I head out to the party. Will I see you there?" she asked.

"Nah, my folks have a big barbeque planned for me at home."

"Okay, Malcolm, you take care of yourself."

"And you do the same."

Denise leaned in to give him a friendly hug and kiss on the cheek. As she pulled away from the embrace she felt his hands still on her waist. He was staring into her eyes and she felt a little off balance. She placed her hands on his arms and held on.

Something was different. He'd given her hundreds of hugs before but something was different. She no longer saw her sweet little prom date or high school buddy. She was looking at a man, a man who was looking at a woman with desire. What surprised her even more was that her body was reacting to it.

She found herself unable to let go of him. Malcolm slowly moved his hands up and down her arms and her body shivered at his touch. He gently wrapped his arms around her, never taking his eyes off of hers. Neither spoke. Only the sounds of their labored breath filled the air.

He pulled her to his body and touched his head to hers. She could feel the warmth of his breath against her skin. He brushed hair from her face and looked at her as if carving her image in his mind. She closed her eyes and moved her head toward his touch, relishing every stroke.

His hands settled on her shoulders, and she found the courage to open her eyes and meet his gaze. His stare excited every part of her body and she gasped as he pulled her in to meet his body.

He lowered his head, his lips stopping just inches from her mouth. She could no longer breathe. Her body was crying out for him to kiss her. She wanted to feel him. Malcolm's eyes darkened as he felt her tremble with need.

Finally able to breathe she let out a rush of air and moved her mouth closer to his. He softly pressed his lips against hers. The first kiss was brief; short but with purpose. He pulled away, watching her reaction to his touch. When she didn't say "no" or slap him, he leaned in again to lightly rub his lips against hers as he began massaging her back with his hands. Passion built inside her, increasing her arousal, anticipating what would come next.

Malcolm deepened the kiss, using his tongue to part her lips. She groaned as his tongue touched hers. He began kissing her passionately. As she placed her arms around his neck the kiss intensified. With every movement of their bodies, every stroke of his tongue, Denise wanted more. It was as if she felt the slide and caress of their tongues and lips throughout her whole body, as if they were making love. Malcolm was releasing months of built-up passion and she was experiencing something she had never felt before.

They continued in the moment, enjoying every touch, every sensation, until voices in the distance interrupted them. Malcolm released her. They both looked around to find a group of graduates walking nearby.

Malcolm cradled her head to his chest, blocking her from their view. She kind of liked that he was shielding her, as if he was somehow protecting her image.

After the group passed by they stood silent for a moment, wrapped in each other's arms until he lifted her chin and planted a soft kiss on her forehead. She smiled as he leaned in close to her ear and whispered, "Thank you for going to the prom with me."

She laughed. "You're very welcome."

He opened her car door and watched as she settled into the driver's seat. Denise was still breathing heavily, her body still filled with sensations, as Malcolm leaned into the car and gently cupped her chin for one last kiss.

"Take care, Denise Rush."

"Take care, Malcolm Anderson."

He closed her door and walked away, disappearing into the night. Denise sat motionlessness in the car, her heart racing. She wasn't sure what had transpired with her buddy, her friend, her pal. Part of her wanted to open the car door and run after him and the other part wanted to just leave the memory a memory.

Taking a deep breath, she leaned back in her seat and stared into the night reliving the graduation ceremony, watching her friends walk across the stage, walking across the stage herself, throwing graduation hats in the air after commencements, proud hugs from friends and family. But nothing would every come close to the memory of the kisses she shared with Malcolm Anderson. She closed her eyes, sighed and just listened to the night. The wind was lightly blowing. She could hear the leaves as the trees swayed, and a dog was barking nearby.

"Wait a minute. There was no dog—"

§

Creasy was barking at the back door. Denise focused on the present with a start.

"Oh shit," she said looking at the clock on the wall. It was seven a.m. "I have to get out of here."

She walked to the open kitchen door. "Hi, boo boo. You ready to come in?" Creasy sprinted into the house.

As she began to close the door she paused for a moment and looked out into the sky. The trees were swaying back and forth from the light wind the weather man promised for the day. One last reminder of the night she shared with Malcolm.

TWO

Denise walked through the first set of prison doors at Tree Mountain Federal Penitentiary for her weekly visit with Gerald.

Clank. Clank. Clank. Denise jumped as the doors slammed shut behind her. She hated that sound. She hated going to the prison every week. And in spite of the brave front she put on in front of her friends, and even Gerald, she hated seeing him behind bars.

Hopefully Gerald will tell me the news I've been waiting to hear and this will be the last time I have to hear the clank of those doors ever again, she thought as she stood in line waiting for security clearance.

At the doubled-paned window she handed the female guard her driver's license. Waiting for the guard to complete her identity check, she looked past the window into the courtyard to see inmates being transported into the prison in shackles and chains.

She shook her head. *All brothers.*

"Here you go, Mrs. Rush." Denise didn't have the heart to say it was Ms. Rush because the person she *intended* to marry was locked up in this filthy prison she was visiting. Instead, she smiled pleasantly, saying "Thanks," and took back her license.

After walking through the security gate, she took the cleanest seat she could find in the visitors' holding area to wait for Gerald's name to be called. Cell phones were not allowed so she closed her eyes and began to reflect on her life. How did prison become part of her new normal?

In the world of radio she was known as the powerful Vice President of Programming at the most popular gospel radio station in Central Texas, Power 105.9. But in the small community of Bastrop, Texas, most knew her as the daughter of Stella Mae. Denise grew up as most middle children, living in the shadow of her older sibling, a brother who most thought would be the golden child of the family, and receiving less attention than the baby of the family, her younger sister Jessica. To the surprise of many, including herself, she became the shining star of the three.

Her mother, a licensed vocational nurse, worked very hard as a single mother to support her small family with very limited means. While at school many of her friends sported the latest and greatest fashions in Nike, Gloria Vanderbilt and rabbit fur, Denise and her siblings modeled Lee jeans, non-branded tennis shoes, and clothes from the sales rack at Sears and the town's general store. Her siblings never let on that their lack bothered them and neither did Denise because she appreciated her mother's hard work. Yet she never felt like she was really part of the *it*-girl crew because of it.

She was very popular and diverse in her class, however. Maybe not *it*-girl status but she was part of every clique and social club. As a child she struggled with her weight so the boys weren't really standing in line for her romantically. But she was well known and could fit in with any crowd. She was the girl who was everyone's buddy, friend, home girl and confidant. She was popular with boys—but because of who she knew. That in turn gave her some level of popularity and attention with the *it* girls, so it worked in her favor.

College was where she began to discover who she was and come into her own. She was a bit sheltered growing up but found a new sense of freedom and independence through her experiences at Prairie View. And it was there that she met and fell in love with Gerald.

He was a Romeo, a non-fraternity group on campus with the reputation for starting fights over campus territory and womanizing. Initially she was interested in his half-brother, Marcus, who was president of the organization. She shared her interest with Gerald in hopes he would hook the two of them up in the same way classmates in high school used her to connect with her girlfriends.

In her quest to gain the attention of Marcus, she and Gerald developed a friendship and enjoyed each other's company. He seemed to take her under his wing in an almost protective way and eventually she saw that Marcus was more of a bad boy than she wanted; he became a non-factor. She and Gerald, however, continued their friendship until all that changed with one look on homecoming night.

Prairie View Homecoming was a big event for the historical black college. No one ever really went for the game—the tickets sold for the long tradition of the Battle of the Bands between Prairie View and Grambling State. Many traveled from all over the great state of Texas to attend the event and Denise had friends from Bastrop in town. It was the first time they'd seen her since high school graduation.

Denise was never really into fashion or makeup because her mother could never afford anything with a brand on it. She never grew up in an environment where makeup was a necessity so her college roommates decided to give her a makeover—hair, clothes, the whole works. When her friends from home saw Denise that evening at the game they were shocked by the transformation. Not only the look but the confidence; shy overweight Denise had been transformed. She expected a level of *what the hell* from her friends because they hadn't seen her in months, but she was quite surprised by the look of pleasure on Gerald's face.

"Hi, Gerald," she said with a huge smile.

"Hello, beautiful!" he said with a smile just as big.

Wrapping his arms around her, he lifted her off the ground and began twirling her around. This was something he'd never done before. Maybe a quick hug or a playful punch on the shoulder. But this flirty behavior had been absent from their friendship.

"You know you're going to be all mine," he said looking deeply into her eyes.

Denise was a little surprised. Up to this point, she still kind of thought of him as the good friend who was going to hook her up with brother Marcus. But in that moment she could see in his eyes there was something more than friendship there. There were real feelings and it wasn't just because she'd had a makeover. He was looking at her like she was the only person within a hundred-mile radius. In that moment she realized she felt an attraction to him too. After homecoming night they became a couple and spent every free moment together. And the rest, as they say, is history.

Gerald was somewhat of a bad boy, at least in front of his brother and the rest of the Romeos, but really he was a smart, gentle guy who was just trying to fit in. He reminded Denise of herself in a way. He didn't really care for their bad boy antics but Marcus was his brother and he was part of the *it* crowd, so Gerald played the game. But outside of that Gerald had all the qualities Denise wanted in a man—what she referred to as Dr. Phil qualities. Understanding, insightful, protective, quiet spirit, attentive, romantic, nurturing, and encouraging, a great listener and great communicator, something every woman hopes to find in a man.

Laughing and having fun together came naturally for them. Their favorite thing to do was people watching. Just getting some ice cream, sitting on a bench in a park or outdoor mall and looking at people walking by. Dissecting their lives or often conducting surveys with complete strangers walking by.

One day she challenged him to find five women who didn't know about Tiffany's, the jewelry store. Her argument was that every girl wanted a blue box from Tiffany's at least once in her life. His was that *every kiss begins with Kay*, as the jingle goes. She won the argument of course: five out of five women agreed with her. As hard as Gerald tried to act in front of his boys, Denise knew the real Gerald, and that was the Gerald she loved.

"Williams," the officer called out, interrupting her trip down memory lane.

Denise followed the officer down the long hallway toward the visiting room. With each step, she was hoping Gerald would greet her with news that his parole was approved and he would be getting out of this place in a few weeks. As she entered the room, she handed her ID to another guard who directed her to table number thirteen. Moments later she saw a group of inmates come in from the hall and finally she saw Gerald, wearing a smile as big as Texas on his face.

"Hey, baby," he greeted her as she stood to give him a hug.

"Hi, honey," she responded with a soft kiss.

No full-blown kissing was allowed. A quick high-school kiss was permitted, but tongue interaction was strictly forbidden. There were occasions, however, when the guards were not looking or they were seated far enough away from the guard's desk to be able to sneak one in. But usually there was a female guard, who Gerald referred to as Butch, that kept a close eye on them. Gerald felt she was either jealous of their relationship or had a thing for Denise.

"How are you, baby? You're looking good as usual." Gerald always made a point of complimenting her; it was one of the many things she loved about him.

"I'm fine now that I see you." They sat down together, holding hands under the table, out of sight of Butch.

"You look like you packed on some more muscles, baby," she said.

"You noticed that, huh?" he asked, flexing his arms.

"You're so silly," she laughed.

"Baby, there ain't much else to do in here but get fine. The weights help me make it through the days while I'm waiting to get home to you... the weights, and God."

"I'm glad to hear you say that." Gerald hadn't been much of a believer when she first met him. He began to attend church with Denise on campus to be near her but, like most prisoners, he really began leaning on God's word and prayer after his incarceration.

"Definitely. I've learned so much about what my purpose is and I realized, baby, just how caught up I was in the world trying to live up to my brother's expectations, thinking the world and the people in it owed me something. I wasted so much time trying to be about that life, hanging out with my friends, focused on the wrong things. Now I realize I wasn't fulfilling God's purpose for me. It took me getting in *here* to realize that. Even though the reason I'm here is not because of something I physically did, I realize I put myself in a position to be implicated. I made bad choices. I made choices without thinking and without seeking God. My life would be so much different if I'd met you sooner. But I know now that, when I get out of here, God will be my captain in everything I do."

"Amen, Gerald. Good for you. What are they saying about your release?"

"Well, baby, it looks like it may be another couple of months."

"Gerald!"

"I know, baby. I'm frustrated too. The review board is backed up and they can't get to my case."

"But, Gerald, how many more excuses are they going to give you for not letting you out? It's been two years since you were up for parole and it's been one thing after another, one excuse after another."

"Baby, you know if I could get out of here, I would. This is not somewhere I want to stay. But I can't force the system. I'm doing everything I can to get to you, baby. We just have to be a little more patient."

"Gerald, I have been patient! I've been patient for twelve years!"

"Denise, you have to remember; I was sentenced to twenty years. Twenty! With the possibility of parole in ten. There was never a guarantee that I would be out in ten years."

"So what are you saying? You're going to be in here for the full twenty years?"

"No, baby, I'll be out of here any day now. I promise; it won't be much longer."

"Gerald, you're in no position to make promises. Every time we talk it's a couple of months! A couple of months is NOT any day now!"

Denise turned from the table and stared out the window. Fighting back tears, she looked out into the courtyard where prisoners were playing basketball and lifting weights. Neither spoke. As they sat in silence, Gerald his face filled with guilt as he witnessed her pain searched for the right words to comfort her, words that would break down the brick wall between them.

"Denise, do you love me?"

"Gerald, don't start with that."

"Look at me, Denise."

She turned her attention away from the window.

"Do you love me?" he asked again.

"Yes, I love you."

"Then a couple of months are just a matter of days. Focus on that. Focus on the life we'll have when I get out of here. I love you. When I get out of here, we'll spend the rest of our lives together. I promise you. I will get out of here, and I will love you the way you should be loved. Baby, God has ordained my love for you and nothing will change how we feel about each other. Not even time. Do you trust me, baby?"

"Yes, I trust you."

"Williams!" the guard yelled.

"Denise, please don't give up," he said as they gave each other one last embrace and kiss, and then the guard was directing him to get in line with the other inmates.

Leaving Tree Mountain, Denise felt more hopeless than when she'd arrived. Gerald's plea not give up was getting more and more difficult. She didn't want to give up, but she was a realistic person. It was getting harder for her not to acknowledge the reality that Gerald's any-day-now release could be years away. She had to make a decision on how much longer she wanted to continue to wait, sooner rather than later.

THREE

"Excuse me. Oh my God, I'm so sorry." Denise apologized to the various people she bumped into as she made a mad dash down Sixth Street toward Maxwell's, the newest happy hour spot in downtown Austin for singles. A flyer had surfaced around town that there was a Friday Happy Hour Super Jazz Singles Mixer and the girls wanted to get there early to grab the best observation booth for admiring the finest black males Austin had to offer.

"Over here!" Denise heard Sabrina's voice as soon as she walked in.

"And why did we have to get the booth right next to the door?" Denise asked.

"Because I want them to see us as soon as they walk in. First impressions. Gurrrl, look, look, look," Sabrina said nudging Denise's sister Jess, who was already sitting in the booth with her. "Um, um, um. Fine as the finest of fine wines right there. Hello!" Sabrina waved as she greeted several men walking through the door. "I'm going to get that number before we leave tonight."

"Sabrina, why are you always getting men's phone numbers and never go past a first date?" Jess asked.

"That's because I don't do second dates, Jess, you know that. Why do we have to have this conversation for the hundredth time?"

"It's not right to get them interested in you if you have no real interest in them."

"I can't help it if I'm interesting, Jess," Sabrina declared. "They know they enter Sabrina's world at their own risk. I tell them straight up from the jump. No strings attached, baby!" Sabrina continued snapping her fingers. "NO STRINGS ATTACHED!"

"Sabrina, you're missing out on your blessings when you use men like that and it gives us good women who want a real man a bad rap."

"Honey... sweet little innocent Jess. I am the blessing, darling. I am the gift. The one-time gift to all gorgeous men in the universe. Wrapped all up in here, you know what I'm sayin?" Sabrina rubbing her hands across her chest and circled her genital area. "It is my gift, my blessing to share with them, for one time, one night only and then it has to be shared with others so that they may receive their blessing. Aren't we supposed to share our gifts with others?" she asked laughing. "That's what I'm doing, sharing and blessing the less fortunate with my gifts and talents. That what the good book says."

"Sabrina, that's sick," Jess said in disgust.

"Hello," Denise said waving her hand in the air. "Sister here. I've been here. Change the subject please." Denise kissed Jess on the cheek and gave her a hug while giving Sabrina a scolding look.

"Hello, sister. Late as always," Sabrina said looking down at her watch.

"Whatever. I'm ready to get my drink on. Why are you already starting in on Jess?"

"She started in on me with that bullshit."

"Leave her alone, Sabrina."

"So, how did your visit with Gerald go?" Jess asked.

"Ladies, can I get your drinks?" the waitress interrupted before she could answer.

"Rum and coke," Sabrina requested.

"Um, can I have a Shirley Temple please?" Jess asked.

"A Shirley Temple? Jess, you ain't ever going to get any *goodie goodie* if you keep ordering Shirley Temples!"

"Sabrina, I don't want no goodie goodie! I want my prince and for your information I have met someone. His name is Larry. We've gone on several dates and I haven't had to give him any goodie goodie. We have a good time together. He makes me laugh. We're just enjoying getting to know each other right now."

"I see you," Sabrina said with a high five. "Honey, well, let yourself be free. But you need to see if he serves it the right way before you know if he'll be your prince. You can best believe that! Cutesy and sweet is cool but if he don't know what he's doing down here," she said pointing below her navel, "he is not a keeper; believe that."

"Sabrina, that's enough! Can I have a lemon drop martini, please?" Denise asked the waitress, who was pretending to ignore the conversation.

"Sooooo… when is Mr. Mannnnn coming home?" Sabrina asked picking up the Gerald conversation again after the waitress left.

"Well, we've run into another delay, it looks like," Denise said.

"Delay, Oh LORD, you mean another denial? Denise, I told you that boy ain't getting out. More delays! How many delays can one man have for something he didn't do?" Sabrina asked throwing her hands up in theatrical Sabrina form.

"Something about paperwork not being ready or the parole board being backed up on hearing cases," Denise said, looking down and fiddling with her napkin.

She didn't want to make eye contact with the girls for fear they'd see the disappointment in her eyes. She also didn't want to see the look of skepticism on Sabrina's face. Yet feeling pressured by the lingering moment of silence at the table, she lifted her head. Sabrina's lips were puckered with disgust, her arms folded, and a leg was swinging back and forth under the table. She looked like she was scolding a child.

"Look, Sabrina. He can't be paroled if there's no parole hearing. That is not his fault. You can't blame him for that. It's not like he's doing something to keep himself in prison. It's just taking a little longer than we thought for him to get out. But he will get out and we just have to make the best of it until then."

"Denise, I am a lawyer! Parole hearings are scheduled at a certain time and on a certain date. How could he not have a definite date for a hearing? And if that is the case, where is his lawyer? Why isn't he doing something about this?"

"I don't know, Sabrina, but I have to stay positive. It's just going to take three more months before something is scheduled. It's really not so bad. That would put him out right around Valentine's Day. It's just three months. We've waited this long."

"Oh, Denise, that's great!" Jess chimed in, trying to cut Sabrina off before she had something else negative to say that would upset her sister. "Think of how romantic it will be to have him home on Valentine's Day, right? You can really plan something special for the two of you."

"How romantic... romantic?" Sabrina interrupted. "That man will just be getting out of prison. That ain't romantic."

"It will be romantic," Jess said again, giving Sabrina the evil eye. "I'll help you plan something special. Just for the two of you. We'll make it a night and a homecoming he will never forget."

"It will be a night he won't forget, alright," Sabrina said sarcastically. "Who wouldn't forget getting out of prison, and child, he ain't going to want no romance.

He will be so happy to be getting him some, you could have thirty candles lit and all he'll see is you with your clothes off and a bed," Sabrina laughed.

"Um, how about we not talk about me anymore? Let's try that," Denise said, desperate to change the subject. "Sabrina, what's up with you and *your* crazy life while you all focused on me? What drama you got going on?"

"Well… we just acquired a big new case at the firm, and if I play my cards right, it will bring the firm lots of recognition and lots of cash for me. The only thing is, I'm going up against Stoney Hunter."

"I've seen him on TV," Denise recalled. "He's a shark, from what they say."

"Yep, hasn't lost a case," Sabrina confirmed. "But he hasn't come up against the Brina baby!" she sang.

"Here are your drinks, ladies," the waitress interrupted.

"Thanks!" they said simultaneously.

"Ooh, that's right on time," Sabrina said taking the first sip. "I'm going down the hall to the ladies room to refresh my face, girls. The next batch of stallions from the six o'clock rush hour should be arriving shortly and I have to be bee-u-tee-ful."

"Oh, that takes work? For some reason we were under the impression you wake up like that," Jess said throwing a little shade.

"No you didn't. Oh, you got jokes. Trust me. It's natural, honey, just reinforcement," Sabrina assured her before walking away from the table in her signature runway model walk.

Denise and Jess watched as a few steps away Sabrina was stopped by a group of men standing near the ladies' room, one of which she'd had her eye on earlier. She made a point of looking over at the girls, making sure they saw her with her new catch. When the gentleman handed Sabrina a piece of paper, undoubtedly with his name and number on it, she winked at the girls. They shook their heads and laughed as they watched the eyes of the men follow Sabrina to the ladies' rooms.

"So, Denise, tell me what's really going on with G," Jess said, using their common nickname for Gerald. "All kidding aside, I know you're disappointed."

"Yes, but I have to keep the faith. He and I have been through so much and I'm going to support him no matter what. He's going to be my husband, Jess, and if I don't support him now, it's a sign that I won't support him when we're married."

"You've been a good woman to him, Denise, and I wouldn't say this in front of Sabrina, but you've been through a lot standing by his side through all of this. But you have to ask yourself how much longer you can wait for him with no guarantees."

"Jess! I thought you were on my side! It's hard enough with him being in jail and having to hear Sabrina's negativity. But I need to know I can count on your support in my decisions to continue making it through this."

"I am on your side and I will always support you, sweetie. All I'm trying to say is this. The level of commitment and support you give to him should really only be reserved for your husband. And besides, so much can change about a person mentally and emotionally over a ten-year period, especially for someone who's been in prison. How do you know he's the same person you fell in love with?"

"Jess, he is the same person. When I visit him and talk to him, I can see he *has* changed mentally and emotionally, but for the better not worse. In fact he's a far better person spiritually now than he was before. And he knows that trying to be like his brother was immature behavior that landed him where he is now. He's not of that mindset anymore. And if nothing else, I am one hundred percent sure of his love for me and the love we have for one another."

"I'm not saying he doesn't love or care about you. I'm sure he does. Who wouldn't love you? You are beautiful inside and out. He would be a fool not to. But the two of you have been separated for ten years. You may think you have the same beliefs and the same things in common because he, like most men, may be telling you what you want to hear. Until he's able to show you, how will you truly know that he's still the one you're meant to be with?"

"Why are you trying to depress me, Jess?"

"I promise you I'm not," she said, holding her sister's hand. "I just don't want you to give up twenty years of your life waiting on Gerald and then realize you could have had something more or someone else."

"Amen to that, sista," Sabrina said, returning to the table.

"Sabrina, what do you have in your hand?" Denise asked.

"A scarf. This is Reggie's."

"Reggie. Uh huh, and who is Reggie?" Jess asked. "When you left, you didn't have a scarf."

"Thank you for jotting down my every move, Jess. If the two of you must know, on the way to make myself more beautiful, I ran in to that fine brotha I told you I would have by the end of the night when we first got here, Jess."

"Sabrina, you said you would have his number, not him. And you definitely didn't say anything about his clothes."

"Well, on my way back from the powder room, I bumped into him." Sabrina turned around to wink and wave at the gentleman staring in their direction from the other side of the bar. "I unwrapped his scarf from his oh-so-fine neck and told him to get it back he had to give me the digits."

"Well... did he give you his phone number?" Denise asked.

"Not yet, but he will."

"Anyway, Denise, I heard the last part of the conversation and I agree with Jess. You cannot waste another ten years of your life lonely, waiting around on a convict. Look at all these fine men in here. You need a man you can touch and feel! Ooh! Like that fine brotha right there! Um, um, um." Sabrina waved at the man walking by their table. "You have needs and those needs need to be fulfilled."

"Gerald has those same needs too and he can't fulfill them."

"Yes he can," Sabrina said with a coy smile. The girls looked at one another and busted out in laughter.

"He wouldn't do that!" Jess reassured Denise.

"All I am saying," Sabrina continued, "is that it won't hurt to take care of your goodie goodie until Mr. Man gets out. He won't know, and what he don't know, won't hurt him."

"But can't a man tell when you've been having sex?" Jess asked. "I mean, I heard something about how they can tell how big the entry point is and something about the wall."

After a moment of silence Sabrina and Denise burst into laughter.

"See that is why yo ass need to give up the virgin act. How you need to be educated about your own body, and you are a nurse, Jessica," Sabrina said poking fun at her. "Besides, I know some exercises that will tighten all that back up and no man would suspect a thing. You could be the Virgin Mary for all he knows."

"Excuse me, beautiful lady," a very attractive gentlemen interrupted, directing his attention to Sabrina. "Will you keep it clean for me?" he asked, caressing the scarf around her neck.

"Absolutely." she responded. "But how will you know?"

Taking her hand he lifted it to his lips and planted a soft kiss on the back side while carefully placing a piece of paper in the palm of her hand.

"Soft skin means soft lips," he whispered in her ear.

Sabrina waited until he exited the bar before unfolding the piece of paper. She paused for a moment. Slowly she held up the paper and looked at the girls. "I got the digits. I got the digits! Now... that's how it's done, ladies!" Sabrina grabbed her glass and they followed, raising theirs in salutation.

"Clink, clink, clink, clink, clink," they said together.

FOUR

The girls parted ways for the evening and Denise decided to take in the latest Vin Diesel movie.

"Gerald may not be here but there is always Vin," she said, laughing to herself as she settled down in her movie theater seat.

Relieved the theater was fairly empty she reclined the seat, grabbing the pillow provided for iPic Sapphire guests, and began to scroll through her Facebook posts. As other moviegoers trickled in, she placed an order with the attendant for food and cocktails.

She began people watching as she often did and noticed a young couple walking in holding hands, smiling at each other as if they were the only two people in the room.

Oh, how cute, young love, she thought to herself somewhat envious of their closeness.

The next couple, a slightly older pair, probably in their mid-fifties she estimated, sat a couple of rows in front of her. She watched as he helped her put on her jacket and she turned to give him a kiss of thanks.

"Aww, chivalry isn't dead after all," Denise said to herself.

As she became increasingly depressed at all the love surrounding her, a much older couple upwards of seventy walked in. The elderly gentleman was holding on to a woman she assumed was his wife, who leaned on him for support. The gentleman was patient with her. It looked like it could have taken them an hour to get to their seat and he would have allowed for it without argument. Denise smiled at the man as they passed her seat. He nodded in return and guided his wife to seats just in front of Denise, carefully making sure his wife was seated and comfortable before he took his seat.

Denise wondered if she and Gerald would ever be that couple. She wondered whether they would still be going on date nights at that age and hanging on to each other's every word like the young couple. Would Gerald still be romantic and caring when he got out or would he be changed forever by the experiences in prison?

As more and more couples filled the theater Denise began to feel a sense of loneliness as if she was the only person in there who was single. Normally this didn't bother her but, after her conversation with the girls, she had a revelation and could see just how lonely she was without Gerald. She had never been a stranger to doing things alone; however, on this night, watching complete strangers in relationships and in love made her question her future with Gerald.

As the final advertisements ran she glanced toward the entrance again to look for her attendant and noticed a very handsome brother walk into the theater alone holding a small bag of popcorn and a drink.

Well, hallelujah, she thought. *Finally I am not the only person alone in the world tonight.* She sat up straight in her chair, running her fingers through her hair. He continued his descent down the aisle and then abruptly stopped. Denise became nervous as he looked her way.

"Oh my God," she whispered to herself as he smiled sweetly at her.

The man waved his arm in the air and Denise waved back when suddenly a twenty-something blonde walked past her toward him, bouncing like a high school cheerleader.

"What took you so long?" he asked her planting a kiss on her lips. They giggled and walked off to their seats.

Completely embarrassed, Denise slumped into her seat and the lights dimmed for the previews. She was in part irritated by what had just occurred and frustrated at the thought of another black brotha mixing his fine dark chocolate with vanilla ice cream. But she was also confused as to why seeing any of the couples had an impact on her emotions.

Why had she let the cheerleader ruin her mood? She was in love with Gerald. Why did she care if the man was with a woman or not. Looking right past her as if she didn't exist? Was it because the woman was white? Was it because she appeared to flaunt the fact she was with a black man, one almost as fine as Idris Elba? And why was she forming perceptions about two people that probably weren't the reality of who they were to each other.

The truth was, the girl could have been from Africa and it still would have bothered her because she was alone. As much as she loved Gerald, her sister was right, she was in fact lonely.

After the movie Denise arrived home to find Creasy anxiously waiting for her at the door. As usual he was all over the place. Excited to see her, and practically bouncing off the walls from room to room as though Denise had been gone for months. As he ran in and out of the room, Denise placed her purse on the entry table and soon after she heard the chime of Creasy's potty bells.

"Okay, I am coming!" she called out to him as she made her way to the back door to let him out before making his dinner.

After feeding Creasy, Denise made herself a much-needed amaretto sour, sipping her drink as she walked to her bedroom to undress the day away. Settling under the covers she performed her nightly ritual of watching a few hours of CNN before taking her nightly dosage of alprazolam or what she preferred to call her *happy pill* to begin her sleep pilgrimage. After Gerald was arrested she had a hard time sleeping and would often lie in bed with thoughts of her whole life swirling around until two or three in the morning.

Typically, thirty minutes after taking the happy pill it was lights out; however, tonight, after two hours of CNN and watching half of *A Walk to Remember*, she found herself awake and crying in bed as Mandy Moore told Shane West she was sick. She had hoped the distractions would take her mind off the loneliness she felt without Gerald but the events of the night made her miss him even more.

More depressed than ever and wide awake she decided to call Sabrina. It was late but she knew Jess would be knocked out and figured Sabrina would still be up and waiting on a booty call or something.

"Hey, girl," she said trying to sound as cheerful as possible but the lawyer in Sabrina picked up on the false tone in her voice immediately.

"Denise, have you been watching that damn movie again?"

"No. At least not the one you're thinking of. Anyway, what are you doing?"

"I'm getting dressed. Denise, I can hear you're not fine so what's going on?"

"Nothing. Getting dressed for what? It's two a.m."

"Scott will be here any minute so tell me what's wrong and talk fast."

Denise growled, "Okay! I'll tell you but only if you promise to listen and not judge. I don't need your critique and your I-told-you-so speech right now. Just allow me to vent. Deal?"

"Oh Lord, this must be about that damn G."

"Promise, Sabrina."

"I will try, girl, but he makes it so easy to have an opinion. What's up?"

"Well I went to the movies—"

"Probably some sad lullaby love story."

"Sabrina! Are you going to listen or not?"

"Okay, I'm listening."

"Like I said, I went to the movies and I was watching all the couples walking in, couples in love, completely captivated and caught up in one another while I sat there alone. I felt like I was the only person in that theater who didn't have someone on their arm."

"Well if it makes you feel any better, Denise, you don't know what's going on in the household of those people. They probably fight just like everybody else, they have problems like the rest of married folks and couples, and they probably have more problems than you and me put together. You have never let the actions of other couples or anyone for that matter affect your feelings. You shouldn't base your happiness on the image of someone else's life."

"I know and I agree. It's just, for the first time, I think it really made me realize how lonely I am. I began missing Gerald terribly and at the same time I think I became angry at him, almost blaming him because he's the reason I'm all alone. Because of *his* stupid mistake."

"You should blame him! You've been putting your life on hold for that sorry—"

"Sabrina!"

"I'm sorry," Sabrina said taking a deep breath. "Please continue."

"I love Gerald and I know we'll have a life together, but I miss the companionship, you know? I miss going to dinner with a man. I miss going to the movies with someone and being able to discuss it afterwards. I mean, I love the time I spend with you guys but you're my girls, my sisters and my family really. I'm missing that quality time with a man."

"Wait, what? Are you talking about vertical quality time or horizontal quality time?" Sabrina asked.

"I can, not, with you," said Denise.

"Look, because I promised you, I'm not going to say anything negative about the convict."

"Ummm, Sabrina, *that* was negative."

"All I'm saying," Sabrina continued, "is eventually you're going to have to make a choice. You're going to have to make a choice between a lifetime of loneliness waiting around on him to get out or—"

"Sabrina, it's not a lifetime of loneliness!"

"Yeah, yeah, yeah, he'll be out in a couple of months, blah, blah, blah. The bottom line is, you are *here* and he is *there* and you cannot put your life on hold because of his bad choices. You have a life to live and be happy in while living it and yes you may love him, but you are NOT happy."

Denise was silent. She knew what Sabrina was saying was true.

"Have you ever considered," Sabrina continued more softly, "the possibility that Gerald might not be the one for you? Have you have never been interested in anyone else?"

"No, not really," Denise said, briefly recalling the attraction she had to the man at the theater. "Gerald has been the only one for me since we first fell in love. I've never wanted anyone else."

"Well if you really think Gerald is the one for you, then fine, wait for the rest of your life if you have to. But accept the fact that you will be lonely and stop crying about it. And stop watching those damn sappy ass movies. Now! If it were me, I think I'd be playing the what-Gerald-doesn't-know-won't-hurt-him game."

"Sabrina, if he ever found out he would be crushed. I haven't done anything nor do I ever want to do anything that would hurt him."

"What would be the harm in just dating other men? You don't have to sleep with them. You just hang out, have a conversation, go to the movies, get something to eat. At least then you're not sitting at home looking at four walls every single night, crying over *The Notebook*, my God."

"I don't want to take any chances."

"Chances at what? Having some free food and drinks?" Sabrina clapped back.

"Falling in love," Denise responded.

"Honey, you've waited for twelve years. I think you've proven you can show some restraint."

"I don't know, Sabrina. It's just two more months. I've held on for so long, I can hold on for two more months."

"Okay, but if I were you, I'd use a man to replace time in those two months and worry about Gerald when Gerald gets out."

Denise paused at the thought before hearing the chimes of a doorbell through the phone. "I guess that's Scott. I better let you go," she said yawning.

"Yes it's him, huntie. I'll call you tomorrow. Are we still on for lunch?"

"Yes, of course, two o'clock."

"Okay, smooches."

"Bye, Sabrina."

Denise hung up and grabbed the amaretto sour still sitting on the nightstand before getting up to do a perimeter lock-down check of the house. After rinsing the glass in the sink she stood staring out the window to see two teenagers, a young boy and girl, playing basketball across the street in the neighbor's backyard. Her first thought was, *Umm, it's two in the morning.* But as she watched them laughing and playfully wrestling for the ball, every now the boy grabbing her and sneaking a kiss before smacking the ball out of her hands, Denise smiled.

She poured herself a shot of Hennessey and stared out the window. *Is it possible to have a friends-only relationship with other men without it affecting my relationship with Gerald?* she pondered. "I could never tell Gerald," she said out loud while walking away from the window to check the lock on the front door. "He would never understand."

She began wondering how she would be able to ensure friendly conversation never went beyond the boundary of friendly conversation.

Maybe Sabrina was right. After all, male and female coworkers go on lunch dates all the time and it's just that, a lunch date, nothing more comes out of it, she thought. *As long as I let them know up front that I'm committed to someone else and that it's strictly a friendship thing, no expectations, what would be the harm ... right?*

"I can do this," she said turning off the light. "I love Gerald and he loves me. No man can ever come between that, no matter how many dates. Right, Creasy?" she asked as the dog jumped on the bed behind her to settle in. "Right. I can do this," she said closing her eyes with some comfort. Only to open them again, staring at the TV with a level of uncertainty.

FIVE

The next morning Denise headed to the corner coffeehouse before work. She decided to sit a moment outside to surf the web and catch up on the latest news and gossip. Waiting for a page to download she looked up to observe the other patrons of the establishment. Some were chit-chatting in line, others were inside at tables talking and laughing while enjoying their cup of joe and, like her, others were reading the morning paper or sitting alone with laptops in their faces unaware of what was going on around them.

After a few minutes she noticed a man seated at a small table across the patio staring at her. She quickly turned her attention back to her computer but she could still feel his stare. Peeking through her eyelashes, she looked again to confirm her suspicions.

Ugh, she thought, keeping her head down to avoid eye contact. Shortly afterwards, an employee walked over to her table.

"Ma'am," the waitress whispered, "the gentleman in the corner would like to buy you another cup of coffee," referring to the man now smiling and waving at her.

"Tell him thanks, but I've had my fill of coffee for the morning," she said, turning down his gesture.

The waitress walked away to deliver the news to her suitor. Denise, peeked through her eyelashes for his response and watched as the employee relayed her message hoping this would be enough to throw him off. The man tipped the employee and began gathering his belongings.

Whew, glad he got the hint. No sooner had the thought entered her mind but the man came walking toward her table.

Oh no. Should she start packing to bolt or sit focused on her computer and pray he wasn't really coming over?

"Hi, I'm David Brewster," he said extending his hand toward her.

"Hi, Denise," she responded, reluctantly shaking his hand.

"May I sit?" he politely asked pulling out the empty chair before she could even respond.

"Actually, I'm right in the middle of a report and I don't mean to be rude, but I really have to get this done and head to work."

"Oh," he responded leaning over her computer. "You work for CNN," he said with sarcasm.

"I just took a break," she said. As if she needed to explain herself.

"Look, I just want to talk to you for a minute. Talk... that's it. I've seen you in here a few times and I thought I'd take a chance and introduce myself today."

"Yes, David, got it. Look, I appreciate the coffee offer but I really do have a report to get to, so if you don't mind—"

"Look," he said interrupting her as if she hadn't spoken, "we're in a room full of people and I'm not Jeffrey Dahmer. I'm just a brother who sees a nice beautiful lady in front of him who he would like the opportunity to get to know. I'm only asking for a minute of your time."

In spite of being a little irritated by his continued presence, she did appreciate the beautiful lady comment and gave in.

"Okay, but just for a minute. I really do need to be heading out pretty soon," she said, still somewhat reluctant to entertain him.

"I only asked for a minute but if you are willing to give me a few I'll take it," he responded with enthusiasm. "So, like I said, I've seen you in here a few times. Most of the time you're alone and I ask myself each time, why is such a beautiful lady sitting alone?"

"Just working," she said trying not to give in to his obvious attempt to flatter her.

"Well I've seen you in here a couple of other times with a female or two but never a male so, being an educated man, I'm pretty sure you're single. Am I wrong?"

"Wow," she replied, "am I being stalked?"

"No," he chuckled, "but it's pretty hard not to notice someone with your beauty sitting alone. Are you married?"

"If I say yes, are you going to walk away right now and never look back?"

"Well, again, being an educated man, if you were married you would not have invited me to sit down to have this lovely conversation with you."

"Touché," she said, having no other response.

"What do you do for a living?"

"I work for a radio station. Power 105.9."

"Really, radio? Huh, interesting."

"Yes, it's a gospel station."

"Yes I know it well,"

"Oh, you're a spiritual man?" she probed.

"Not by man's standards, but I have a relationship with a higher being, and you beautiful lady still haven't answered my question."

"Oh, I'm sorry, what question is that?" she asked, ready for the whole encounter to end.

"Are. You. Married?"

"I thought you were an educated man," she said smiling and taking a sip of her coffee.

"That I am, but I just want confirmation," he responded in like manner.

Her initial thought was to lie but she answered truthfully. "No. I'm not married."

"Are you seeing anyone?" the man continued, noticing hesitation in her response.

"It's complicated."

"What is it about the question that makes it so complicated?"

"It's too complicated to get into with a stranger and you're just asking way too many questions, way too early in the morning. I think our few minutes are just about up."

"Oh no, so soon. I'm really enjoying your company, Ms. Complicated. Do you have any kids?"

"Umm, okay! Gotta go now. Nice to meet you, Mr. Brewster," she said as she began gathering her things.

The man laughed. "Okay, okay. Do you work on this side of town?"

"And still more questions," she said putting the rest of her items in her briefcase. "Shouldn't we be talking about the weather or something neutral for a first conversation? I think we're getting a little too personal for having known each other all but," she looked at her watch, "ten minutes."

"I might run into you again and I just want a little background information for our next discussion. I assume you live nearby since I see you in here so often."

Shocked by his forwardness, she said, "Again, way too personal. I do have a car, Mr. Brewster. See right over there," she said pointing directly behind him. "Most people use them to drive wherever it is they need to go. Like I now need to go and drive to work," she said walking away from the table.

"But do you?" he asked following her.

"Do I what?" She was irritated that he didn't leave the conversation at the table.

"Live nearby. Here, let me get that for you," he said reaching to open the car door for her.

Denise let out a laugh, avoiding his question as she put her things in the back seat. At the same time, she couldn't help noticing he really wasn't a bad looking man. Six feet tall, slim, Morris Chestnut Chocolate and somewhat entertaining. A real Clydesdale, using a term women used to describe men back in the day.

"Well," he prodded as he leaned into the car window to give it one last try. "Can I call you sometime?"

"Well now, Mr. Brewster, you don't have my number," she said flirting back a little herself as she turned the ignition key.

"Let's change that," he said, picking up on her interest.

"Goodbye, Mr. Brewster," she said with a wave as the car began to roll.

"Aww, that's how you going to do me?" he asked spreading his arms out. "That's okay, I know you like me cuz you gave me more than a few minutes," he yelled out as Denise pulled away from the curb.

Denise looked into her rearview mirror to see him still standing on the sidewalk as if he were waiting for her to turn around. Part of her wanted to give him her number but the bigger part of her still kept Gerald's feelings in mind. However, she caught herself smiling quite often on the rest of the drive into work.

As attractive as Mr. Brewster was, she wasn't ready to open up that door yet and, even though he was nosey as hell, she'd enjoyed the attention and conversation. But she certainly wasn't going to tell the girls about the little encounter. If Sabrina knew that Denise was even slightly attracted to a man other than Gerald, she would have her on a dating app by the end of the day.

The encounter with Mr. David Brewster, however, made her think that maybe Sabrina was right. Maybe it wouldn't hurt to lift a few sanctions and allow herself a little conversation, drinks or dinner with a man and still keep her commitment to Gerald.

Regretting that she didn't give him her number, she remembered that he said he saw her in the coffee shop frequently so she resolved they would see one another again. She wondered, however, if he would be receptive to her again after she drove away leaving him on the street rejected.

"I'll see him again," she murmured as she arrived at work. "What would be the harm in just giving him my number and meeting him for a drink? I have no intention of ever sleeping with him or any other man." *Why am I talking to myself?* she thought as she pushed the elevator button.

Later that day as she stared out her office window, Denise reflected on her conversation with David Brewster. She began imagining what it would be like to have an encounter with him. Closing her eyes, she leaned back in her chair and drifted into la la land as she began to imagine a world with Mr. Brewster in it.

She opened the door to her home to find him waiting patiently on her doorstep. "Hello, you."

Mr. tall, dark, sexually handsome. A man most women, especially Sabrina, wouldn't have hesitated giving their number to the instant he asked for it. She was wearing sexy lingerie from Victoria's Secret. Black lacy bra, with fringe running the length of her torso hovering just above her panty line. Satin thong of the same color with fishnet pantyhose and black Louboutins. Her body was ready for the taking.

"Hello, you," he responded with a smoldering stare. "My, my, my! You sure look good tonight," taking a verse from the popular nineties song. "And you sho damn fine," he finished before kissing her.

"Sorry it took me so long to answer," she said in her sexy whisper voice. "I just got out of the shower and I threw this on. I fully intended to put on something a little more decent," she said winking at him.

"Trust me," he said pursing his lips. "What you have on is fine. Can I come in?"

"I don't know. I don't usually let people I just met in on the first date."

"I won't bite."

"Well, I don't know." She turned around and began her runway walk into the foyer. "I don't usually let people that don't bite in on the first date." She turned to face him.

"I tell you what. If you let me in, your every wish is my command," he continued, still standing in the doorway.

"My *every* wish?" she asked, needing clarification.

"Yes, every wish, and your wish will be my pleasure."

"Well... since you put it that way," she said walking toward him.

Pulling him in by the tie, she teased him with a kiss before turning and walking him into the living room to issue her first command. She knew he watched from behind, mesmerized by every inch of her, as her body swayed from side to side causing the fringe to dance against her body.

Turning to face him, she began to slowly unravel his necktie taking the ends and pulling him close. She leaned in and nibbled softly on his lips before kissing him passionately. Unable to contain himself he lifted her off the ground. She wrapped her legs around his waist as he deepened the kiss, pressing her back against the wall, kissing her lips, her neck, her breasts. After allowing him and herself a little pleasure, she pulled away, pretending she didn't want it. But he knew full well she was loving every minute of it and her sweet coy smile excited him even more.

He let her down off the wall and she walked over to the couch.

"Come here," she commanded. He stopped where she pointed and she slowly began to unbutton her shirt.

"This little piggy went to the market," she said with the first button. "And... this little piggy... stayed home," she said biting her lips and looking up at him.

"And what of the next little piggy?" he asked.

"Well, this little piggy right here," she said pointing to the next button. "You see, this little piggy says I have on too many clothes."

At that, David unhooked her bra, kissing her intensely as it slid down between them, Denise moaning with pleasure and excitement.

"And the next?" he asked, intrigued by the game she was playing.

"Well, this little piggy," she said as she opened the next button and turned to sit on the couch. "He just had to have a taste of this spot right here," she said licking her fingers before rubbing them against her vagina.

David leaned over her and began to massage the area. He softly rubbed it with his fingers as he enjoyed the expressions and sounds of pleasure coming from her. Then as those sounds intensified, he pulled her pantyhose down to follow her instructions, tasting her with his tongue. Denise could feel passion building inside of her as he came up to suck on parts of her body, nibbling his way to her breasts, sending her into a near climatic state.

He paused briefly to unbuckle his pants.

"No, no, no," Denise said slowly shaking her finger sideways.

"Come on, baby," he whimpered. "Don't do me like this."

"Little piggy didn't say so," she said, still shaking her finger at him.

David placed his lips around her finger and began sucking it just as intensely as he had sucked her breast.

"This little piggy can't wait anymore," he said kissing her passionately as he pulled her on top of his now naked body, "Oh! Yes!" she cried.

"Does it feel good?" he whispered.

"Yes," she groaned.

"Do you want more?"

"YES," she said louder, wrapping her arms around his neck.

Knock, knock, knock.

Denise heard a knocking in the distance.

"Denise, your meeting with Mr. Hamm is in five minutes," her receptionist announced.

"Ugh," Denise moaned. "Okay," she said disappointed that la la land was interrupted.

SIX

Denise arrived bright and early at the coffeehouse the next day hoping she would have another opportunity to run into Mr. Brewster. Try as she might she just couldn't get him out of her head and the sexual fantasy she dreamed up didn't help. To her own surprise she wanted another opportunity to be in his space. It had been a long time since a man had showered her with compliments and attention. It was a huge ego boost to say the least. She began to wonder if maybe Sabrina was right. Maybe it wouldn't hurt to just have a companion. Gerald was her one true love and nothing and no one would change that. So maybe she should just give it a try.

Denise had business that afternoon but she wanted to put in a little extra time and effort getting dressed in hopes of impressing her suitor. Walking into her closet she scanned the color-coordinated racks and fixated on a little red dress she'd purchased for a cocktail event. It was perfect for what she was wanting to accomplish. She may have been out of the dating game for a minute but every woman knows you can't go wrong with a red or black dress. The dress was a red wrap threaded in gold. The right amount of cleavage showing to catch his eye, but still professional enough to keep the business happy.

After hair and makeup she added the finishing touch to her ensemble—the shoes—settling on a pair of beige Prada's. After modeling in the mirror for a few minutes she was ready to face the world and David Brewster, looking cute and feeling confident.

Arriving at the coffeehouse earlier than normal, Denise purchased her usual caramel latte and chocolate croissant, and glanced around the restaurant. He wasn't there yet, which she was happy about because she needed a moment to sit down and get herself together.

"How long have you worked here?" she asked the barista making her latte.

"Umm, about a year," the young girl responded.

"Oh, are you pretty familiar with the regulars that come in?"

"Yes, ma'am, I see you in here often."

"Oh, well, maybe you know David Brewster," Denise continued with her inquisition. "He's slightly taller than me. Dark skin, grayish well-trimmed beard."

The barista stared at her blankly. "Ma'am, I don't know names. I just see people and serve coffee."

"Oh," Denise said. "I guess it's a silly question anyway. Never mind. Can I get the croissant warmed please?"

"Sure," the barista responded, in a manner that left Denise feeling ridiculous.

Denise located a table near the door making every attempt to look busy in case David Brewster walked in. But the truth was her thoughts were consumed by the passionate encounter she'd daydreamed about, the two of them enthralled in a moment of passion. The flashback gave her a warm sensation.

What am I doing? she asked herself. *Why am I having these kinds of thoughts about this man, and why am I sitting here waiting on him to show up as if we were dating. He's just some guy I know nothing about. Get yourself together, girl.*

She finished the thought yet remained at the table anticipating his arrival. But where was he? An hour passed and still no David Brewster.

She decided to act as normal as possible and began reading Yahoo News headlines. To the onlooker her composure was calm, cool and collected; however, in actuality she was nervous as hell.

The coffeehouse was beginning to clear as the morning crowd died down and Mr. Brewster was still a no-show. Two hours passed and she was feeling somewhat agitated as if she was being stood up, at least in her mind. He said he came here often, so where was he? By now she had consumed two lattes at five hundred calories each, her entire caloric intake for the day. Her body couldn't afford to wait on David Brewster too much longer. Her business meeting would begin in half an hour and his arrival at this point would only be enough time to say "hi, how are you doing" and "bye, good to see you."

After giving it another ten minutes Denise, disappointed and facing the inevitable, gathered her things together to head off to work.

"Maybe he didn't have time for coffee today. I guess I'll try again tomorrow. I'm sure he'll be here tomorrow," she reasoned with herself.

Tomorrow came and Denise settled on the back dress. She sat in the restaurant again looking cool, calm and collected but again David Brewster was a no-show.

Like the day before she gathered her things to leave the coffeehouse but before stepping off of the sidewalk, she looked left and right down the street to see if just maybe he was walking up it. But he was not. Sighing with disappointment and regret she slowly crossed the street toward her car. As she reached it she heard someone calling out her name in the distance.

"Denise!"

Spinning around with excitement she searched through the crowded sidewalk to find where the voice was coming from and, more importantly, if it was coming from David Brewster.

She turned toward the voice and saw a white male waving in her direction.

"Denise!" he yelled out again as a brunette brushed passed her.

"Hello, my love," the brunette responded as they embraced right in front of her.

Denise turned back and got in her car to quickly leave. But she sat there for a moment, hands gripping the steering wheel, watching others go about their day, trying to hide her disappointment and not rationalize why he didn't show up. Because, in the grand scheme of things, Mr. Brewster didn't matter. He was just a guy she met at a coffee shop, a guy in fact who actually got on her nerves.

In spite of her efforts she'd developed multiple theories and scenarios to explain his no-show. It was better than to accepting the realization that she was to blame for the missed opportunity. After a few minutes of contemplation, she remembered they'd met on a Thursday so maybe that was the only day he came to get coffee.

I mean, it's possible, she thought. And in the end she was happy with that explanation.

She didn't go to the coffeehouse on Wednesday but that evening she decided to google Mr. Brewster to see if she could find out any information about him on her own.

Not having very much information to go by other than his name made it very difficult to do a general search for him on the internet. Trying to find him on the net, however, turned out to be the same challenge as finding the man himself. He was obviously not from Texas. A few name matches were found but in order to view the information, payment was required. There were several David Brewster's but she wasn't about to pay the extra money. She'd already invested enough time in her efforts and wasn't about to invest finances.

Denise woke up the next morning somewhat dreading going to the coffeehouse, but she managed to find the strength to find the perfect ensemble to impress her missing-in-action suitor.

Grabbing her keys to head out for the day, she stopped in front of the mirror to take one more glance at herself.

"What do you think, Creasy?" His ears perked up. "Hot or not hot?" Creasy glanced at her once before resting his head on the side of his bed.

"Well, this will have to be good enough because I am over it," she said turning from side to side in the mirror, twisting her waist enough to see her backside to ensure the fabric clung to her curvy figure as designed with no static cling. After adjusting her breasts in her bra to form the perfect V, she placed her hands on her hips and let out a sigh.

"Here goes nothing," she said to Creasy lying nearby in his bed and walked out the door.

The coffeehouse was emptier than usual making it that much easier to see that Mr. Brewster was not there. Denise wasn't sure if that was or a good thing or bad thing. The temperature outside was perfect for enjoying her coffee and after all it was where she'd initially met him. It was the perfect place for him to spot her. She decided she wasn't going to spend any more energy or tactical operation time on David Brewster. If he didn't show by the time she finished her coffee, she was done.

She had the perfect vantage point to see everything and everyone on the street. She people watched for a while. Everyone was busy going about their morning. People walking by the restaurant. People strolling along the sidewalk peeping into adjoining retail shops. Some taking their dogs out for the morning walk. She must have seen over one hundred people within the court, over one hundred people and no David Brewster.

Had she dreamed him up? She was starting to think the man was a mythical being in spite of having had a full-length conversation with him just a few days ago. It was very strange that on her third attempt there was still no sign of him. Most coffee lovers were pretty loyal about going to the same location when it came to their morning coffee, and he'd said he noticed her several times. So where was he now?

After another twenty minutes, Denise sipped the last of her coffee and let out a sigh.

What am I doing? she wondered. *I've been running to this coffeehouse like a desperate lonely woman to impress a guy who I know absolutely nothing about and quite frankly actually got on my nerves. I have a man. I have no intention of having anything remotely serious with this man. So why am I torturing myself like this?*

Gathering her things together to leave the coffeehouse and vowing never to return, she walked onto the sidewalk upset, embarrassed and ashamed. Upset that she allowed herself to build up her hopes, embarrassed that she'd put so much energy into something she really didn't want to begin with and ashamed because she loved Gerald and if he even suspected any of this it would devastate him.

She walked away from the coffeehouse, head hung low, looking back one last time to see if just maybe he was there. That was the last thing she remembered before she heard a distant voice and felt pain. Opening her eyes as if she'd just come out of a month-long coma, she saw several strangers huddled over her.

"Are you alright ma'am?" someone asked.

"What happened?" She was lying on the sidewalk.

"Seems like a minor case of the preoccupied mind," a gentleman answered.

With the help of those standing around her, Denise gathered her strength and stood on her feet.

"Are you okay?" she heard the gentleman's voice again. "You had a pretty good fall."

"Oh, my God!" she said. "I remember turning to look over my shoulder. I must have run into you, sir. I am so sorry. I wasn't watching where I was going."

"That was pretty obvious," the man joked. "Here, let me help you get your things," he politely suggested as the rest of the crowd began to move along with their day. Still trying to catch her breath, Denise looked down to see the contents of her purse spilled out across the sidewalk.

"Oh no, thank you, I got it," she said kneeling beside him, frantically grabbing everything in sight hoping there were no female products in plain sight.

"That's okay. It's the least I can do for knocking you out cold. Looks like I'm not the only one in a rush this morning."

Denise stood and finally got a good look at the man who had stayed with her. She was taken aback to realize she'd slammed right into Blair Underwood's twin. He was handsome. He was very, very handsome. So handsome that thoughts of David Brewster quickly dissipated.

"It was totally my fault. I apologize for plowing you down, sir."

"Oh, no sirs please. The name is Richard. Richard Barnett. Nice to meet you, Mrs...."

"Oh, Ms. and it's Denise. Nice to meet you, Richard, and thank you again. I am so sorry. My mind was clearly focused on the wrong thing and if there are any damages, I'll give you my card. Just let me know what I can do."

"Damages," the man laughed. "I'm fine. I mean, no offense, but I wasn't the one on the ground. Like I said, it's no big deal. Why don't you let me buy you a cup of coffee? Or tea? I mean, to calm your nerves."

"Thanks but I think I've had enough coffee this morning," Denise said declining his gesture. "Besides you said you were in a rush so I don't want to take up anymore of your time."

"It's the least I can do after knocking you down."

"You're too kind, but let's just put the blame where blame is due. All on me."

"Come on, just one cup. I have time," he persisted.

Denise pondered the offer for a moment as the man began walking toward the coffeehouse backwards, waving his hands and arms for her to follow.

Somewhat reluctantly Denise gave in and the two returned to the coffeehouse. As he went to the counter to order beverages, Denise ventured outside to acquire the same table she'd camped out at to wait for David Brewster earlier. As she took her seat she quickly scanned the coffeehouse to make sure Mr. Brewster had not arrived.

"Here you go," Richard said handing her the tea.

"Thank you. If you don't mind, I need to just send a quick text to my assistant to let her know I'll be a little late."

"Sure," he responded.

Denise finished her text and began to have a pleasant and surprisingly enjoyable conversation with the man who had saved her life. They discussed everything from the weather and sports to work and even relationships. He was single and owned a sports apparel store on the east side of Austin. He'd graduated from Lanier High School, home of the Vikings and as it turned out they both graduated as class of '89. He attended Austin Community College and after receiving his associate degree in business he decided he didn't want to work in corporate America and opened his own clothing store. After enjoying his company for over an hour Denise glanced at her watch.

"Oh my God, I guess I better start heading to work. Good thing I have a little clout at that place because I'm extra late. Thank you again for the cup of coffee," she said smiling sweetly.

"Again, it was no problem. I'm just glad I was there to help. Are you feeling okay from the fall?" he asked concerned.

"Yes, I'm fine. Thank you. So would it be okay if I called you sometime?" she asked. The words rolled off her tongue before she could stop them. Embarrassed she covered her mouth. "I can't believe I just asked you that. Forgive me for my forwardness. What I meant to say was maybe I enjoyed the conversation and maybe we will bump into each other again sometime." She began quickly grabbing her things.

"Whoa! Slow down. I don't want you running out of here slamming into someone else. That pleasure is reserved for me," he quipped. "I would love for you to call me sometime."

"Great, that's great," she said standing up and feeling very embarrassed.

"Would you like my number?"

"Oh yes, yes, of course," she said fumbling for her cell phone.

By this point her anxiety level had spiked and she felt as if she was about to literally pass out a second time. She had never been that forward with a man, but then again, for as far back as she could remember Gerald was the only man she had ever been with, and he had approached her.

"Can you just enter it in?" she asked handing him her phone.

"Absolutely."

Denise stood by awkwardly while he finished entering his information into her phone.

"Denise, it was very nice to meet you and I look forward to hearing from you soon," he said handing her phone back to her. Their hands touching briefly during the transaction.

"Nice to meet you, Richard."

"Goodbye, Ms. Rush, and be safe out there. No more running into strange men," he laughed.

"Roger that," she said holding out her hand for a parting handshake.

Denise left the coffeehouse and made it to her car without injury. On the drive to work she reflected on how awful her week had been while chasing after David Brewster.

What a difference a day makes, she thought. "Can I give you a call sometime?" She repeated the words out loud. "Where in the world did that come from?"

Wherever it came from Mr. Barnett had obviously knocked down an unstable brick in the wall she'd placed around herself to keep men out. That thought ignited a more uncomfortable thought. If he was able to knock down that wall, would it be the beginning of the end for her and Gerald?

SEVEN

"What's up, girlie girl girl?" Sabrina answered in her usual larger-than-life self. "We still on for happy hour tonight?" she asked before Denise could tell her why she was calling.

"Of course," Denise responded, "but that's not why I'm calling." Denise couldn't wait to tell her about her Blair Underwood lookalike. She'd been on the fence about Mr. Brewster, but Richard was something to brag about.

"Is Snow White going to be there?" Sabrina asked referring to Jess.

"I'm not sure. She said she was going to try and meet us. I think she has a date."

"What! Ms. Purity Forever has a date?"

"Yeah, she's been seeing this guy for a few weeks now. They seem to be hitting it off really well."

"Are they hitting it off or is he HITTING IT?" Sabrina asked sarcastically.

"I can assure you he's not hitting anything; they've only been out on a few dates. My sister hasn't even mentioned if the subject's come up."

"Then he's either a nerd or gay; take your pick," Sabrina concluded.

"Why is it when a guy doesn't make a move within the first three hours, you think he's gay?"

"Because they are, Denise. I don't make the rules. That's just the way it is."

"Oh my God, this is not even why I called," Denise said, suddenly uncomfortable about going into detail about her encounter with Richard Barnett.

Sabrina was her girl. No one could make her laugh harder than Sabrina, no one was as real as Sabrina and no one had been that ear to hear Denise vent as much as Sabrina. Yet, as much as Denise leaned on her, she had to be very strategic when she did so. The phrase "leading the witness" was an understatement when it came to Sabrina. A person could get two words out and she already had a case built on speculation around it.

"Denise, what's up, girl? We meeting tonight or what?"

"Yeah, yeah, Studio Grill. Six p. I'll see you there."

"Well, what did you have to talk to me about?" Sabrina asked.

"Nothing, girl. I'll tell you later," Denise responded, hoping that would be enough to throw Sabrina off her scent. Denise could tell she knew there was more but for some reason she didn't persist.

"Hmm, hmm. Alright, girl, bye" was all she said. Denise was relieved.

Denise decided to have a glass of wine and go through snail mail before meeting the girls for happy hour. Among the month of accumulated bills and news ads she was surprised to stumble upon a letter from Gerald. She was surprised because they alternated weeks when they wrote one another and, although delayed, it was her turn to write him.

Laying the letter on the table she took a sip of wine and stared at it. She was hesitant to open it, afraid that if she did it would contain the dreadful parole denial words Sabrina loved to tell her would eventually be written. Or maybe it would say the hearing got pushed back again. Maybe it would say nothing at all. Maybe he just decided to write. But it was her turn to write so why was he writing? She sipped her wine again, flipping the letter between her fingers as she contemplated what it could say, as if her mind could tell her what it said without her opening it.

After a few more moments, and a few more sips of wine, it dawned on her that maybe the letter was news of his release date. Suddenly she became excited. She ran to her office and pushed open the door in search of her letter opener. Checking the computer desk.

"Rats." It wasn't there.

She checked both kitchen junk drawers and glanced around the room. Still, no letter opener.

"Oh my God," she said to herself. "Do you have to be so anal about everything? Just open it." She ripped it open.

Hey Baby,

I know it's your week but, Baby, I am missing you and thinking about you so much I just want to surprise you and write you sooner to tell you. With each passing day I hope you find comfort in knowing we will soon be together. So far we are still on schedule for my release in February, Baby. I haven't got a firm date set yet on the parole hearing, but I should be hearing something soon.

You don't know how much I wish that I could be with you on Christmas. Just knowing that once I am out of here we will have so many more Christmases to celebrate keeps me going.

I pray every day that you are safe, well and happy. And that God will carry you wherever you go, protecting you from all harm because I don't want to have to kill nobody when I get out of here, lol. I would be crushed if anything ever happened to you. You are my world. I love you.

How is our temporary child? Is he still bouncing off the walls? I know you said you were going to get him clipped but I keep telling you to let that dog be a dog, Honey. You can't just go around clipping off a man's junk! That is his prize possession. He will be scarred for life. You already scarred him with that name, Creasy. What is that? The guys in here call him Crissy. Please let me do the naming when the real child comes along, Baby.

I miss you, Baby. I can't wait until I can have you in my arms. You better rest up. Rest up good, Baby. Because when I get out of here… you know I am going to be lovin on you for several days. Make that weeks!

As soon as I get out I want to start planning our lives together. I don't want to wait another minute. You are my Boo! I want to make sure the whole world knows it. I love you, Girl, more than you will ever know. I apologize for all that I have put you through with me being in here. I know it is hard being out there, and I know that you are all alone because of my stupid mistake. I know because it's torture for me being in here alone without you. It must be so much worse for you though. Having to lie in that big bed every night. Thinking about the fine brotha you got waiting to taste every inch of your body (smile). I know you wake up in night sweats just thinking about it (laughing).

I will be home soon, Baby, I miss you. Take care of yourself because I need you in order for my heart to continue beating. I can't wait to hear from you.

Write me soon, Boo, and send some pics. Please don't give up on me, Baby.

I Love you, Baby.

– Gerald

After reading the letter Denise gently folded it back together and held it to her chest. Tears began to flow as she became overwhelmed with emotion.

Reaching into her closet, Denise pulled down a pink satin memory box inscribed with the words "The best things in life are the people you love, the places you go and the memories you make," a quote from an unknown author that she once saw online. It was the perfect sentiment to have engraved on top of the box that housed the special memories she shared with Gerald.

After unraveling the rubber band securing letters she'd received over the years, she carefully placed the newest addition at the back of the stack and once again secured them with the band. Depression sat in. As much as Denise held on to the thought of Gerald getting out and them running off into the sunset, she often thought he might never get out, at least not soon enough for her not to give up on waiting. Feelings of love and loneliness sat in. Before the thoughts could gain momentum she took a deep breath and gathered her purse and keys to leave the loneliness within the four walls of her home and headed out to meet Sabrina.

Denise arrived at the Studio to find Sabrina cuddled against her next victim.

"Eh, um." Denise cleared her throat.

"Oh, hey, girl. It's about time you got here. Denise meet, uh…"

"Darryl," he said helping her out.

"Yes… Darryl. Darryl, this is my girl, Denise."

"Nice to meet you, Darryl," she said greeting him with a handshake.

"Well, I am sorry, Darryl, but it's girls night out so we'll have to part ways for the evening. It was certainly a pleasure to meet you."

"The pleasure is all mine, Ms. Diva. Be sure to use that number, okay?"

"Okay," Sabrina responded insincerely, waving her hand to shoo him off.

"Girl, you never quit, do you?"

"He's the one that needs to quit. Did you smell his breath? Talk about a yuck mouth!"

Denise laughed. "When I walked up you were all hugged up with him, laughing and carrying on with Mr. Yuck Mouth."

"I had to laugh to pull in some fresh air. I was suffocating. What a waste. Fine as Shemar Moore with yuck mouth!"

"Have you ordered?" Denise asked looking around for a waiter.

"No, but I'm about to. What are you having?"

"Um, I'll take a cosmo."

"Okay. I'm going to go to the bar and order. We'll probably get it faster."

While Sabrina was getting drinks, Denise thought about the letter from Gerald. *Please don't give up on me, Boo.* Was she giving up on him? She made a decision to start seeing other people. Why? Maybe a part of her was afraid they would never reach that happy ending.

Reaching into her purse for hand sanitizer, she saw the paper with Richard's number tucked into the corner. She thought back to her meeting with Richard. How, without hesitation, she'd asked for his phone number. How would Gerald feel about her getting another man's phone number? How would he feel if she actually called the number? He had once told her it would be okay if she needed someone to fill the lonely nights. Of course she vowed that would never happen, committing to wait for him as long as it took. She had no intention of breaking that promise. Her conflict was whether or not asking for a man's phone number and ultimately going out with him violated that promise.

Still waiting on Sabrina she pulled the phone number out of her purse. Staring at it as if it was the pathway to sin. A vision of Gerald's disappointed face suddenly entered her mind and in that moment she decided not to make the call. Making that call would be like playing with fire, and she did not want herself or Gerald to get burned.

I can't do this to Gerald. I can't be unfaithful, she thought.

"What's that?" Sabrina asked, grabbing the piece of paper. "2815569840 please call me, Richard. WHAT! Look at you! That's my girl," Sabrina said with joy, making the announcement for everyone within earshot. "It's about damn time you broke the chains and started living again."

"Sabrina, I haven't broken any chains," she said grabbing back the piece of paper. "Gerald and I are still together and still very much in love."

"Then what's up with the digits?" Sabrina asked, grabbing the piece of paper again.

"That? Well, I don't know what that is. That was a spur of the moment weakness and it should have never happened. And for the record, I haven't called him and before you snatched it out of my hands I was about to tear it up."

"Oh no, you are not! You are going to call this number and you are going to go out on a date with this man."

"Sabrina, what are you going to do? Make me?"

"Yep! Denise, stop always trying to do what's right for Gerald," she said rolling her eyes. "If Gerald was doing what was right for you he wouldn't be in jail, leaving you lonely and depressed all the time. Be the bad girl for once in your life."

"A… I am not depressed and B… Gerald didn't do anything wrong, remember?"

"I thought you were going to at least pursue other friendships while you're waiting around for Mr. Never Going to Get Out."

"I mean I considered it. And I was going to call Richard, really I was. But I got home today and there was a letter from Gerald and—"

"And that letter just messed up your whole little head, didn't it? Took you out of focus on your life."

"No, it put me back into focus. Gerald loves me, Sabrina. He misses me just as much as I miss him. I know it's not an ideal situation, but the last thing he said in his letter was for me not to give up on him. I feel like going out on a date with any guy would be like me giving up on—"

"Blah, blah, blah," Sabrina interrupted, waving her hands in circles. "Well I think you would be a fool not to call this guy back. At least talk to him. You don't have to have sex with him, just talk, Denise. Have a little fun. If you're as in love with Gerald as you say you are, then what are you so worried about?"

Denise flashed back to the daydream fantasy she had about David Brewster. The intensity of sexual desire in that fantasy made her realize she wasn't sure she would be capable of avoiding temptation in the right setting. It was too risky.

"I would just rather not put myself in a situation where I would be tempted to do the wrong thing. It would be too risky."

"Honey, I hate to tell you this, but you need a good risk," Sabrina said, pulling her cell phone out of her purse.

"What are you doing?"

"I'm calling Richard," Sabrina said dialing the number.

"No, Sabrina, don't!" Denise shouted reaching for the piece of paper.

"Yes I am! Trust me. You'll regret it if you don't. SHH! It's ringing."

Denise was panicking. She wasn't ready to have a conversation with the man. She wasn't sure she was going to have one at all let alone right now. She buried her head in her hands praying for him not to answer and for the right words to say if he did.

"Hello." She heard Sabrina's voice.

"OMG," Denise said, looking up to Sabrina's coy smile.

"Hello, is this Richard?" Sabrina continued. "Yes, I'm the personal assistant for Ms. Rush. She asked me to call you. Would you mind holding while I put the call through to her? Okay great, hold just one moment please." Sabrina muted the phone and held it out to Denise.

"NO!" Denise whispered, waving her arms back and forth as if she was sending a distress signal. In a way she was.

"Take it," Sabrina growled.

"Ugh, I can't believe you," Denise said growling back and grabbing the phone. "You are unbelievable." She unmuted the phone and said, "Richard, hi. This is Denise. Denise from the coffeehouse."

"Yes, glad to hear from you," he said. "How are you doing?"

"I'm great. Did I catch you at a bad time?" she asked rolling her eyes at Sabrina who was laughing hysterically.

"No not at all. I've been waiting for your call so no time could be a bad time. I'm impressed. You must really have some clout around there. Not everyone can have their personal assistant make calls for them."

"Yeah, I'm sorry about that. How are you?" she asked, not sure of what else to say.

"I'm fine. You know, work, work and work."

"Ask him out," Sabrina hissed across the table. Denise threw an evil look her way and continued.

"Well I was just wondering if you would be free for a drink some time tomorrow, or you know, whenever?"

"I would love to have a drink. How does six p at the Elephant Room sound? Tonight?"

"Tonight? Are you sure? I mean I don't want to change any plans you already had or impose. I'm actually out with my girl right now so tonight is not good. How about tomorrow?" She was shocked he was so quick and eager to meet.

"No imposition. How does the Elephant Room sound to you? Do you like jazz?" he asked.

"Uh, y-yes, sure, okay, six p Elephant Room. Tomorrow. And yes, I love jazz."

"Okay, then six it is. I can't wait to see you again."

"Okay, great. Six p. Great."

"Stop repeating everything, Denise, my God," Sabrina said. Denise held a finger up to her lips.

"Okay, well I guess I'll see you tomorrow." She was ready to get off the phone.

"Tomorrow it is," he confirmed.

The call ended and Denise sank into the booth as Sabrina celebrated.

"That was the most excruciating conversation I have ever had," she said to Sabrina as she gulped down her Cosmo.

"So that went well." Sabrina motioned to the waiter. "Um, can we have two buttery nipples and another round of Cosmo's please?" She turned back to Denise. "So the Elephant Room huh? Classy."

"Yes. We're going there tomorrow for drinks. I can't believe I just did that."

"Did what?" Sabrina asked. "All you did was accept a drink offer. It's not like you're going to sleep with the man. It's just drinks."

"I know it's just drinks, but Gerald—"

"Oh Gerald Shmerrild. How is he going to know unless you tell him? Stop worrying about stuff he never has to find out about. You're going to go and you're going to have a good time."

"Ok, I need an objective point of view. You're not helpful."

"I'm being objective, damn it." Sabrina went on the defensive. "Why is it when miss Virgin Mary gives you advice you consider it? But when I give you advice, you need an objective point of view?"

They both paused for a moment and burst into laughter.

"In all seriousness, Denise, I see the loneliness on your face and I hear it in your voice. I just want you to have a little fun, that's all. I know you love that man. Only God knows why, but I know you love him. I'm saying just go have the drink. It will get you out of the house instead of you sitting at home watching that godforsaken movie for the ten thousandth time."

"Okay, Sabrina. I'll meet him tomorrow."

"That's my girl! Now where the hell are those buttery nipples? We need to celebrate!"

EIGHT

Tomorrow came and Denise spent the whole day anxious about her date with Richard. After dropping Creasy off for a day at the spa in the mall grooming center, she treated herself to a facial, manicure and pedicure, capping off her afternoon with a full body massage by Ricardo, her favorite sexy Italian masseur.

Ricardo had no limits and, if desired, he would massage any place you wanted him to massage. Denise of course didn't want the special favors he offered other customers; however, she had to admit, only to herself of course, that his touch gave her satisfying pleasure. She couldn't cheat on Gerald ever, but a massage from Ricardo was the closest thing to it.

After her near sexual experience, she purchased a blue off-the-shoulder cocktail dress with a little bit of sparkle and just enough slit at the thigh to pique the interest of onlookers. It had been a long time since she'd dressed up for a man. After purchasing the dress, she picked up Creasy and headed home to rest a little before the evening event.

While soaking in the tub with a glass of wine she decided to check her voice mail, something she never did on a regular basis so the box was full as usual. Those who knew Denise knew her preferred method of communication was text. Especially if a quick response was desired. The first eight messages were telemarketers, which was the main reason why she never bothered with voice mail, but message nine was from her sister Jess.

"Hey, girl, I hope you get this message before I leave. Larry and I are going on a cruise to the Caribbean. We leave on Sunday. I hope you get this message before then. Love you! I am so excited. Call me back."

"A cruise! Wait, what!" Denise said needing more information. No one had met this man yet and now her sister was going on a cruise with him? She grabbed the phone. As she waited impatiently for Jess to answer, thoughts of every ID investigation show she had ever watched flashed through her mind. "What is she thinking? No one has vetted this man for her to be—"

"Hello?" Jess answered.

"What's this about you going on a cruise?" Denise asked in big sister tone.

"Yes," Jess replied with excitement. "Can you believe it? Jamaica, the Caymans and Cozumel. The cruise sails out of Galveston so we are going to go to and hang out in Kemah, spend some time at the boardwalk and then we leave for the cruise on Sunday for seven days."

"Jess, I'm happy you're excited but I'm a little concerned about you going off on a cruise with a man you hardly know."

"You mean someone *you* hardly know," Jess clapped back. "I know him, Denise. I've been dating him for several months now. He's a good guy."

"Several months is hardly ample time to *really* know someone, Jessica. Why can't you guys go somewhere close, like San Antonio to the Riverwalk? They have a boat ride."

"Really, Denise? Sis, you know how long I've been waiting to find someone. The perfect someone. I've been very careful and selective. You more than anyone should know how careful I am with men. Do you honestly think I would be taking this trip if I didn't feel one hundred percent sure I could trust him? He's a good, no, great guy. So great that he understands and respects my celibacy and got us separate cabins. He was willing to do that to make me comfortable on this trip. That says a lot about him and his character, don't you think?"

"I mean, I guess," Denise said with hesitation.

"Denise, he's the one. I can feel it. I am sure of it. He's a wonderful man, and when we get back I promise I will introduce him to you. We'll do dinner, okay?"

"You sound really happy and I'm happy for you, sis. I just want you to be careful. You know some guys pretend to be all sweet and innocent and in a split second they become Scott Peterson."

Jessica laughed. "I can assure you he's no Scott Peterson. That's funny, in a morbid kind of way. Denise, I'll be careful. I promise. I have to go, but if it makes you more comfortable I'll call and check in to let you know I'm okay. Deal?"

"You better call, every day. Morning noon and night or I will have every news outlet and the military and the triple-X version of Vin Diesel out looking for you."

"Stop!" Jess responded as they both burst into laughter. "I gotta go, but thank you for your blessing, sis. We'll be back on Sunday, okay?"

"Okay. I love you too, Jess. Have fun and just be safe, okay?"

"I will. Love you. Bye."

After they hung up Denise suddenly became very emotional. She was happy for her sister but her sister's happiness was another reminder of how alone she was without Gerald. "Maybe one day Gerald and I will have our cruise," she said with a deep sigh, no longer relaxed enough to enjoy her bubble bath.

§

Arriving promptly for her date, Denise spotted Richard standing outside the restaurant doors.

"Hi, how are you?" she asked somewhat nervously as he gave her a hug. "It's freezing out here. Why are you standing outside?"

"Waiting for you. I didn't know if you remembered what I looked like so I wanted to be sure some other guy didn't grab your attention."

"Oh okay." She was not amused but impressed by the gesture.

"Let's get you inside," he said opening the door for her. "You look beautiful."

"Thanks," she responded, flattered that he noticed.

As they entered the restaurant the hostess smiled and asked how many.

"Just two," Denise answered, her eyes skimming the restaurant for seating.

They followed the hostess who led them toward a table that couples in love would enjoy. Denise wanted a more public atmosphere and asked to be seated in the middle along the wall. As they walked behind the hostess Denise spotted a very public table that was near the band. It was close enough to enjoy the band, yet far enough to have a conversation without talking over the music.

When they reached the table Richard placed his coat on the back of his chair and sat down. Denise, a bit stunned, stared at him blankly. The fact that she was still standing and he was seated was a bit of a red flag. Without incident or conversation, she shrugged it off realizing not all men actively practiced chivalry. He had stood outside in the cold and opened the door for her after all, so she wasn't going to make a big issue of it but she definitely made a mental note.

"Is this okay?" he asked after noticing she was still standing.

"Yes, it's fine," she said pulling out the chair across from him.

"Are you sure this is table is okay? You seem like you don't like it."

"No, this is fine," she insisted.

"Well, you don't seem happy."

Denise stared at him. Her mind was saying, *Oh no you didn't*, but verbally she reminded him that she picked the table and mustered up a fake smile hoping he wouldn't ask the same irritating question again.

As she began to remove her coat she struggled to get her arm out. Richard glanced at her providing no assistance.

"You got it?" he asked.

"I guess so," she said still struggling as Richard turned his attention back to the band.

Wow, she thought. She stood to better remove her coat and in doing so accidentally bumped into the gentleman sitting nearby.

"Oh I'm so sorry," she apologized.

"It's okay," the man replied asking asked if she needed help. Before she could even answer he stood up, helped her remove her arm from the coat and placed it on the back of her chair.

"Good looking out," she heard Richard comment.

"No problem man," the gentlemen responded winking at Denise. But not in a flirtatious way, more of an I-got-you kind of way. A way she was expecting from Richard but he for some reason was clueless and unbothered by the fact that another man had just helped his date with her coat.

Embarrassed, Denise turned to the gentleman, smiled sweetly and said thank you before sitting down.

"You okay?" Richard asked.

Denise, now irritated, responded with a simple "I'm fine." She took a deep breath as a waitress approached.

"You want something, hun?" the waitress asked handing Richard a beer.

"When did you order your drink?" Denise asked.

"While you were taking off your coat. I didn't know what you wanted."

"Really," Denise said, more irritated than before. Turning her attention back to the waitress in an effort to keep from going all-out-Sabrina on him, she answered, "Yes, can I get a Cosmo, please?"

"Sure! I'll be right back."

The band played and Denise, now annoyed and ready to leave, tried to change the mood and make the best of the situation. He was already on his third strike with the chair, the coat and the drink.

"They sound good," she commented trying to break the ice.

"They aight," he responded. That's it. Just two words. *They aight*. Denise was in shock.

The waitress returned with her drink and asked her if she wanted to start a tab. Looking at Richard she asked, "Did you start one already?"

What she expected him to say was, *Sure, just put it on my tab*, instead he looked at her and said, "Actually I paid cash for mine. I don't like doing tabs."

Her mouth literally dropped.

"Oh I thought since this was our first date we were going Dutch," he said seeming to think his behavior was normal.

"Oh," she said but really wanting to use some expletives.

"Is that okay?" he asked. "I mean, I just thought—"

"Sure," she interrupted flashing him a fake smile. "No problem," she said handing the waitress cash.

"You need change, hun?" the waitress asked, who now wore a facial expression that read *Dis Negro right here*.

"No, I'm good," Denise responded still fake smiling.

After a couple more songs the band took a break. Up to this point the two had not a real conversation so Denise again tried to take the initiative.

"So do you like the band?" she asked.

"They aight," he said again. "Have you been to this spot before?" he asked, finally saying more than two words.

"Yes. My girls and I come here every now and then."

"Oh," he responded sarcastically.

"Why you say it like that?" she asked noticing.

"I don't know. It seems a little boujee, but it's aight."

And that was the nail in the coffin. If Denise hated anything in the world, it was for someone to call or imply that she was boujee.

"Why is it boujee?" she asked, ready to read him.

"You know, prices too high for the drinks and food, people walking around all stuck up like they better than everybody else."

"Oh I see," she said nodding her head as if to agree, but far from it. "So, because people dress nice, act like they have some home training and have a little money they are boujee."

"Well, some people act like just because they have a few extra dollars in their pockets they better than the next brother."

"I would agree there are some people that might act a little too proud when they have a little extra but in general that's not the case. You're making an assumption. People have what they have, live the way they live and buy what they want to buy just like you do. Why do they have to be boujee because you don't have it to spend?" Denise asked.

Richard was silent.

"I'm sorry I didn't hear you," she said knowing full well he'd not said anything.

"Oh I gotz mine, believe that," he finally spoke. "I'm just saying I don't forget who I am just because I have a little change in my pocket."

"Well who says the people you refer to as boujee have forgotten who they are? Black people have evolved beyond the days of *Good Times*. Our community uses the word boujee as a derogatory phrase to describe blacks with money because they don't have money. Why just because a black person prefers to speak a little better, dress a little better or live a little better gotta be boujee? Why just because a black person prefers to go to a concert, play or opera on the weekend instead of the corner tree to play dominoes and drink forties gotta be boujee? Why because a black person prefers to travel the world instead of going on a trail ride as an adventure gotta be boujee?" Denise asked ending her dissertation and quite possibly the date.

"Damn," he said. "Well I guess you told me."

"How old are you?" she asked.

"Forty-two, look a-hear," he said without taking a breath in full ghetto mode. "You got a man or what, baby?" he asked as if the last thirty minutes never happened.

"Yes I do actually and why I am wasting my time on this right here I have no idea. What happened to the guy I met on yesterday?"

"I am that guy, baby."

"Umm no, not the same guy," she responded moving in the opposite direction of his lean.

"Look, boo, I know what you're looking for. The same thing all women look for. You are looking for a real man, and that's me, baby. You would be a fool not to acknowledge what we could have together. You sitting there all pretty. We would have some pretty offspring," he said placing his hand on top of hers.

Denise quickly removed her hand from his grasp and stood.

"Look, you have the wrong female. I am not sure what type of females you're used to, but I am not the one. This will be our first and last date." She stood to grab her coat.

"Wait, baby, don't leave," he made one last plea.

"No, I'm good. Have a good night," she said walking away.

NINE

The next day she woke up eager to feel God's presence after being in the presence of one of the devil's offspring the previous night.

Sunday service was business as usual. The preacher preached and shouted and sang his message as Sundays before. Reminding the congregation that Jesus died on the cross and rose on the third day, saving us all from our sins. Every Baptist minister she had ever heard ended their sermon with "Jesus died on the cross and rose on the third day." No matter what the topic. They could start out the sermon discussing backbiting and envy but at the end of the sermon they would all make sure we knew Jesus died and rose on the third day. She had heard it so often she figured it must be some type of code they learned in Seminary. "Make sure you end your sermon with 'Jesus died and rose on the third day.'"

"Amen," she said, joining the rest of the congregation.

"So tell me about last night." Sabrina prodded, nudging her side.

"Shh, we're in the Lord's house! We can talk about this later."

"I just want to know... Did he *Make it Last Forever?*" she asked, singing the old Keith Sweat tune.

"Shh!" Other members turned to scold them for talking.

"Shh," Sabrina responded. "So tell me, what happened," she continued in spite of their looks.

"I'm not talking to you anymore until church is over."

"What! He hit it didn't he. Aww, suki, suki now."

"No, he did not hit it, Sabrina! Now be quiet."

The service ended and the girls made their way out of the sanctuary.

"So fess up! How did it go?"

"Nothing like what you're thinking. I'll tell you all about it at the restaurant."

"Tell me now, D!" Sabrina demanded.

"No, Sabrina. Where do you want to have lunch, Boudreaux's?"

"That's fine. Okay, just tell me if he hit it."

"Bye, Sabrina," Denise responded, waving her off.

As planned, they met at Boudreaux's Sports Bar and Grill. The Cowboys game was scheduled for kick-off in thirty minutes so the place was pretty packed. After a twenty-minute wait they were seated at a table near the entrance. Sabrina insisted on the location because the table was the only elevated table in the bar. Perfect for anyone wanting to be noticed, which made it the perfect spot for Sabrina.

"Okay, so tell me what happened."

"To make a long story short, it was a complete waste of my time. Very entertaining but a complete waste of my time."

"Denise! You probably didn't even give the poor boy a chance."

"Oh, trust me. I gave him a chance but he blew it right from the start. The minute we walked into the Elephant Room he became a totally different person. G-h-e-t-t-o as hell! He started calling me Boo and telling me we were meant for each other, blah, blah, blah. He paid for his drink and told the waitress I was paying for my own. Proceeded to tell me we were going Dutch."

"No he did not!" Sabrina responded.

"Yes he did. Told me we were meant to be and that he could basically do what he wanted to do and I could do what I wanted to do as long as we backed each other up. I was like, what the hell?"

Sabrina was rolling in her seat with laughter. "Woo, girl, you are going to make me choke. Oh my God. I wish I could have been there. Sounds like ole boy was a trip."

"Ole boy was a fool. That's what he was. And he was serious! Then he asked me if my current boyfriend was hitting it right."

"Ah, hell to the naw!"

"Yes! He was seriously out of his mind. He told me I would be a fool not to acknowledge what we could have together."

"So that went on the whole night?"

"Uh, hell NO! I got out of there when he started talking about how pretty our offspring would be!" Sabrina could barely contain herself.

"Well, Denise, don't let that one experience keep you from going out and having a good time. At least it was comical if nothing else. And anything is better than you sitting at home all night watching that damn movie for the hundredth time."

"You're right and as bad as it was, and trust me it was bad, I had at first said that was it, I tried it and it didn't work. I was determined to end my little experiment right then and there. But I did enjoy being out of the house. So it wasn't all bad and I decided I would give it another shot. Besides, if all the men I pick up end up being like brother man from the fifth floor, Gerald won't have anything to worry about." They both laughed at the image. "I don't think I'll have to worry about compromising my relationship with Gerald in the least bit."

"Child, Gerald better hope you don't pop up on Mr. Right, or he *will* be scared."

"Gerald is Mr. Right, Sabrina," she responded annoyed.

§

Denise spent the next few weeks going from one meal to the next with one guy to the next. She was surprised at the amount of men who were trying to pick her up once she made herself open to the idea. Ever since she made the decision, men were coming from all directions.

Jess told her it was the work of the devil. He was working to get her to commit sin. She said Denise was committed to Gerald and only Gerald, but when she opened the door to let other men in, the Devil came in too.

Sabrina told her men were approaching her because they could tell when a woman was in heat. She said they have the ability to smell it in the air.

Denise partially agreed with Jess. She had been so committed to Gerald that she'd ignored the flirtations of other men. Whenever she did notice a guy checking her out, she would look away or walk in a different direction to avoid the situation all together. But now, she was scheduling dinner plans and booking appointments on the regular. She was even brave enough to ask them out. Men were approaching her everywhere she went and she was driving from one side of town to the next. Sabrina would often belt out Ludacris's *Area Codes*, when they went out for drinks and had begun addressing her as Jezebel. Denise stood assured that even with all the activities, she was still very much in love with Gerald and that nothing would ever come out of her rendezvous.

She had established rules and guidelines for dating to prevent herself from being tempted in an effort to maintain her commitment to Gerald. Rule number one: one date and one date only. Rule number two: no kissing. Rule number three:

no holding hands. And rule number four: no going back to anyone's place. She would only agree to meet them in public places and no one was to ever, ever, ever come home with her. So far the rules were in place and things were going well.

After her disaster of a date with Richard, she accepted a dinner invitation from fifty-two-year-old Rodney Stanford, a retired railroad technician. They met in the produce section of H-E-B in Bastrop. Rodney was an associate minister of a local church in the area. Recently widowed, he spent most of his time working and raising his teenage daughter. They had recently returned to the area from Florida. After their initial meeting Denise ran into him on several other occasions and finally mustered the courage to ask him out on a date. He happily accepted.

They agreed to meet at Carrabba's Italian Grill, her favorite restaurant. They arrived at the restaurant about the same time and he walked over to her car and opened the car door for her. As they walked toward the entrance of the restaurant he commented on how nice she looked and politely opened the door. She was impressed from the start. As the hostess guided them to their table Mr. Stanford allowed her to walk ahead of him and, like a gentleman, when they arrived he pulled her chair out and waited until she was seated comfortably before taking his seat.

They were seated at a table near the back of the restaurant, which revealed an extraordinary view of Town Lake. Denise peered out of the window to see tour boats moving to and fro on the calm water. Bundled passengers were laughing and having dinner as they enjoyed the view of Christmas lights strung along the trees at the back of the beautiful homes overlooking the lake. Shortly after being seated the waitress arrived and handed them two menus as she explained the daily drink and meal specials. Denise ordered water out of respect for the minister, who had explained to her that he no longer partook of alcoholic beverages.

They had pleasant conversation over appetizers, discussing the usual topics of weather, work, family and common interests. Although Mr. Stanford worked in Austin, he didn't know much about the city itself so Denise gave him a quick overview of what the capital of Texas had to offer. After explaining the history behind the infamous Austin bats located under the Town Lake Bridge, their meal arrived. Denise couldn't help but notice how polite Mr. Stanford was in comparison to brother man from the fifth floor. He seemed genuinely interested in hearing everything she had to say. She was enjoying her time with him.

He told her that he'd been married three times and had three children from his second marriage. His third wife was killed in a car accident, leaving him to raise his very young stepdaughter as a single father. The child's biological father was never involved in her life and he had been the only father she'd known. He had made a vow to his wife that he would assume sole responsibility for his stepdaughter if anything ever happened to her. As far as he was concerned, she was his daughter in every way that mattered and he would always be there for her.

Denise admired him for taking on that responsibility. Most black men found it difficult to care for their own children let alone someone else's child. It was commendable. However, she was a little alarmed by the fact that he had been married three times.

He explained that he and his first wife had married out of high school and neither were ready for the commitment; the marriage ended after six months. His second wife was a marriage of obligation that lasted six years and three kids. She had become pregnant early in their relationship and he tried to do the right thing by asking for her hand in marriage. He was new to his ministry and felt it was something he had to do. In the end they both realized it was wrong to stay together for the sake of the kids when the love was not there, and they divorced after ten years. It was his last wife who was the love of his life. From the moment he met her he knew that she was the one. She was the one Whitney Houston sang about in her rendition of *I Believe in You and Me*, he explained. And he loved her more than he loved his own life. Tragically she was taken from him after six years of marriage.

After they had eaten their salads, he began to share pictures of his kids while waiting on the main course. Mr. Stanford had many pictures of his daughter in his wallet. Her name was Michelle; she had been named after her great-great grandmother. Denise proudly showed off her four-legged son, Creasy. While looking through the pictures of Michelle, Denise being a woman, couldn't help but notice how severely damaged her hair appeared in each photo. She politely asked him what beautician he had been taking her to for hair care services.

"I watched my wife on many occasions perm her hair before she passed and I have been taking care of it ever since. I don't like a lot of people handling her so I prefer to do it myself."

"Hmm, and how is that going?" Denise asked.

"Oh it's going good. I usually try to perm it every two months. Her hair used to be long and thick but I let someone do it one time and they broke it all off. Now I just do it myself; that way I know that it's taken care of."

"Oh," she said. "A hair dresser caused the damage."

"No, someone I was dating once."

"You've never considered taking her to a professional hair dresser?"

"No. I would just rather just do it myself. That way if it breaks off it will be because I broke it off and not somebody else."

"Hmm," she said again and then to herself, *Mental note: we got a stubborn one.*

Changing the subject Denise began to ask about his ministry. She was interested in understanding what led him in that direction because she believed Gerald was destined to follow the same path. From their last conversation she got the impression that he was beginning to realize the same for himself.

Denise explained to Mr. Stanford that she was actively involved in various aspects of her church and that her main area of focus was the youth department. She told him about the new boys' ministry program she'd developed at her church and shared with him how exciting it was to see young men interested in knowing what God expected of them as men in Christ.

"Is this an all women's church?" he asked. "I mean do you have a woman in the pulpit?"

"No, why do you ask?"

"Well," he said, in a disapproving tone. "Why aren't the men teaching the boys' ministry?"

"It was something God placed on my heart to begin. I found a book to use as a guide, discussed it with my pastor and began teaching the lessons. Yes, there are men in the church capable of teaching the classes and they participate on some of the topics, especially the topics pertaining to their bodies. I just thought it would be a good idea to add the ministry to our church program because there are so many young men getting in trouble because they don't live Godly prosperous lives. If we instill a foundation in them while they're young, about what God expects of them, then it's my hope they'll take it with them when they become responsible for themselves."

"Well, I think the idea sounds good and all. I just think boys should be taught by men in the church and girls should be taught by the women. A woman can't teach a boy how to be a man. Only a man can do that. It's also out of order with

God's word. And I wouldn't allow my son to be taught by a woman. I wouldn't care if she was my wife or not."

Denise sat back in her seat, surprised by his chauvinistic comment.

The atmosphere had become unpleasant and uncomfortable. She looked out the window. Even the Christmas lights shining from the yards overlooking the lake seemed dim to her now. This man had just taken something that she was excited about and basically told her she going against God. How could she be going against God if she was helping bring the children closer to God? *This is what he asks of us. To live our lives in a way that encourages others to seek him.* The more she thought about what he'd said, the more furious she became. Neither of them spoke.

Their pleasant and enjoyable conversation was gone in an instant. Now she was being judged by someone who had been married three times.

Didn't the Bible say till death do us part? Where were his morals when he divorced his first and second wife?

"May I ask you a question?" she asked.

"Sure. You can ask anything you want."

"Were both of your parents involved in raising you?"

"Yes, my mother and my father."

"So would you say your mother played a role in helping you become the person you are today?"

"Sure she taught me some things and some hard life lessons, but when it comes down to being a man, a woman can't teach that. Look, I just feel like as a woman in the church you should be teaching the girls how to dress pretty and wear makeup. Women teaching a man how to be a man goes against Scripture."

"Oh, I see. So based on what you're saying God had no intentions of having a woman teaching or providing any guidance or instruction to a man."

"Not according to Scripture," he responded. "Women are supposed to teach girls, and men are supposed to teach men."

"So tell me this. Why is it when men grow up and mature, most of them thank their mother, or grandmother for that matter, for helping them become the person they are. My mother raised my brother as a single mother with two other children and he is a great guy. Any woman would be lucky to have him as a husband because of the values that our mother and grandmother instilled in him."

"I don't doubt that," he said clearing his throat. "Like I said, women have their place, but I have to live my life according to Scripture and the Bible says women are to teach the girls. I won't go against what the word tells me even if other people don't like it."

"But how do you know your interpretation of the Bible is the right interpretation? Because nowhere in the Bible does it say a woman can't teach a boy. If that's the case we shouldn't have women teaching Sunday school because according to you we're going against the word."

"No what I said was women have their place."

The waitress returned with the main course and Denise asked her to bring the check.

"I'm sorry ma'am. We tried to get it out as quick as we could. As you can see we are really swamped tonight."

"Oh, it's not a problem. You are fine, sweetie," Denise assured her. "I would just like the check and a to-go box." Puzzled the waitress turned to leave.

The two sat quietly while Denise anxiously waited for the waitress to return. Mr. Stanford attempted to make small talk and Denise pretended to be interested in what he had to say, all the while fuming. The waitress returned and Denise quickly handed her cash and a tip. She explained to Mr. Stanford that suddenly she wasn't feeling so well and needed to leave.

"Oh, let me walk you out," he offered.

"Not a problem. See my mother taught me how to walk by standing in front of me and holding her hands out. According to you, that is her only purpose in life and she taught me well. So I tell you what I'm going to do. I'm going to take the knowledge that my mother rightfully gave me and walk right out that door," she said pointing to the entrance. With that she took another sip of water, and then she got in one last jab before her exit. "And if you keep doing your daughter's hair she's going to be bald in a year."

TEN

Cautious about continuing her quest to remove all loneliness, Denise reluctantly ventured out on yet another date.

His name was Albert Washington. Albert was an employee at Austin's International Airport where he transported passengers to and from airport terminals and parking lots.

He was *high yellow*, as they used to say referring to his light skin color, and he had the most beautiful head of hair she had ever seen. Jet black, silky, long and wavy, reminding her of a young El DeBarge back in his heyday. And although she would never admit it, there had been an instant attraction.

§

With a bad day at work behind her she popped Betty Wright's greatest hits CD into the car stereo and headed for home with plans of curling up with a good book and a glass of wine.

While waiting at a light near the airport she sang background vocals on Betty Wright's *After the Pain*. It was her favorite Betty Wright track. She used to say it was her anthem, her theme song, so to speak. Before Gerald, her heart had been broken by so many men that she and Betty often had empowerment sessions over wine and bubble bath. She often listened to Betty just to survive the time apart from Gerald.

The car windows were down and the music blared loudly into the earth's atmosphere as she belted out each verse of the song. "After all I been through, I should be through with love but there's a God up above," she sang at the top of her lungs. A metallic blue Jaguar caught her eye and she paused for a moment to follow its movement as it crossed the intersection.

"Ooh... nice," she commented while appreciating the lovely vision crossing her path.

She continued to follow the vehicle as it turned the corner and she suddenly noticed the gentleman in the next lane was smiling at her.

"Nice voice," he said.

"Sorry, was I too loud?"

"No you sounded great. It was cute."

"Thanks," she said, too embarrassed to say anything more or sing another verse. Turning to face the light, she prayed that it would soon turn green before he had an opportunity to continue the conversation.

The light was still red and out of the corner of her eye could see him. He was still there. Still smiling at her. She could see the glare of the sun bouncing off three gold teeth in the front of his mouth, or "the grill" as the young people called it today.

Catching the color change, she hit the gas and took off down the road to catch the next light before it turned red. Halfway down the block the color changed to red before she could gather up enough speed. "Damn timing system," she said, hoping the gold tooth man had turned somewhere in between.

Determined not to turn and look his way, she could feel her neck stiffening as she gripped the steering wheel. Her hands twisted along the steering wheel as if she was in the middle of a Nascar race and the checkered flag was about to drop any minute. Unfortunately there was no checkered flag waving to start a race. Instead, she could see the airport van he was driving creeping slowly beside her through the rearview mirror.

"I just wanted to let you know that I think you are absolutely gorgeous!" he yelled across to her.

"Thank you for the compliment," she responded, mad at herself for not rolling up the window.

Before he could say more the light turned green and Denise pressed on the gas with no hesitation. She had made up her mind that she was going to run the next light. She didn't care if it turned red or not. As she raced down the road, halfway down the next block, the traffic light changed from green to yellow.

"I can make it," she told herself pressing harder on the gas.

Her speed increased rapidly as she neared the intersection. The light was still yellow and she was going for it.

"Don't stop," she said speaking to the car in front of her as if the driver could hear her command. "I'm gonna make it," she sang to herself.

Seconds away from victory she saw him. Mr. Police Officer. He was perched on his motorcycle across the intersection behind a parked vehicle.

"Damn it!" she yelled, slamming her brakes just as the light turned yellow. The sounds of her tires screeching filled the air as everything that was loose in her car flew forward.

After reaching over to pick up items thrown from her purse, she peered out the window to see if the officer was coming to give her a ticket. She was sure he knew she was going to run the light and would give her a ticket based on intent. But he hadn't moved. He just sat there, staring at her, daring her to make the wrong move. She could see the look of anger and disappointment on his face. He was disappointed that he was not going to be able to make his quota for the day. Not on her dime anyway.

"You ain't getting your ticket quota on me, Mr. Police Officer," she sang out loud, teasing the officer and staring at him as if they were in a bull fight.

Suddenly she was startled by a dull honk from the car in the next lane. Grabbing her chest she turned to find yet again, the gold tooth man.

"Damn," she said to herself. He was still smiling and there was still that darn glare from the sun. It seemed to be following him around. She swore she saw a sparkle come out of his gold teeth. Like the ones seen on toothpaste advertising commercials. Or, God forbid, a diamond inlaid in the gold.

"Can I call you sometime?" he asked.

"I don't think so," she responded politely.

"Please! I like what I see and I just want to talk to you a little bit. It's hard to talk with all the lights."

"Yeah, darn things keep turning green, huh," she said sarcastically.

"I'll make you a deal. You give me your number. We can have one conversation and if you are still not interested, we'll leave it at that. Deal?"

"Will you stop following me if I say yes?"

The man laughed. "Yes, I promise."

After taking a deep breath she decided to give him her number. He thanked her profusely and made his exit toward the airport. After glancing over at the officer still perched on his bike she turned the sound up on her stereo and enjoyed the rest of her ride home with Betty.

ELEVEN

After finishing her glass of wine, Denise completed a final check of the perimeter before heading to bed. As her head hit the pillow, she realized she was going to have a tough time falling asleep. Even with the glass of wine, her mind was racing in a million directions and usually when that happened it meant a night of tossing and turning.

Rolling over on her back she stared at the ceiling. Every now and again car lights would run across and down the wall, and she began to think about Gerald. She wondered what he was doing, wondered if he was safe and if he was missing her.

Turning on her side, she continued to watch the car lights pass, unable to close her eyes and unable to take her mind off of her sweetheart. She was wide awake. Glancing over at the clock she reached out to see what time it was.

"Twelve thirty. Ugh," she moaned in frustration. She knew if she didn't get to sleep soon she was going to have a hard time getting out of bed. Rolling over she turned the TV on and reduced the volume and stared blankly at the images on the screen.

A few moments later, the phone rang and Denise sat up quickly at the sound. She rubbed her eyes for a second to focus and locate the receiver. Not remembering when she'd even dozed off she glanced over at the clock to see that it was twelve forty-five in the morning. The last thing she remembered was counting car lights. She was at sixty. Still a little dazed from sleep she laid back down after the last ring.

"They'll call back in the morning," she said to herself as she fell back asleep.

Five minutes went by before she heard the ring again. This time her eyes opened immediately.

"Gerald," she said reaching for the phone. Because of the hour and the quick call back she was sure it was him. Maybe calling to let her know he was out. Who else would call in the middle of the night?

She reached over and grabbed the phone. "Hello?"

"Hello, Denise?" a voice spoke and it was clearly not Gerald's.

"Yes. This is Denise." She was scowling.

"Hi, this is Albert."

"Albert?"

"Yes Albert, Albert Washington, from the other day."

Denise couldn't believe it. It was nearly one a.m. What was he doing calling her at one in the morning?

"I apologize for calling so late. I wanted to call you earlier but I misplaced your phone number and I've been searching for it for the last couple of hours. I finally found it and I wanted to call. I didn't want you to think I was a flake by not calling. Are you up? Did I wake you?"

"Yes, you did. It's too late to be calling." She was totally annoyed.

"I know. Again, I apologize, but I wanted to be able to tell you good night and let you know how happy I was that we met when we did."

She had to admit that what he said was pretty sweet, calling her to tell her good night. She just wished he had called a lot earlier, when most of the world was still awake!

"That's very sweet of you, and I don't mean to be rude but can we talk tomorrow? Preferably before ten p.m.?"

He apologized again and told her he'd be looking forward to it.

The next day he called at the decent hour of eight p.m. and surprisingly they talked for five enjoyable hours. Denise found him easy to talk to and even though he was ten years younger than she was, he seemed very mature for his age. He was really articulate and well spoken. He could hold a decent conversation, which was uncommon with most guys his age. If the conversation wasn't about hip-hop or sports, most twenty-something males were unable to carry on a conversation with a thirty-something female.

Albert told her that he was a child of the foster care system for most of his life and he never knew his mom or dad. Currently he was living with friends and had moved from Houston to Austin in an attempt to get on his own two feet.

They spent quite a bit of time discussing their religious beliefs and at one point during the conversation he started praying. He prayed for her and thanked God for bringing her into his life. Denise was very impressed.

He asked if he could spend more time with her and, feeling good about their conversation, she agreed. Plans were made for the two to meet at Dave and Buster's around seven the next day.

After discussing a few more topics ranging from music to politics, the gold tooth man caught on that Denise was getting tired. She'd been yawning for the last hour.

"Well, I guess I better let you get some sleep," he finally said. "I know you have to go to work tomorrow."

"Don't you?" she asked.

"I, uh... I'm off tomorrow."

"Oh," Denise responded. "Well then I guess I'll see you tomorrow at D and B's, at seven, right?" she asked, trying to push him closer toward the end of the phone call. She was trying to avoid another topic of conversation.

"Uh... Denise?"

"Yes?"

"Can you pick me up at my place tomorrow?"

Whoop, there it was! She knew it was too good to be true.

"What happened to your car?" she asked. There was irritation in her voice.

"I don't have one."

"But I saw you driving a—"

"The company van, remember?" he said before she could finish.

Denise suddenly remembered the big blue van that followed her for several blocks when she first met Mr. Twenty-something.

Taking the phone receiver she banged it on her head a few times. What had she got herself into? She had always had a problem with women who actively drove grown men around. She was not a taxi driver and could never understand why a grown mature man would ask a woman to pick him up here and take him there, especially if he was trying to court her.

"So can you pick me up around seven?" the gold tooth man asked again.

Denise took a deep breath and reluctantly agreed to pick him up at his apartment. She decided since it would only be the one date she would compromise. That, plus the fact that they'd just had a pretty good conversation. It earned him some cool points. Besides that, she figured he was young and trying to get on his feet, so maybe she should cut him a break.

The next evening she picked him up at his apartment and he introduced her to some of his twenty-something roommates before they headed to a backyard barbeque at another one of his twenty-something friend's home.

For the most part she enjoyed herself. There were females there and women could always have a conversation about shopping, music and men, things women talk about even if they're ten years younger.

The gold tooth man hung outside with his twenty-something male homeboys where Denise could only assume they were discussing sports, cars and the latest screwed up jam by Swishahouse.

After the barbeque they headed to Dave and Buster's for a few drinks and more conversation. Denise agreed to shoot a few games of pool with him and he agreed to play *House of Dead* with her. She was no professional at pool, but if that ball was right in front of the hole, she could do some serious damage. But she was a pro at *House of Dead*. Once she spent twenty bucks and managed to beat the game with the help of some nearby kids.

Enjoying her time with the gold tooth man they finished their last game of pool. The best two out of three where she won by default. Throughout the evening he had showered her with attention, hanging on to her every word, pulling chairs out for her, opening doors, holding her hand as they walked through the building. They disagreed on many things because of their difference in age no doubt, but he respected her opinion on every subject.

After complete annihilation of the ghostly beings in *House of Dead* they decided to make their exit to rejoin several of the partygoers from the barbeque at an underground casino on the city's northeast side.

As they walked through the crowded room full of adult gamers, Albert grabbed her hand and led her through the crowd. He touched her in an almost protective way, making sure she wasn't pushed or knocked over by other patrons who may have had a little too much to drink.

The warmth from his hands sent a surge of fire throughout her body that she didn't expect. He was twenty-something. Attractive as he was she didn't expect any fires to ignite. This was just going to be a playful date. Something to do; something she would laugh about down the road when she and Gerald were happily married.

But there was something about the way he touched her. Something about the way he spoke to her. Something about the way he stared directly into her eyes when he spoke to her. He, surprisingly, made her feel like she was the only person in the room. And she suddenly realized that she was feeling something for the gold tooth man. Something she had not felt on the previous fiascos. A spark.

TWELVE

Around ten p.m. they walked toward the door of what looked like an abandoned grocery story. It had been painted grey, and bars were attached to each door and window.

"Are you sure this is okay?" she asked him.

He didn't seem to be phased in the least bit. But she was nervous. The north side was not the best area of town to be in, especially after hours. It had been infested with drugs and prostitution over the last few years and several recent murders had occurred in nearby blocks.

"We'll be fine, sweetie," he said, rubbing her shoulders for reassurance as if to say he would protect her.

"I've seen the news reports about places like this. Underground casinos getting raided and people going to jail, including the people caught gambling."

"We won't stay that long, but I've been here many times. Trust me, it's safe."

Denise was holding on to his hand for dear life, trying to figure out how she got herself into this situation. She couldn't blame him. She knew what she was getting into it. He said underground casino. For some reason she had the image of Harrah's in her head: bright lights, lots of buzz and nice cars. What was she thinking? She was in Texas where gambling was illegal. It wasn't until she got to *the hood*, she was hit with reality. She was not in Vegas.

The gold tooth man rung the doorbell located outside the protected door and shortly after an Iranian man peered through the gated window.

"We're closed," he said.

"I just need a pack of gum," the gold tooth man responded. Shortly after that, Denise heard a buzz and the gold tooth man grabbed the door handle and pulled open the door.

What was that? Was that the special access code? *I just need a pack of gum.* Were they at a drive-in grocery?

They entered what appeared to be a small convenience store filled with chips, cigarettes and drinks. But they didn't stop to buy gum as the gold tooth man had indicated at the door. Instead, he led her past the shelves toward a back room.

Once they reached the entryway of the room Denise couldn't believe what she was seeing. There were slot machines, card tables and a roulette wheel. She couldn't believe it. Who would have thought this nice little Iranian store in the middle of the hood contained a replica of Vegas?

"Wassup, boy?" the gold tooth man's friend greeted him. She recognized him from the barbeque.

"Nuttin, man. Just hanging with my girl."

His girl? When did she become his girl?

"Well shit, does she know how to gamble?"

"I don't know. Do you, baby?"

Baby?

"Yes, a little," she responded.

Everyone was walking around like there was no threat of cops bursting in at any minute. Having a good time and drinking with not a care in the world.

The gold tooth man handed her a twenty dollar bill and placed her in front of a slot machine and told her to have a good time. He stood next to her as she placed the bill in the bill acceptor.

Taking a deep breath she somewhat reluctantly pulled the handle.

"Do you want anything to drink?" he asked.

"Yes, a Miller Light please." She definitely needed one as she watched the drums roll up the display.

When the gold tooth man returned he found that Denise was ahead by forty-two dollars.

"Wow, I see you've gotten the hang of it."

"I've gambled before," she said grabbing the neck of the bottle. "Just in safer and more legal establishments."

He laughed out loud as he grabbed a stool and sat next to her.

Denise was ahead by two hundred dollars and all fear and nerves had been erased by the sounds of the machine as she hit it big.

There was a man sitting next to her who had won the jackpot on one of the quarter machines. Denise gave him a jealous eye as he cashed in his winnings. She was determined to keep playing until she was cashing in herself.

After losing fifty dollars she decided it was time to snap back to reality and cash in her winnings. She was starting to get a little uncomfortable each time the door opened, wondering when the cops were going to show up.

"Can we go?" she asked. The gold tooth man was still sitting next to her. "I have to drive you back home and then head to Bastrop and it's getting kind of late."

"Sure. Let me just tell the boys bye and we can head out."

"Okay."

Denise sat on the stool that he had occupied for several hours and then they safely left the building, without handcuffs.

Over the next few weeks Denise continued phone conversations with her young suitor. He called her each evening just to say good night or ask her how her day had gone. So far, the second date rule was still intact. He had asked a couple of times, but she made excuses, telling him she was going out of town or that she already had plans, which was the truth in most cases.

One night he told her that he and his roommates were being evicted from their apartment. The rent was several months past due and although his friends had places to go he had nowhere. He had no family to speak of. He never knew his mom or his dad so he literally had no place to go.

Denise was concerned about him. She wanted to find a place for him to stay and suggested that he speak with her pastor who knew many people in the community. She hoped that maybe he could find a place for him to stay. But he assured her that he would be fine.

"I have always been on my own," he said. "It's nothing for me to stay at the Salvation Army until something better comes along."

"You don't have any friends that you can go live with?"

"Well one, but he says I can't move in until I find a job."

"Find a job! What happened to your job?"

"Oh, I thought I told you. I had a couple of accidents in the van and they had to let me go."

"No. You didn't tell me. What does that have to do with your friend letting you stay there?"

"He says I have to pay rent, but as soon as I find a job I can move in with him. I can just stay at the Salvation Army until then." He asked her to pray for him and wished her a good night.

A few days later he called to let her know that he'd been staying in the Salvation Army for the past few nights and that they had a program he was using to help find a job and a place to stay. Even though he assured her he was safe she couldn't help but be concerned about the young lad. He just couldn't seem to get a break and she wanted to do something to help him.

She recalled a recent bible study in which the topic was helping others. She remembered the passage where several men took their friend to Jesus but it was so crowded they had to lower him in through the roof. They were determined to help their friend no matter what. And the lesson encouraged others to do the same.

After discussing the situation with her pastor, she decided to help her new friend get on his feet. Over the next several weeks she agreed to take him to the workforce center on her way to work to help him search for jobs and learn skills that the volunteer programs offered. He even attended church with her on several occasions and she offered to buy him lunch before dropping him off at the Salvation Army. She didn't consider her time with him as a second date. More like a mission of mercy and she was enjoying his company. In a way she felt young again. He made her feel attractive and, if nothing else, he was keeping her busy.

She continued helping him for several weeks and initially he seemed to appreciate everything she was doing. He would call her, excited about his day and what he had accomplished at the workforce center, and she was happy that she was able to bring joy to the young man's life after having grown up with so many disappointments.

As time went on things began to change. His outlook on his future changed. She started to see that she was doing most of the work and realized she was more excited about helping him than he was about helping himself.

He started canceling interviews or just not showing up and on a couple of occasions he missed lock down at the Salvation Army and was forced to spend the night in the bus station.

Denise's efforts to do her Christian duty were turning into a burden and she was beginning to question whether or not she should continue to help the gold tooth man.

"What's going on, Albert?" she asked one evening when he called to tell her good night.

"What do you mean?"

"I'm trying to help you but I'm starting to feel like I'm being used."

"No. I'm so appreciative for everything you've done."

"Do you still want a job?"

"Yes, but I don't have a way to get around town to attend the interviews. I can no longer afford a bus ticket. That's why I've missed the curfew because I either have to walk to the SA or get someone to take me and I end up getting there too late. I've been trying to hustle and sell some CDs to get some money for a ticket but that's not going well either. I don't want to be a burden to you, Denise. You're a good woman and I'm trying to be a man and take care of this on my own."

"Look, sometimes we can't do it on our own and we need to ask for a little help. I'm going to take you to the bus station tomorrow and I'm going to buy you a bus pass for the month," she said sympathizing with his situation. "You have to be able to get around to find a job and the bus is the only way you can do that. Plus you should not be staying in a bus stop when the Salvation Army is available to you. So that's what we will do."

As promised she picked him up after work and they went down to the nearby H-E-B where she purchased a bus pass. He seemed very appreciative of the gesture and gave her a hug. He promised her that he would pay her back as soon as he got on his feet.

On the ride back to the Salvation Army he asked if he could use her cell phone to check on a couple of friends in Houston.

"Sure," she said still trying to be helpful.

"May I speak to Veronica?" he asked the person on the other end.

Denise was a little surprised, but okay, maybe it was a cousin.

"Hey, girl. It's Al. Albert, girl, what you doing? Oh you know me, doing big thangs, doing big thangs."

Denise looked over at him, shocked to hear the words coming out of his mouth. Doing what big thangs? He couldn't even afford a seventeen-dollar bus pass but he was telling people he was doing big "thangs."

The gold tooth man had laid the passenger seat back and it was nearly lying on top of the back seat. One arm was resting on the open window frame and the other supported her phone attached to his ear.

His hat was turned to the side reminding her of a scene from a rap video and he was leaning back in *her* seat. Talking on *her* phone with a bus pass that *she* paid for, riding around in *her* vehicle on his way to nowhere. Suddenly, she was beginning to see his age and she had to ask herself what in the world was she thinking.

"Well, girl, you know why I can't stop calling you," he continued his conversation. "You know. It's always going to be like that. Alright, I'll talk to you later."

He hung up the phone and asked Denise if he could make one more call. Denise agreed with much hesitation.

"Yo, Ty." Ty was the person he was supposed to move in with once he got a job. "You got that money for me? Man, I really need that money. I have some things I'm trying to do and I need that money. Monday, okay, bet that."

After hanging up the phone he handed it back to Denise, who had a look of confusion on her face. She was confused by what she'd just heard and confused about what type of person she'd invited into her life.

"Isn't Ty the person you were supposed to be moving in with?"

"Yeah."

"Why does he owe you money?"

"He took a couple of CDs a few weeks ago and he's supposed to be getting me the change."

"Oh," Denise responded.

"So what's up, baby? What we listening to hear?" he asked pushing the buttons on the stereo.

"Brian McKnight," she responded. Brian McKnight was her favorite singer. Her husband as she liked to call him. She often listened to his single *Home* because it reminded her of Gerald and she couldn't wait until he came home.

"Brian Mc who?" he asked.

"Brian McKnight."

"You need to get some real music up in here," he said as he pushed the FM button on the stereo and began scanning the channels.

"Beat 105.9 where the beat never stops," piped through the speakers as he turned up the volume.

The next sound Denise heard was the gold tooth man. "Lean wit it, rock wit it, lean wit it, rock wit it…"

She glanced over to see his arms stretched out in front of him as he bounced his shoulders up and down to the beat of the music. He was bobbing as if he were in a Dre and Snoop Dogg video.

"Do you think we could turn it down a little bit?" Denise asked shouting over the music.

"Oh… yeah! I'm sorry, baby," he said adhering to her wishes.

They pulled into a parking spot located right in front of the Salvation Army and Denise placed the car in park.

"Well, I guess this is it. You're all taken care of," she said. She unlocked the car doors as a clue that he needed to make his exit but instead Albert reached over and turned the ignition key.

"What are you doing?" she asked grabbing his hand.

"I just want to turn the car off for a minute and talk to you." Albert took a deep breath. "Denise, I have to tell you the truth about something."

Oh Lord, she thought, bracing herself for what was to come next.

"You know I like to date older women. I've told you this, right?"

"Yes, you did, Albert."

"Well, I can't believe I'm going to tell you this. But you're just so nice I don't think I should continue lying to you about it. Something about you just makes me want to tell you the truth."

"What's the truth, Albert?"

"God! Okay, um… I can't believe I'm going to do this. Okay, well you know how I told you my age right?"

"Yes, you're twenty-six."

"No, I'm not twenty-six."

"How old are you?"

"I'm… The truth is… I'm twenty-two."

"What?" Denise screamed, wanting to jump out of the car and run into traffic.

"Yeah, I'm twenty-two."

"You have got to be kidding me!"

"No, I'm not kidding you. I tell women I'm older because they won't give me the time of day if I tell them the truth."

"But regardless of what you think or how you feel, a woman has the right to make the decision as to whether or not she wants to date someone, and in my case, someone fourteen years younger."

"I know but I'm mature for my age. You've even said that and most people say I act like I'm thirty."

"But you're not thirty," she said angrily. "You're twenty-two."

Holding her head Denise suddenly flashed back to the image of him "leanin and rockin wit it."

"Does this change anything?" he asked.

"I would say this changes everything."

"Why? It doesn't have to change anything. I'm still the same Albert you fell in love with."

"Fell in love with? Who...? Albert, just go please. They are about to lock the doors and I wouldn't want you to miss out on a bed."

"Denise."

"Please just go."

"Okay, I'll call you later."

Denise didn't respond. He closed the door and she pulled off as quickly as she could and that was the last time she spoke to the gold tooth man.

THIRTEEN

"Hello?" Denise answered the phone praying it wasn't Albert.

"Hey, girl, where you been?" Denise sighed at the sound of Sabrina's voice.

"Oh, here and there."

"So, how's the dating thing going?" Sabrina asked.

"It's not. I feel sorry for the single women of the world. There's not much to choose from out there. The available guys either don't want to work, have no goals and expect women to take care of them, or pretend they're the type of person you want to be with until their true colors begin to shine and you figure out they're just sheep in wolf's clothing, you know? The kind that play the 'good Christian guy' role on one hand while they sip wine out of their closet with the other."

"Denise, you can't blame all men for a few bad dates. Besides, look where you're meeting them, on the street, at the grocery store. If you want a good man stop picking up scrubs."

"I have a good man, Sabrina. Gerald is a good man. And you are the last person to criticize where I pick up men, sister girl. You met your last one where? I believe at the dumpster."

They both laughed.

"This was a mistake. I don't know what I was thinking. I wanted to meet one nice guy. Just one! Someone who I could hang out with, no strings and no sex attached. Someone to occupy the time until Gerald gets home."

"Ahh, chickadee, don't just give up. Be more selective in your choices."

"I have one more date tonight and if doesn't turn out well, that's it, I'm done."

"Where did you meet this guy?"

"He works for the station. We work together on different projects occasionally. Last week he asked me if I wanted to go to a Spurs game with him and I agreed."

"That's great, Denise. Go to the game. Have a good time."

"My expectations are low but if he gets on my nerves, I'll just focus my attention on Tony Parker to pass the time."

FOURTEEN

In her last and final attempt to meet a suitable man for friendly company, Denise headed out for her date with Paul Baker.

This time, she made no effort to dress up for the occasion. There was no purchase of fancy shoes and she didn't run down to the mall to find a sexy dress. They weren't going to a fancy restaurant or having a romantic evening out and she didn't feel the need to impress him or anyone else.

Paul and Denise were going to a basketball game courtesy of the station. Employees would often give away group seats to the ninth or tenth caller and many times the winner failed to pick up their winnings so they were offered to employees on a first-come first-serve basis. Paul scooped up the tickets and during a business lunch invited Denise to join him.

She was dressed in a freshly cleaned pair of Baby Phat jeans, casual V-neck cotton shirt and Spurs hat. Her hair flowed down to her shoulders as she rushed out the door with her on-the-go Mary Kay look to head to San Antonio for the game.

When she arrived at the AT&T Center, Paul greeted her as planned outside their seat section. She was impressed with his promptness, but then again, it was a basketball game and he was a man.

"They're always on time for something that's important to them," she said to herself.

Denise had explained to Paul that she preferred taking different cars. The excuse she gave was that she would probably be running late and didn't want to hold him up. Truth be told, she needed a getaway car in case things went south.

Paul greeted her with a friendly hug as the crowd piled past them into the auditorium. He was dressed from head to toe as a diehard Spurs fan. Tim

Duncan Jersey, black jeans to match. A Spurs hat, similar to hers, and the typical noisemakers to cheer his team on filled his hands and armpits.

Pitiful, she thought to herself.

"So, Denise, ready for a good game?"

"Yes I am. Who are they playing again?"

"The Pistons."

"Ahh... right, the Pistons. They're my favorite team, you know."

"What! You're from Texas and your favorite team is the Pistons?"

"Yep, I'm from the old school. I was a big fan of Bill Laimbeer, Dennis Rodman, Isiah Thomas—"

"The Bad Boys, eh?"

"I beg your pardon! Isiah Thomas was not a bad boy! He was the one who kept the others under control."

"He was a bad boy. You know what they say about the quiet ones. They just didn't glorify his actions like they did the others. And he used to whine and cry all the time."

"Whatever, Paul. On that note we should go find our seats."

"You can't handle the truth," he said laughing as he guided her through the crowd and up the stairs to their seats.

"Wow, great seats!" Denise said impressed as they seated themselves third row from the court.

The two sat down and chatted while they waited for the game to begin. They mainly discussed office politics, office gossip, and upcoming events and projects. Denise was impressed by the fact that he didn't get too personal with her. It was more of a buddy-buddy type of conversation and she felt no pressure from him to turn it into more.

"URRRRRRRRRR, let's get ready to RUMBLE…" the announcer's voice piped in through the speakers. Fans stood on their feet to cheer the players on as they made their entrance onto the court.

Denise was enjoying herself for the most part and the evening was going much smoother than her previous encounters. That was until the Spurs were down by twenty. Paul became completely focused on the game at that point. He had been standing for more than twenty minutes as if he were the coach about to call the next play. Pacing as much as he could with the amount of people present, biting his nails and throwing up his hands at bad calls or missed shots. When he did sit down, which usually occurred only during the time outs, Denise would make an attempt at trying to hold a conversation with him. Any attempt ended abruptly ended as soon as the game went into play.

She knew from past experiences with Gerald that one thing a woman can do that will surely irritate a man is to try and have a conversation with him while he's watching the game.

Hey, wait a minute, she thought. *He asked me out. How would I be irritating him? He should be entertaining me.*

A time out was called and the Spurs reduced the gap to a six-point difference. Paul sat down a little calmer than before and asked Denise if she was enjoying the game.

"Yeah, I didn't think the Spurs were going to come back for a minute there," she said trying to sound interested.

"Oh yeah, they'll bounce back no matter what," he assured her. "Are you hungry?"

"Umm, I guess I could eat a snack."

"Okay, the time out is almost over so here," he said handing her money. "I want a hot dog and some peanuts. Get whatever you want."

Denise sat there for a minute, as he stood up to rejoin the game.

"What the hell," she said to herself. "Why do I have to go buy the food?"

The game was approaching half-time and the Spurs were down by ten. Paul had not realized she hadn't moved. He was on his feet along with the rest of the diehard fans yelling and clapping. "Defense." *clap, clap,* "Defense."

Finally accepting the fact that he was not going to be rejoining their conversation anytime soon, she headed to the concession stand to fetch his food. As she neared the end of the aisle she could hear his voice above the rest of the crowd. "C'mon ref. That's foul, man!" Irritated at the sound of his voice, a part of her wanted to keep walking right out the door and to her car.

San Antonio was a good hour-and-a-half drive from Bastrop and she would love nothing more than to head home. But she had his money.

"Darn it," she said unrolling the dollars he'd given her.

Instead, she decided to make the most of it, walking as slowly as she could in the opposite direction of the concession stand.

Denise wandered around the AT&T Center for several minutes before finally heading back toward the concession stand.

There were many activities going on around the center in conjunction with the game. Various fan contest and giveaways, a car exposition and tons of vendor booths. Some of the Silver Dancers were on hand to take pictures with gawking fans. The line was around the corner for that event. Men and boys alike piled in to capture a moment with the beauties.

The walkways were becoming more and more crowded so Denise made her way over to the concession stand. She figured it must be getting close to half-time and Paul would want to gulp down his meal before the game began again.

Shortly after she found her place in the long and chaotic line for food, she heard the announcer pipe in over the loud speaker announcing the half-time show as a multitude of fans piled out of the stadium.

As usual she picked what had to be the slowest line in the entire building. It never failed. There could be twenty lines open at the grocery store and she always managed to pick the one with the price check.

"Prom night. Class of 1989. You wore a red velvet dress, trimmed with studded diamonds and matching tiara. Your hair was flowing just below your shoulders and you were wearing that oh so sexy red lipstick with a gloss shine that made you look totally irresistible."

Denise recognized the voice and she instantly felt a chill travel up her spine. She smiled at the flashback of that night.

"Malcolm Anderson!" she said turning around to give him a hug. "Look at you! Wow! You look great and blessed I might add. Taller than I remember."

"Yes, I've gotten a lot taller than the little nerdy boy you remember. You're just as beautiful as that night. I take that back, even more beautiful if that's possible."

Denise smiled at the compliment as he brushed her hair away from her face.

"Time has definitely treated you well," he said, continuing with the ego boost. "Very well."

"Well, thank you for the kind words, but there hasn't been that much time between us," she said nudging his side.

"I know! Can you believe it! We're coming up on twenty years."

"It's hard to believe, but then *I* have attended every class reunion, and *I* still live in good ole Bastrop. Unlike some people who move away, dropping off the face of the earth never to be heard of again. That is, until you signed that multimillion dollar contract and your face was splattered all over the local news as our hometown hero. You would be amazed at how many of our former classmates are still around."

"Well, if you're referring to me as the person who was never to be heard from again," he said nudging her side, "I was around for a while after graduation. But when pops died, I didn't have any reason to stay."

"I had heard that he passed. I was so sorry to hear that, Malcolm. He was always, always so kind to me."

"Yeah it was tough. A few months after he passed I realized I had to bounce if I was ever going to have a life."

"Bounce is right. Detroit Pistons, huh? You go, boy!"

"Yeah, I'm trying to do a little something something. God has definitely blessed me in ways I would have never dreamed of. Today included," he said grabbing her hand. "So what about you? What did you end up doing after high school?"

"I attended Prairie View. Got my master's in Communication, and currently I'm Vice President of Programming for Power 105.9."

"Really? I had you pegged for TV. Like, news anchor or something. You definitely had the looks and you definitely had the gift of gab."

"Shut up! Actually when I initially started out I wanted to be a DJ."

"Yeah, I remember that! What was it you used to say when we were in the school? I would call you and you would say, 'I can't talk right now; I'm in the studio.' You would say you were producing a recording for New Edition or somebody."

They both laughed at the memory.

"Well through God's spiritual guidance I realized my gift was better suited for behind the scenes in the planning aspect of the field. Not to mention it pays more."

"So are you married? Kids?" he asked.

Denise knew the question would come up soon or later.

"No marriage, no kids. What about you?" she asked quickly trying to divert the attention off of her.

"Nope. Came close once upon a time though."

"What happened?"

"She didn't want a family. She enjoyed her freedom too much and didn't want to commit to the relationship."

"Oh I'm sorry to hear that."

"It was hard at first, ya know? All break ups are. But after a while I realized she was not the person God intended for me. I accepted the blow and moved on eventually. Do you live in San Antonio?" he asked to change the subject.

"No, I'm still in Bastrop unfortunately."

"Yeah, you did say that. Bastrop is not so bad. We are who we are today because we lived in Bastrop, Texas. Small town life is a much better environment to raise kids in than big town USA."

"Yeah, that, and the fact that there's absolutely nothing to do in small town USA! We didn't have a choice not to get in trouble because there was nowhere to go to get into trouble."

"You got that right," he said laughing.

Denise was having such a good time. For the first time she was having a conversation with someone, an actual conversation, with dialog that had nothing to do with music, romance, gold teeth or shady illegal casinos. It was almost like no time had passed at all between them and she completely forgot where she was and what she was supposed to be doing. At that moment, the only thing she was interested in was Malcolm.

They continued reminiscing about different events that occurred throughout their four years of high school. They laughed about different hair styles, different clothing styles, old teachers and past loves.

"Whatever happened to your ace? You know that girl you used to hang around with all the time. Um... Sabrina, I think was her name."

"She's still my ace. And we still hang around with each other all the time. She lives in Austin and she's doing very well for herself. She's a lawyer!"

"Is that right?"

"Yes! She's a high-powered attorney, partner I might add, at a firm downtown. Walker and Wheeler."

"It doesn't surprise me. She was always popping that neck around trying to claim justice for all the sisters in da hood."

Denise was laughing out loud. "Whatever, man!"

"How's your family?" he asked.

"Well, my mom passed away in two thousand and my grandmother passed shortly after her, in two thousand three."

"Denise, I'm so sorry to hear that. They were both very good people."

Denise was touched by his concern. She could hear genuine sorrow in his voice and she knew he was truly sorry for her loss.

Denise had lost all of her elder family members, her great-grandparents, her grandparents and her mom. She never knew her dad so in many ways she had lost him too. It was just her and some of her aunts, uncles and cousins. When she thought about her future with Gerald and children, she would often become sad knowing that they would never know the two most important people in her life. Her mother and her grandmother with the help of God all played a role in shaping her to be the person she had become. Her children would never be able to enjoy the experience and wisdom of those who were instrumental in her upbringing.

Malcolm could tell the conversation was getting to her. He reached over and stroked her hair. Then his hand moved to her back. It was so... intimate... and nice.

"That must have been so hard for you to handle."

His touch excited her. A surge of desire swept through her body. He softly ran his hand down her spine.

"It was—" Denise responded, not able to finish her sentence as her body shivered.

"It was what?"

"Cancer in both cases," she managed to say. "So, how is it? Living in Chicago I mean," she said trying to change the topic.

"Oh I don't live there. My home is in Austin. I have an apartment in Detroit for when we're in season, but when I have my own time I'm in the capital city."

"Look at you, Malcolm. I'm so happy you're doing well."

"Denise! Denise!"

Her stomach turned at the sound of the voice. She turned to find Paul waving his arms at her as if he was shoveling dirt.

"Come on, half-time is almost over!" he yelled across the crowd. "Did you get the food?"

"Is that your man?" Malcolm asked.

"Oh no! He's just a co-worker," Denise said making sure he understood. "He's *just* a co-worker."

"Oh! Well I better let you go."

"It was so good running into you, Malcolm."

"You too, Denise. I'm so happy to see that you're doing well for yourself but I always knew you'd be successful. We should get together sometime and catch up. Is it okay if I call you?"

"Yes! Please do and we definitely need to get together soon," she said accepting the invite.

Malcolm pulled out a piece of paper from his back pocket, ripped it in half and scribbled his phone number on one piece. He gave her a pen and she wrote down her number on one piece of the paper as he wrote down his on the other piece. They exchanged papers and he gave her a quick hug. Promising to contact her very soon before walking away from the moment.

Denise finally made it to the counter and purchased the food Paul had ordered and returned to her seat to find Paul, still on his feet, still playing back-up coach for the team. She slid into her seat and placed the tray on her lap. He hadn't even noticed she was back.

She nudged his side to get his attention. Paul sat down and she handed him the tray of food.

"What took you so long?" he asked.

"Sorry, I ran into an old classmate and got sidetracked."

"Dang, brother is starving."

"Sorry," Denise apologized again.

As soon as he had finished the last bite he was back on his feet screaming at the ref for another bad call. The Spurs were ahead by twenty, but it was still a close game. Everyone around her was immersed into the game. Cheering and screaming out names of players, everyone except Denise. She was as excited as they were but for a different reason.

§

"Good morning," Denise greeted her assistant.

"Good morning, Denise. How are you?"

"Great and you?" she asked, still on a high from running into Malcolm.

There was no dragging out of bed that morning. No hitting the snooze button and no dozing off on the way in to work. She spent her morning recalling every word of their conversation, wishing they had more time to talk. For the first time in a long time she was excited about the day, even if she never saw him again.

"Here are your morning messages, and Mr. Rodriguez would like to have a meeting with you around eleven to discuss upcoming promotions."

"Okay, I'll be in my office until then."

"Oh, some packages arrived for you; they're in your office."

"Okay, thanks."

When Denise opened the door to her office her mouth fell to the floor. There were flowers spread all throughout her office. Each bouquet was beautifully arranged in a finely crafted crystal vase along with a teddy bear holding a small envelop with numbers written on each of them.

"Samantha!" she called out to her assistant in disbelief.

Samantha walked in with a smile almost as big as Denise's.

"Samantha! When? Who? Who did this?"

"I don't know. The truck just pulled up and brought in all of these flowers. Took him a good twenty minutes to bring them in and set them up. The guy said to tell you to open them in number order. You must have made a big impression on somebody. Will there be anything else?" she asked picking Denise's briefcase and purse up off the ground.

"No. No, Samantha. Hold all my calls for a bit, okay?"

"Sure thing!"

Denise walked over to the vase with the envelope marked number one. Vase one was arranged with red roses and baby's breath. Ribbon was strung throughout the roses and it was finished off with a red ribbon tied around the vase.

Denise pulled the card from the teddy bear and took in a good whiff of the aroma. Red roses were her favorite and to top it all off they had bloomed. The most beautiful blooms she had ever seen.

Anxious to see who had gone to such lengths to put a smile on her face she read the card. "Roses are red." That's it. That's all it said. "Roses are red," and there was a smiley face at the end of the statement.

She went to vase number two. Purple violets! Purple was her favorite color. The card read "Violets are blue."

Vase three was located on the windowsill. "Not even the smell of a rose" was written on card three. She took in a deep breath, savoring the scent of the yellow roses and moved to card four, which read "Could ever be as sweet as you."

"Roses are red, violets are blue, not even the smell of a rose could ever be as sweet as you," she said bringing the message from all four cards together. Denise could barely contain the emotions building inside of her.

There were two more vases and she still didn't know who had done such a wonderful thing. "Gerald?" she wondered. But how could he have? He would never have enough money to afford something this extravagant. So who could have done this?

Like the others, a teddy bear was attached to a vase containing roses, pink roses to match the pink teddy bear. "One day I hope you will come to understand how seeing you was just what I needed."

Denise held the card to her chest. She knew who her admirer was.

Still holding the card to her chest she walked over to her desk and sat down. The last vase contained what had to be two dozen coral roses with white carnations carefully placed throughout the surrounding greenery. Taking a deep breath, she read the card. "Please do me the honor of meeting me for dinner tomorrow evening at Turlock's. I have reserved a table for two at eight p.m. I can't wait to see you again."

The card was signed Malcolm Anderson.

FIFTEEN

The next day, Denise met up with Sabrina and Jess for an afternoon workout. She couldn't wait to tell them who she ran into. She wasn't sure she was ready to tell them about the flowers and the dinner date but knowing them they would ask her enough questions to force her to reveal the information.

As usual they started their workout by walking three miles on the treadmill, discussing the latest on the soaps. *The Young and the Restless* was their favorite. They all had the hots for Nicholas Newman.

After the soap update they played twenty questions with Jess. They had not all been together since her cruise and Sabrina wanted details.

"So, Snow White," she said coyly, "are we still pure?"

Denise gasped for air. "Sabrina!"

"You want to know too, Denise. Don't act funny. Well?"

"Yes, Sabrina. I am still celibate."

"How can you go on a romantic cruise, with a man I might add, and still come back a virgin?"

"Because Larry is a perfect gentleman and there was so much more to do. It was so exciting, guys! From the minute we got on the boat it was one adventure after another."

"Well you know what I want to know," Denise interrupted. "Is Jamaica everything I dreamed of?"

"That and more. We traveled to Negril, walked along the beach, hung out at Margaritaville for the afternoon. Then we went out on wave runners. Then we snuggled in hammocks overlooking the crystal blue waters. The images you see on TV are exactly what you experience when you're there."

"Okay, something is wrong with him. There has to be," Sabrina deduced. "There has to be something wrong with a man who takes a woman on a seven-day cruise to some of the most beautiful places on earth and she still comes back a virgin. Either something is wrong with him, or something is wrong with you, girl."

"Nothing is wrong with Larry, and nothing is wrong with me. He understands I'm saving myself and we both want to wait. We decided on the cruise that we're going to wait."

"Wait till when? Hell freezes over?"

"Sabrina, stop!" Denise interrupted punching her in the shoulder.

"No, not till hell freezes over. But we're going to wait until our… wedding night!" Jess screamed holding out her hand to reveal a two-carat marquise cut diamond engagement ring set in twenty-four carat gold.

"What!" Sabrina and Denise said together in shock.

The girls stopped the treadmills and squealed, attracting the attention of other patrons.

"Oh my God, Jess, it covers your whole finger!" Denise said admiring the beauty.

"Not quite but isn't it beautiful?" Jess asked, barely able to contain herself.

"Do you need confirmation? Larry proposed and I said yes!"

"Oh my God, Jess. How did this happen? I can't believe you said yes! How long have you known him? Do Mom and Dad know?"

"Calm down, Denise. Yes, Mom and Dad know. I told them as soon as I got back and they're happy for me. You know Dad is a pretty good judge of character and he has a good feeling about Larry, so he's happy for me."

"Jess, I haven't even met this guy yet! How can you marry someone I've never met?" Denise turned to Sabrina. "Why aren't you saying anything? Usually I can't stop you from taking jabs and now you have nothing to say? Will you back me up please?"

"Denise, if she wants to marry the man, more power to her. What is there to say, I'm just happy the girl is going to finally get some," Sabrina answered restarting her machine.

"Sabrina, that's not the point," Denise snapped turning back to her sister. "Jess, I don't want you to make a mistake that you'll have to live with for the rest of your life. It's easy to get into a marriage but it's not easy to get out of one. Divorce can take a lot out of a person, especially when there are kids involved."

"Who said anything about kids and, for that matter, divorce? I think you're jumping way ahead of the game, sis. The wedding won't be until December next year. Larry and I will have plenty of time to get to know each other better, and you'll have plenty of time to get to know him better. I can't believe you're not happy for me."

Tears were forming in her eyes as she returned to her treadmill. There was an uncomfortable silence between the three for the remainder of the workout.

After they had finished their three miles and lifted a few weights they headed back to the locker room to shower for lunch.

"I'm not in the mood to eat," Jess said. It was clear her conversation with Denise was still upsetting to her.

"Jess, we always eat after our work out," Denise said disappointed.

"I know but you guys go on ahead without me," Jess responded as she stepped into the shower.

Denise looked at Sabrina for support.

"Don't look at me," Sabrina said throwing her hands up before she stepped in the shower to wash off.

Denise didn't want to leave things the way they were. Her sister meant the world to her. She was only concerned she might be rushing into a situation she may not be able to get out of.

Denise finished her shower and quickly dressed to catch Jess before she left.

"Jess," she called out running toward her as she was about to leave the gym. Sabrina was walking slowly behind to give them a chance to talk.

"Jess, I'm sorry. I am happy for you. My baby sis is getting married and for so long it's just been me and you. Now there is someone else in the picture and I'm going to have to share you. That will take some getting used to. You'll have this whole other life with less time for me and it scares me. I don't want to have to let you go."

"Sis, you don't have to let me go. We will always be sisters. We'll continue to get together as we always have. Yes I'll have a husband and yes we'll probably have kids, but I love you, and I'll always make time for you."

"Promise?"

"Promise."

They hugged and Jess agreed to go out to lunch as usual.

SIXTEEN

The girls headed for soup and salad as they normally did after a workout and Sabrina began to ask questions about Denise's date with Paul.

"Jess, girl, your sister has been having some wild nights her damn self," Sabrina said with laughter.

"Whatever, Sabrina. Jess, I will have to tell you about that later. Trust me it will take way more than a lunch hour to give you the full effect of the events of my life during the last few weeks."

"How was the game the other night," Sabrina asked nudging Denise.

"Denise, you went to a game? Basketball?"

"Yea, Spurs versus Pistons."

"Cool, how was that?" Jess was back to her normal perky self.

"The game was great," Denise answered, trying not to provide too much information.

"Yea, I bet it was," said Sabrina.

"What's that all about," Jess asked.

"Well rumor has it that the next day after the game, Denise received dozens of roses," Sabrina not so quietly whispered in Jess's ear.

"Is that right, dozens?"

"Dozens. Apparently in all different shades and colors!"

"Spill the beans, sis," Jess demanded.

"First off, Sabrina, how do you know what goes on in my office?"

"Don't worry about all that. Just answer the question."

"Well," Denise treaded carefully, "you'll never guess who I ran into at the basketball game."

"Um, let's see, a basketball player?" Sabrina made a sarcastic guess.

"Very close. Right on the money, actually, but you'll never guess who the basketball player was?"

"I hate when people ask you to guess. You know we won't get it anyway, but you keep asking us to guess. We have to go back to work soon, Denise. Who did you see at the damn game?" Sabrina asked impatiently.

Denise gave her a glare. "Sabrina, how do I hate thee… let me count the ways."

The girls laughed.

"You know you love me more than life itself. Come on, spill it."

"Okay, you're right. You'll never guess. It was none other than Mr. Malcolm Anderson."

"Shut up! The nerd from high school Malcolm Anderson?" Sabrina asked.

"Yes, well, not the nerd as you so eloquently put it, but yes Malcolm Anderson, the one and only. He looks great, guys," Denise said excitedly and started spilling all. "He got rid of the glasses. No more pimples. The boy's been working out and looking fine and dapper, I must say."

"I have to see it to believe it," Sabrina said folding her arms.

"Denise, what was he doing at the basketball game in San Antonio?" Jess asked. "Didn't I hear he got picked up by the Pistons?"

"Yes he did, but he had a weekend off, so he came home to take it easy for a bit."

"Home, he still lives in Bastrop?" Sabrina asked surprised.

"No, he lives in Austin. He left Bastrop after his father passed away. He has an apartment in Detroit for obvious reasons, but Austin is where he lays his head when he can."

"Wow, sis, you seem really excited about running into him. Maybe there's a little fire burning that you don't want to admit to—"

"Yeah," Sabrina interrupted, "because if I remember correctly you were supposed to be going to the game with a co-worker. Um, uh, what happened to that?"

"You said the key word, co-worker. That's all it was. Paul was all into the game and that was the only thing he was interested in. I ran into Malcolm when I went to the concession stand. Running into him was great. We didn't get a chance to talk too long but those few minutes with him washed away all the bad memories of the previous disasters I got myself into. It was nice to see a familiar face and relive the old days a little."

"Wait a minute! Hold up!" Sabrina yelled putting her hands up as if she was directing traffic. "We have been here thirty minutes and you have not once mentioned the convict."

"Sure I have," Denise said realizing she hadn't.

"Oh no you haven't, ma'am. Ole boy must have really made an impression on you, girlfriend."

Denise was feeling a little guilty. Although Gerald crossed her mind each day, she had to admit her thoughts were consumed with her encounter with Malcolm, especially after receiving the flowers.

"I was just letting you guys know who I ran into, that's all. Gerald's name would have come up sooner or later." She was trying to convince herself as well.

"Denise, please. Gerald has always been the center of attention for you. Every conversation began and ended with Gerald. You didn't mention him at the gym either," Sabrina pointed out.

"Sabrina, why you gotta bring up old stuff? For you information, Gerald is still scheduled to get out in February and I am still very much in love with him and I am still very much counting the days until his arrival."

"I can't tell," said Sabrina. "Let me ask you this. Did you tell Mr. Man about Gerald?"

Denise had no response.

"Uh, uh, dat's what I thought! Did you and Malcolm exchange phone numbers?" she continued.

Still no response from Denise.

"Um, hmm, dat's what I thought."

"Are you done?" Denise asked, waiting for the third degree to end. "No, I didn't tell him about Gerald because we didn't talk for more than fifteen minutes and the subject never came up."

Denise suddenly remembered Malcolm did ask her if she was married and although she told him the truth, that she wasn't married, she neglected to tell him that she was committed.

"You lie, you lie and you lie," Sabrina said shaking her finger. "I can see it all over your face."

"I am not lying! We did not have that much time to talk but yes we did exchange phone numbers because he wants to catch up... as old friends. That's it. Nothing more, nothing less."

"Denise, who are you fooling? Ain't no man going to send you that many roses and want nothing more than to play catch up."

"How many roses did he send you?" Jess asked finally getting a word in.

"Uh, I lost count," Denise lied.

"Uh huh, five dozen roses and a dozen carnations," Sabrina revealed.

Denise gasped for air. "How in the heck to you find out all my information?"

"Nunya." Sabrina waved her hand.

"So when are you going to see him again, sis?"

"Tonight, eight p.m., Turlock's."

"Denise, tonight is Tuesday. You never go out on a weeknight," Sabrina noted.

"Thank you for telling me my schedule, and besides we're not going out. We're just meeting for dinner to catch up. I am allowed to eat aren't I?"

"All I'm saying is convict Gerald better watch out. Daddy Malcolm might be moving in."

"Malcolm is not moving in. Where do you come up with this stuff, Sabrina? We are just meeting for dinner. We'll talk about old times and play catch up, that's it."

"Yeah, you keep saying that—"

"Hello, counselor," a gentleman's voice interrupted.

The girls turned to find a gorgeous tall brother standing behind them. Noticing a change in Sabrina they realized that the fine piece of chocolate must be the infamous prosecutor Sabrina was up against in her newest case.

"Hello, Mr. Prosecutor," Sabrina responded clearing her throat.

"How are you?"

"Things are good, and you?"

"I'm good. I've been watching you girls over here for a while now. I noticed you ladies when I first came in but you looked like you were having such a good time I didn't want to interrupt."

"I have a good time at everything I do," Sabrina assured him. "Is there something I can help you with?"

"No, I just wanted to say hello. I'll save the work for our meeting later. Hello, I'm Stoney Hunter," the man said reaching for Denise's hand.

"Uh, uh," Sabrina cleared her throat again. "Yes, these are my friends, Denise and her sister, Jess."

"Nice to meet you, ladies."

"Likewise," they said simultaneously.

"Well, I'll leave you friends to your lunch. Sabrina, this afternoon I would really like to focus on our options concerning the case."

"I thought we were clear on our options, Mr. Prosecutor. My client is innocent. What more is there to discuss?"

"Well, I thought I would give you another opportunity to make things a little easier on your client."

"Oh you did, huh?"

"Yes, but let's not discuss that here. We're meeting in my office around seven tonight, correct?"

"No, how about we meet in my office around eight?" Sabrina responded, making every attempt to show him she was in control.

"Yes, ma'am, eight it is. Ladies... again, a pleasure meeting you both."

Jess and Denise leaned over in their seat as he walked away.

"Oh please, close your mouths! He's just a man, honey, just a man," Sabrina said, trying to pretend she wasn't attracted to him.

"Sabrina, girl, he is gorgeous," Jess commented as she came out of hypnosis.

"I concur," Denise said. "I didn't notice a ring on his finger either."

"He is very single, but I am immune to his appeal. I have a client to defend and I will not allow Mr. Hunter to distract me from proving my client's innocence."

"I don't see how you can work with him and not get distracted. I wouldn't be able to remember my name let alone the facts of a case. I would be like, yes, your honor, whatever he says, your honor," Denise said and Jess laughed.

"That's why you are the VP and I am the lawyer. I can handle him. Trust me," Sabrina said grabbing her glass of wine. "He is no match for the Brina."

SEVENTEEN

Creasy was perched on the floor watching Denise as she tried on multiple outfits. With each outfit change came the earring change and the shoe change. She couldn't make up her mind what impression she wanted to make.

"This one's too sexy," she said about the little red dress. "It's too formal," she said about the black one. With each change she explained to Creasy why it didn't work.

"I can't be too sexy because I don't want him falling all over me, but I don't want to look like a plain Jane because I want him to like what I have on without being attracted to me, if that's even possible. Oh, I don't know what to wear."

Creasy followed her every movement as she tried on this shoe and that shoe talking to him all the while. Finally she settled on a sheer red cowl-neck tunic and a pair of black cuffed capris.

True to form the Texas weather was unseasonably warm for November so she wore red Prada sandals to match her red Prada purse. Black hoop earrings accessorized her earlobes and a gold necklace with the initial S hung from her neck.

The necklace was her mother's. S for Stella. When her mother passed away she was wearing the gold chain and it was given to Denise before the ambulance took her away. Attached to the letter was an angel. She never took it off. Her mother was that angel watching over her.

"Okay, girl," she said to herself as she stood in the mirror for one final glamour check.

"Rule number one: one date only. Rule number two: NO touching. And rule number three: under no circumstances is he to come back to the apartment."

Running her fingers through her hair, she pursed her lips and blew a kiss at her reflection for final approval of the look, and then headed toward the door.

As she grabbed the handle she suddenly flashed back to graduation night. The tender kiss he gave her was vivid in her mind and remembering the surge of heat that ran through her body from his touch. She glanced back at the mirror.

"And rule number four: don't fall in love."

Turlock's was the top of the line for fine dining in Austin, Texas. A glass of wine ran a patron twenty-one dollars and one could expect to pay a minimum of fifty dollars per plate on a meal. It was the type of restaurant that was only visited on special occasions for common people.

Denise handed the valet her keys and stepped onto the sidewalk just in front of the entrance.

Denise stood frozen.

"Is everything okay, ma'am. Ma'am?"

"Yes, everything is fine." She continued standing, watching as people came in and out of the doors.

What's wrong, girl? Go in! her body was screaming.

But she was afraid to move, afraid to open the door, opening the door to what could be the end of her and Gerald.

"Stop being silly," she said interrupting her own thought. "It's just a date. My God, you act like you've slept with the man and you're about to tell him you are pregnant."

That's right, it just a date. Get a grip, Denise thought, as she mustered up the courage to grab the door handle.

Once she entered the restaurant the hostess guided her to a table near the window overlooking Town Lake where Malcolm was waiting patiently. He spotted her right away and rose to his feet to greet her.

Tipping the hostess he politely pulled the chair out for Denise to be seated.

"Thank you. Have you been waiting long?"

"Oh, only about twenty minutes. But twenty minutes that felt like an hour."

"I'm sorry," Denise apologized.

"No, no apologies. I've just been so anxious to spend time with you; it felt like this moment would never get here. You look gorgeous."

"Thank you. You look pretty dapper yourself."

"Will there be others joining you?" the waitress interrupted.

"No," he responded without looking in her direction. He could not take his eyes off Denise.

"What can I get you to drink?" the waitress asked, looking at Denise.

"Uh, I would like sangria and some water please."

"And you, sir?"

"I'll have a rum and coke please."

"No problem. I'll be right back."

"So how was your day?" he asked.

"Oh you know, the usual, business, business, business for eight hours and I managed to squeeze in a workout. What about you?"

"I managed a workout too and I spent the day visiting old friends," he said smiling.

"How long are you in town?"

"I fly out later tonight. We have a game in Seattle Wednesday and I have to be back in Detroit for practice tomorrow."

"Wow, how do you deal with flying back and forth so much?"

"It's not that bad. I often feel like I'm living life on an airplane, but hey, it's a small price to pay for a spot on the Pistons. So tell me, Denise. What has life been like for you? I mean after high school?"

Denise told him about her life at Prairie View. How it took some getting used to. Being free to do whatever she wanted to do, when she wanted to do it. That type of freedom was hard for her to grasp at first and she almost let it get the best of her. Not studying, traveling from one frat party to the next.

Growing up, her parents had always kept her on a tight leash. She didn't get to go to parties or hang out at the mall or movies like other kids her age. Most of her childhood consisted of activities with her sister or cousins. Family slumber parties at her grandparents' house, searching for doodle bugs, making mud pies and hanging out in trees. Most times she and her sister pretended they were on *Solid Gold* to pass the time. They were honorary *Solid Gold* dancers, as yet undiscovered. It wasn't until her senior year that she was finally granted a little bit of freedom but even that was limited.

She purchased her first car, a hatchback Ford Pinto, for which she paid three hundred dollars, money she earned from her part-time job at KFC. To her that green Pinto was a Cadillac. Back then, the cars were made with better quality and nothing could dent that car. On one occasion Sabrina and Denise were heading out to hang at the basketball courts and Sabrina accidentally turned too short while leaving her house. Her Buick hit the Pinto. Sabrina was furious. The Buick had a permanent dent shaped like a bowl, while the Pinto was still intact.

As intact as it could be anyway. Denise fixed the car up as best she could. She installed a stereo system with home stereo speakers and cassette tape player all by herself. Not exactly factory installed but it worked!

The hood on the car wouldn't close so she purchased a thick chain and strung it through a hole, chaining it to the bumper of the car. Her brother had a battery stolen out of this car and she was trying to prevent the same thing from happening to her. That and she didn't want the hood to fly up as she was driving of course.

A flat piece of wood lay on the floorboard of the car to cover a hole that revealed pavement. To add a touch of flare she accessorized the interior with seat covers, with matching dashboard and steering wheel protectors.

That was her car and it was great. No one could tell her any different. It gave her just the freedom she needed for as little as three hundred bucks. She later sold the car for fifty bucks just to get it out of the yard.

Even with the newfound freedom she was still far behind other classmates who had experienced more of the street life than she... dating, sex, heartbreak, betrayal. Adjusting to college was a big challenge. That was until the day she fell in love with Gerald. Everything seemed to come into perspective for her the day he told her she would be his.

Denise and Malcolm continued chatting over appetizers as he described his life after high school and the death of his father. His mother passed when he was very young and his father raised him as a single parent. His father never remarried due to the risk of another woman not loving his child. Malcolm was all he had left of his wife and he was devoted to raising his son to be a contributor to society. When his father became too ill to continue with the upkeep of the shop, Malcolm stepped in to help out.

Although Malcolm's father had always dreamed he would one day take over the business, he urged his son in his later years to sell the shop and pursue his own dreams if anything ever happened to him. Malcolm tried to keep the business going after his father's death but soon realized it was not where he wanted to be. He heeded his father's wishes, sold the shop and left Bastrop.

Their meal arrived as the two began to reminisce about different recollections of their high school days. Class dances, class fights and classic breakups provided endless conversation.

Denise was enjoying her evening. Finally, she was able to go out with a nice guy and just talk. He was so easy to talk to. There was never a pause or awkward moment. He listened. He listened to every word she had to say and she hung on to every conversation he initiated. She was having a great time with her old friend and there was no place she would rather be and no one else she would rather be with at that very moment.

"So what made you come back to Texas?" she asked. "Growing up we all agreed when that last bell rang, releasing us from the grip of senior year, we would be packing our bags for bigger and better things. The vow was to leave Bastrop and never come back, remember?"

"We were all going to do bigger and better things," he laughed, recalling the memory.

"We all left alright... and we all came back."

"You came back and I live in Austin," he pointed out.

"Please, Austin is just a bigger version of the country."

"I think we all came back for the same reason, Denise."

"Well, please tell me because I have yet to figure out why God brought me back to this place," she kidded.

"Austin really is a beautiful city. You have to admit that. It's clean. Crime is low. And when a person begins to mature and grow spiritually, they desire the simple things life has to offer."

"I agree. When a person finally realizes life is not one big party, they begin to make the right choices in life, begin to establish roots and focus on what's important."

"Exactly. See we're here, girl." he said pointing his fingers from his eyes to hers. "I decided I wanted to establish my roots here. There is no other place I would want to live than the great state of Texas."

"Well, I wouldn't go that far. If I had it to do all over again, I would pack up and move right now. I would be in New York City."

"New York City?"

"Yes! I love New York. I love the fast pace, the bright lights, the people, the shows, the museums. You can't beat it. There's always something to do and see in places like that."

"Yeah but that was before you began to mature spiritually and seek the simpler things in life."

Denise laughed out loud. "Yeah, I agree. I would much rather have a family and raise kids right here in good old Central Texas."

"So tell me, Denise, because inquiring minds want to know."

Here it comes. Denise knew the words he would speak next.

"Why have you never been married?"

There it was, those six words that every man has to ask. The one question they want every female they meet to answer. It's like at birth their father programmed the words into their brain and there's a trigger that floats around in their brain that says, "Okay, ask it now."

"I hope you don't mind me asking."

That was different.

"I mean, you're beautiful," he continued. And she was glad he did. "Inside and out, so what gives?"

"Why have you never been married, Malcolm?"

"Ahh, but I asked you first," he responded.

Denise was not ready to tell him about Gerald. For the most part, she was ashamed to tell him she'd been waiting around on a guy who'd been in prison over ten years. When said out loud it sounded kind of pitiful. Anyone hearing her story would think she was nuts.

Most people wouldn't be able to understand why such a confident, career-minded, well-bred woman would waste time on someone who would have a life of struggle even if he did get out because he would be a convicted felon.

Sure he could get out, start his own business and educate himself on the stock market and make some changes, but on the other hand, he could get out and start selling magazines on a street corner with no chance of ever getting a decent job because he had a record.

So in answer to the burning question on the lips of ever man, she said, "I just haven't found the right person," and added quickly, "now your turn," trying to divert attention away from herself.

"Well, I think I told you at the game I was close but she wasn't willing to commit. She did all the right things. She was interested in the things I was interested in and we did a lot of activities together as a couple. Plays, concerts, movies, dinner, times were great between us. We could talk on the phone for hours and discuss any subject under the sun. The sex was great—"

"TMI," Denise interrupted.

Malcolm laughed and continued. "I would have done anything for her. I did anything for her. And she did many things for me. Whenever she needed me, I was there for her and vice versa. She had two kids and I was there for them too. But no matter how great things were, she just wouldn't commit to a long-term relationship. One minute she loved me and things were great and the next she didn't want to be in love, didn't want a boy friend and didn't want a commitment. It was a constant roller coaster and there were a lot of games being played, by her for the most part."

"Oh, I am so sorry, Malcolm."

"Yeah, my ego was bruised and abused over and over again, but I believed she really loved me because of her actions and the things she did. I figured she'd been hurt and was just having a hard time opening up, but eventually she would and we would be together."

"So what made you finally decide to get out of that situation?"

"One day out of the blue she said she didn't want to be committed to the relationship any longer. That was it, after three years of stringing me along, she was done playing her little game and it was over. Maybe she got bored, maybe she found someone else, who knows?"

"That's awful," Denise said. "Anyone who plays with another person's emotions like that is an awful person. It's emotional abuse."

"Yeah, and there was a lot of it. She was great in a lot of ways but in other ways she was stubborn, prideful and unappreciative as well as insensitive to my feelings. I tried to overlook those qualities because she was so good at everything else. You take the good with the bad in a relationship, ya know. She wanted to remain friends in the end, but her friendship came at too high of a cost, so I had to move on."

"Good for you. You are too good to be played like that. No one should be allowed to play with your heart. Shame on her."

"Yeah, by the end of it all, at final break-up time, I was just done. A little angry, at myself mostly, for wasting so much time on someone who wasn't worth it. She was not the person God intended to be my queen." Denise liked the way he said *my queen*.

"I am so sorry you had to go through that," she said. She could tell the memory was getting to him a little. She'd been through several merry-go-rounds in her lifetime before meeting Gerald, so she knew the emotional drama he'd been through all too well.

"Enough about me. Do you have room for dessert?" he asked changing the subject.

"Oh no, I'm stuffed," she said rubbing her stomach.

"Well, I know it's getting late and you have to rest for work tomorrow. I'm sure Turlock's wants their table back. Waitress," he motioned as she was passing nearby, "could I have the check please?"

Malcolm paid for the meal and escorted Denise out of the restaurant.

After handing the valet attendant their tickets they leaned against the wall and stood in silence both unsure of what to say, lost in their own thoughts.

They had talked so much and now they were at the end of the date portion of the evening and both were at a loss for words. Denise didn't want the evening to end but knew that it would be best to preserve her rules. Malcolm wanted to invite her for coffee but didn't want to push his way into her life so soon.

"Malcolm! I didn't thank you for the beautiful flowers!"

"No thanks needed. I heard from a little birdie that your breath was taken away."

"From a little birdie? Samantha? My receptionist?"

"I'll never tell."

"Well, I'll have to have a talk with her and let her know that she just can't be telling every strange guy she meets my innermost secrets."

As the cars pulled up, Malcolm walked her to her vehicle.

"Malcolm, thank you for such a lovely evening."

"The pleasure is all mine. I am so glad I ran into you at that game."

"I am too. Don't be a stranger."

"Not a chance," he assured her.

"I better let you get to your flight," she said, trying to take the awkwardness out of the situation.

"Denise," he said, grabbing her hand as she turned toward her car.

Oh no, she thought to herself. Her breathing became labored.

Turning her to face him he reached his arms around her waist and pulled her to him. She laid her head his chest. She didn't dare look up for fear the moment would end much like it had ended on graduation night. Taking in a deep breath filled with the scent of his cologne, she had to admit to herself that she was enjoying his touch.

"When is your flight?" she whispered, finally able to get the words to come out.

"In two hours," he responded just as nervously.

"Malcolm, two hours," she said looking up at him. They were still embraced in each other's arms. "You're not going to make your flight in time if you don't get out of here."

"It's not a big deal. My bags are packed in the trunk and all I have to do is head straight to the airport."

"What about your car? Do you need a ride? I can drop you off."

"No, that's sweet. Thanks for asking but I have a private garage at the airport and I leave my car there."

"Wow, must be nice Mr. Big Time Basketball Player," Denise said nudging his side.

"Well, you know, what can I say?" He rubbed his mustache as he mimicked J.J. Walker from *Good Times*.

The valet attendant was about to open the door for the Denise, but Malcolm insisted on having the honor. Relieving the attendant of his duty, he opened the car door and held out his hand for Denise.

"Have a safe flight and good luck on your game tomorrow," she said as she slid into her seat.

Kneeling beside her he reached for her hand. His touch was warm and he rubbed it in a way that excited Denise. A surge built up inside of her that needed satisfying as he softly kissed the back of her hand. She turned to face the passenger window. She did not want him to see the desire in her eyes. Gently grabbing her chin he pulled her face to his and softly kissed her lips.

"I have a feeling you just gave me all the luck I need."

EIGHTEEN

Denise and Malcolm spent every free moment together they could after that evening. Breakfast with Denise, lunch with Denise, dinner with Denise, movies with Denise.

Whenever he could get away from Detroit he was on a flight to Austin International Airport. The free time from games and practice were reserved for Denise.

Denise broke the second date rule multiple times over, justifying her weakness by stating the other rules were still intact. He had not been to her home, there was no physical activity taking place and she was doing everything in her power to not fall in love. His time in Detroit was a big help. The weeks where he had games and practice allowed her the time she needed to return to her senses as far as Gerald was concerned. The other factor that kept her from melting was Malcolm himself. He was the perfect gentleman. He hadn't tried to cross the line with her or pressure her into anything more than good company.

Though there were moments where her body wanted him. The times when he would brush the hair out of her eyes. The times when he would hold on to her at the end of the night. Every time he smiled and said something sweet enough to make her melt.

The rules may have been intact but the Do Not Fall in Love rule was in grave danger. She could feel herself drawing closer to him. Excited when he was coming to town. Enjoying how his life mission seemed to be making her happy whenever they were together.

When they weren't together, there were hourly phone calls, periodic text messages and touching emails. He would call just to hear her voice. He called to make sure she was okay. He called to see how her day went, and he called to keep her company at night. Each call offered encouragement on a bad day and sweet compliments on the good days.

Denise felt very blessed to have come in contact with such a wonderful man. Most women may never experience the kind of devotion he had given her over the past month. He was exactly what she needed to remove the emptiness that Gerald's incarceration brought to her life. The loneliness that filled her heart and soul as she longed for Gerald day in and day out. She missed Gerald but didn't realize how much she missed the tender interaction between a man and a woman until Malcolm walked into her life.

They had been spending time with one another for a little over a month and Denise still had not mentioned Gerald. She knew she would have to one day and as much as she enjoyed the time they shared together, deep down inside, her heart was and would always be with Gerald.

Gerald was scheduled for release in two months and fourteen days. February fourteenth was the scheduled release date. Valentine's Day. In his last letter he asked why she hadn't been to visit him in a while. "Good question," she said to herself as she read his thoughts. Rather than write him back with lies about how she had been so busy at work she couldn't get away, she decided to make the trip and see him. He was right, she had not been to see him since September.

As much as she missed him the real excuse was she was afraid to face him. She knew he would want to know why. Why the distance? Denise was not a liar. She and Gerald had always agreed to discuss their feelings openly. Owning up to mistakes instead of making excuses to justify their behavior. But how could she explain her behavior over the last month?

"Well, love of my life. I've been busy hanging out with a high school class mate that I am slightly attracted to. Oh yeah and here's the kicker, baby, I am starting to fall for him."

If he asked the question she would have to be honest.

"Without trust a relationship cannot survive," she would always tell him.

Lying was something that did not come naturally to Denise. The few times in high school she attempted to lie to her parents she achieved great failure. No matter what she did they seemed to instantly know she was lying, or they found out about it later.

She would have to be honest with Gerald. Besides, she hadn't slept with Malcolm. Just a few dates and good conversation. There was no harm in that.

Okay it was more than a few, twenty dates, with forty emails and close to three hundred text messages, but it was all done under the pretense of friendship. And she reasoned with herself that they weren't really dates. More like catching up with an old high school friend. Sure. It takes twenty dates to catch up with an old friend? Obviously she had a hard time convincing herself so she knew there was no way she could convince Gerald it was nothing more.

She was about twenty minutes from the prison and thought it would be a good time to start praying. She thanked God for arriving safely and prayed that on her visit with Gerald she would find him in good spirits. Just before the prayer ended she asked for a little grace in the situation, just in case she was faced with the dreaded "Tell me everything about your life the last couple of months."

Just in case, she tried to come up with ways of avoiding the question or at least diverting it in a different direction without having to lie.

NINETEEN

"Oh, umm, I've been busy with work mostly. No, goofy," she said smacking her forehead. "You can't say umm." Taking a deep breath she tried again.

"Well," she cleared her throat, "what have I been doing? Umm you know… dang it," she said smacking her head again.

You're doomed, she thought.

She arrived at the prison and the officer led her to the waiting room.

"Visitations are packed today, ma'am. Lots of folks trying to get in visits before the holidays are over."

Denise found a seat in a corner of the room. The location provided some form of privacy in case things blew up in her face. There were several visitors waiting patiently for their names to be called and others standing in front of a TV hung high against the wall.

Denise could hear the announcer.

"Detroit twenty-seven. Mavericks ten."

"What? The Pistons," she said softly. Walking over to the TV she immediately spotted Malcolm on the court. The sight of him warmed her heart. She couldn't help but smile as she watched him at his best.

In high school Malcolm was a tall, lanky fellow. It was hard for her to believe that he had grown into this six-foot-four well-defined man. She could definitely tell the brother made working out an art form. Coated with the smoothest cocoa brown skin she had ever come to know, she'd spent many nights in recent weeks imagining her hands gliding across his smooth chest, admiring every sexy curve.

He wasn't a hairy man, which was a big plus for Denise. She was completely grossed out by men who not by their own doing were completely covered in hair from head to toe.

Malcolm's best feature? His smile. His smile could light up the whole room. Especially when he saw her coming toward him. It was like the sunshine appeared from underneath the cloud of basketball, practice and traveling, and the moment he saw Denise he could breathe fresh air again. At least that was how his smile made her feel.

He was a well-trimmed man. Not one hair from his head, mustache or goatee was ever out of place. He looked great. He was gorgeous. As much as she tried to deny it to others, she couldn't hide it from herself. She was definitely attracted to him.

She continued to watch as he dribbled the ball down the court for another shot. Weaving in between players of the opposite team as he glided toward the goal to score. Unstoppable some teammates called him.

The crowd around her stood to their feet as Malcolm stopped mid-court with four seconds left on the clock. He went up for the shot in an attempt to make a shot before half-time. Out of nowhere a player from the other team sprinted up behind him in an effort to divert the shot. The next thing she saw was Malcolm lying on the ground holding his leg in what appeared to be excruciating pain.

Denise jumped to her feet.

"Oh my God," she said covering her mouth.

"Oh he'll be alright," said one of the visitors.

She was trying her best not to scream. The visitor didn't know the real reason she was so concerned. Pushing her way to the front of the circle, she watched in horror as the team doctors rushed to where he lay.

"Denise Rush," the guard called.

"Just a minute," Denise responded.

"Sorry, ma'am, I need you to come with me now or you forfeit the visit."

"Oh my God," she whispered burying her head in her hands.

"Ms. Rush," the guard called again.

"I'm coming."

Reluctantly Denise walked toward the guard, making one last glance at the TV before the visitation door closed shut. The walk was the longest she had ever taken. All she could think about was Malcolm. Was he alright? Did he get up? What did this mean for his career? She felt tears coming on as she neared the visitation room.

Okay, you have to get a grip, girl. She had been so ready to put on a good face and now she was a wreck. She could see Gerald through the window as she neared the door. He stood smiling as the guard pointed in his direction.

"Hey, baby," he greeted her, wrapping his arms around her and squeezing her as tight as he could. She buried her head on his shoulder and began to cry softly. She wasn't sure why she was crying. She didn't know if she was crying because she was happy to see Gerald or crying because her heart and mind were with Malcolm.

"What's wrong, baby?" Gerald asked, lifting her chin to meet her eyes.

"It's just been so long since I last saw you. I missed you." That wasn't a lie; it had been a long time and she did really miss him.

"I missed you too, baby," he said giving her a sweet kiss. "Words cannot explain how much I miss you." He leaned in for another quick kiss. Kissing was not allowed so he had to make it quick before the guards saw it.

Denise buried her head in his chest again and began crying again.

"Baby, stop crying. You're going to be tired of me when I get out in a few weeks."

"No, I won't be tired. That day can't come soon enough."

"How are things back home?" he asked still holding her in his arms. They were rocking slightly, almost dancing. Denise kept her head buried in his chest. She knew if she looked into his eyes he would see that there was something more going on inside her. Confusion. She wasn't confused about how she felt about Gerald. She loved him with all her heart and soul. She was confused about what she was feeling for Malcolm. In a few short weeks he had swept her off of her feet and a million different emotions were running through her body. Emotions she had not felt for anyone other than Gerald in years.

"Things are great," she said trying her best to hold back the tears. "You know the usual daily tasks. Work, hanging out with the girls and taking care of the baby."

At least she wasn't lying. She had definitely been to work, definitely hung out with the girls and Creasy was an everyday task.

"Everything's fine," she said again, praying that he wouldn't probe any further. "How have you been?" she asked trying to divert the attention off of her.

"I'm great! Especially now that I see your lovely face. Guess who wrote me?"

"Who?"

"Remember Jonathan McKinley?"

"The name doesn't sound familiar."

"Remember when you used to come watch me play ball at the Y and there was a guy that I would always ball with? He was in the reserve."

"Yeah I remember him. I didn't realize you guys kept in touch."

"Really we don't. I mean he hasn't been to visit me or anything. He wrote when I first got locked up and I hadn't heard from him since. Anyway, I got a letter and he wanted to let me know that he had started his own detail business. He said he heard I was getting out soon and he wanted to let me know that if I needed a job to get me started, there would be a position for me."

"That's great, Gerald."

"Yeah, I can't wait to get out of here. I want to start taking care of you. I mean I know it's not a job at Trump Tower and I won't be making very much money, but it won't be forever. I'm going to do everything I can to make sure I'm able to provide for you. Baby, you have always been there for me. You have placed your life on hold for me and I know that was hard. I have a lot of making up to do and I'm going to do whatever I have to do to fulfill my role as a man in the eyes of God and I intend to make him and you proud of me."

Her eyes begin to swell with tears. She looked into his eyes and stared into his soul where she found love. A deep love that reminded her that this was the man she loved. This was the man she wanted to be with for the rest of their lives. Nothing else mattered. Gerald would be out in a few weeks and they were finally going to have the lives they were destined to have. Things with Malcolm had to end.

TWENTY

After leaving Gerald, Denise drove home, no longer confused. No longer wondering where her life was going and who would be in it when all was said and done. Gerald reaffirmed their love that day and she couldn't wait for their lives to begin.

She was halfway home before Malcolm crossed her mind. Wanting to know if he was okay she activated the Bluetooth system in her car and dialed his number.

"Voicemail."

Hanging up she checked her cell phone to see if he'd left her a message while she was visiting Gerald. There were messages from Sabrina and Jess, who had scheduled a girls' night out, but no Malcolm.

After arriving home she checked the answering machine as soon as she got settled and still no word from Malcolm. Starting to get worried she scrolled through the caller ID to see if he had even called. Maybe the accident was worse than she thought. She tried his cell phone again, which went straight to voicemail. This time she left a message asking him to call her as soon as he could.

"Why are you so worried about Malcolm?" she asked herself already knowing the answer. Malcolm was a friend. He had been a great friend over the last few weeks and her only concern was for her good friend. That's it. Nothing more, nothing less. Or so she tried to convince herself. In the end she knew what she had to do. She had to tell Malcolm about Gerald. She had to tell him the truth.

It was about three in the afternoon and the girls had made reservations for six, so Denise decided to relax in the Jacuzzi for a while. The events of the day had worn her out. She went to Tree Mountain afraid to face the man she loved. Confused, worried and scared. She imagined the visit being a complete mess and instead it turned out to be one of the most defining moments of their relationship.

The Best of Luther was playing through the surround sound as she poured herself a glass of red wine and headed toward the Jacuzzi.

After taking a quick sip, she slipped her dress off of her shoulders, letting it fall to the ground as she stepped into the tub. Submerging her body into the warm water and bubbles.

A sense of pleasure came over her as the jets pushed the warm bubbly water and lavender oils across her naked skin. She moaned softly as she cupped water in her hands and rubbed the oil along her torso and breasts as her legs swayed to the sounds of Luther.

"… and a house is not a home when, there is no one there to hold you tight and no one there you can kiss goodnight…"

Leaning back on her bath pillow she closed her eyes humming along with the crooner until she drifted off to sleep.

About thirty minutes later she was awakened by the ringing of the telephone.

"Malcolm," she said opening her eyes at the first ring.

Jumping out of the water as quickly as she could without breaking her ankle, she ran across the deck to answer before the voicemail picked up. Stubbing her toe along the way she dived onto the couch and dug frantically for the phone.

"Where is it!" she shouted in frustration.

The answering machine picked up. "Hey, I can't get to the phone right now…"

"Got it," she said grabbing the phone from underneath the sofa.

"Hello! Hello!" she said hoping he hadn't hung up.

"Hey, you."

"Malcolm! Oh my God, are you alright? I saw what happened on TV, and I've been trying to call and you weren't answering your phone. Are you okay? Are you hurt? Where are you?"

"Calm down, girl."

"I'm sorry. I was just so worried. What's going on?"

"First of all, it makes me feel good to know that you worry about me and, secondly, I am fine. My knee is a little bruised, along with my ego, but I'm fine."

"What happened? I saw you go up for the shot and the next thing I knew you were on the ground."

"When I came down on my foot, I landed the wrong way sending me to the floor. When I fell my knee touched down first and another player fell on my back which increased the intensity of the pain. But I'm fine, a little ice and heat therapy and I was back in the game. I'm just so happy to know that you actually watched the game."

"Yeah," she replied. "I thought the guy had knocked you down."

"Well, I saw him coming and I was trying to avoid landing on him but hurt myself in the process. Where did you watch the game? I know you didn't actually turn to ESPN yourself," he said laughing.

She didn't go into details as to how or where she ended up watching the events unfold and she was glad he didn't ask why she didn't know he returned to the game.

"Never mind that," she said trying to avoid having to lie. "I'm just glad you're okay. I couldn't get in touch with you and I started imagining the worse."

"We had a meeting after the game and I hopped on the plane right after. Just landed at Bergstrom. Are you up for dinner?"

"Oh I'm sorry, the girls and I have plans." She wasn't lying at least.

"What about after your dinner? I would love to see you."

"Well you know tonight is girls' night out so there's no telling what we're going to get into or what time we'll finish. When are you going back to Detroit?"

"Tomorrow night. We have practice on Monday and I'll probably be in Detroit all week because we have games on Tuesday and Thursday."

"Oh, Malcolm, I am sorry." Really she was relieved. The less time he spent in Austin the better. She would run out of excuses for avoiding him soon.

"That's okay. Hopefully there will be other opportunities. I may call my boys up and see if they want to get together tonight. It's been a minute since I've seen them because a certain female has been occupying all my time."

"Well, the nerve of some people," she said going along with his playful insinuation. "Well, I better start getting ready to go. Malcolm, I'm so glad you're okay. I was really worried about you."

"I'm sorry. Next time I'll send you a signal to let you know I'm okay."

"A signal? Like Batman," she laughed.

"Hmm… let's see. During the game Monday night, you'll see me make a gesture and that will be the gesture I will send out every game to let you know I'm thinking about you."

"What kind of gesture?" she asked intrigued.

"I'm not going to say, but when I do it, you'll know it's meant for you."

TWENTY-ONE

As usual Jess and Sabrina had already arrived and ordered drinks by the time Denise arrived.

"Hello, ladies," Denise greeted them.

"Hey, sis," Jess responded with her usual enthusiastic self.

Sabrina however could be counted on to bring sarcasm to the situation as she looked down at her watch.

"I know, I know, I'm late again, Sabrina. I've had a long day. Leave me alone."

"What's going on, sis?" Jess asked rubbing her back. Jess could always be counted on for comfort.

That question ignited a mountain of emotions before Denise could even get comfortable in her seat.

"Everything. My whole world seems to be crumbling down around me and I feel like I'm on the verge of making either the biggest decision of my life or the biggest mistake of my life. In my heart I've chosen what I believe is the key to happiness and in my head I sometimes wonder if I've chosen the key to regret, and either way I'm creating a situation where someone is sure to be hurt in the end."

Sabrina and Jess sat in silence staring blankly at Denise.

"Damn, Denise," Sabrina finally spoke, "do we have to kill the mood before we finish our first drinks?"

Denise buried her head in her hands and started crying. Jess threw an evil eye at Sabrina as she searched for words to comfort her sister.

"Sabrina, you know, everyone is not as strong as you," Denise said sobbing before Jess could remove the tension. "Some of us have feelings and connections with other people that affect our lives daily," she continued, barely able to get the words out.

Jess hissed at Sabrina again.

"Ah, honey, I'm sure whatever is going on God will work out a way that's best for everyone," Jess said turning toward Sabrina, who was doing everything possible to stay out of the conversation.

"Say something," Jess mouthed to her.

"What?" Sabrina mouthed back. Jess squinted her eyes in disapproval.

"Denise, sweetie, don't cry," Jess said. "Whatever you decide, I know you will follow your heart and when you follow your heart you can't go wrong. It's our head that gets us in trouble. Right, Sabrina," Jess added in an attempt to force Sabrina to participate in the conversation.

After a small pause Sabrina took a deep, disgusted breath and finally spoke. "Denise, what happened?" she asked. That was the best she could do.

"Gerald will be out in less than a month and I-I just don't know what I'm going to do."

"You and Malcolm are just friends, right?" Sabrina asked.

"Yes, nothing has physically happened between us but I have to be honest with myself about the emotional attachment we've developed. Malcolm sees this as a long-term thing and it just can't be that for me. I'm in love with Gerald. Nothing can ever happen between me and Malcolm and I have to find a way to end things with him. But how can I do that in a way that won't make things difficult for him. He will be crushed."

"Denise, do you love him? Malcolm, I mean, do you love him?" Jess asked.

"Do I love him?" she repeated the question as if she hadn't hear it right the first time. Part of her did love him. The part of her that longed for daily attention. The part of her that longed for conversation. The part of her that missed being touched and caressed in such a way that her body became consumed with desire. But the part of her that longed for him confused lust with love and she didn't want to make a decision to leave the love of her life based on those circumstances. No matter how long he was in prison.

"I guess, I mean, I know I care for him deeply. Gerald has just been away for so long and I wonder if he and I will even be compatible once he gets out. The world has moved on and I'm going in one direction and I just wonder if he'll be going in the same direction I am. What if I end things with Malcolm and then things aren't what I expected with Gerald? Malcolm will never take me back. I wouldn't even ask him too. That's why I say someone will be bound to get hurt in the end, no matter what I do. Including me."

Denise began to cry again as Jess wrapped her arms around her shoulders. Looking over at Sabrina with a what-in-the-hell expression on her face, she whispered, "Say something," low enough without actually making a sound.

"What?" Sabrina whispered back, throwing her hands in the air. She cleared her throat. "Hmm, umm. Denise, girl, you want a drink?"

Jess's jaw dropped in disbelief.

"No, Sabrina," Denise responded rising from her sister's chest. "I don't want a drink! I'm going home, guys. I'm ruining everyone's night and I'm just not up to the bar scene."

Denise gathered her things to go as Jess tried to convince her to stay. Sabrina knew at this point she better say something or she wouldn't be getting her buzz on anytime soon.

"Look, Denise," she said softly, grabbing her hand. "Sit down."

"Sabrina, I can't take anymore of your sarcasm. Not tonight."

"No more sarcasm, just advice from one sister to another. Sit down please."

Denise took a deep breath and returned to her seat.

"We can't tell you what you should do. Only you can live your life and you have to decide who you want to wake up next to for the rest of your life. Whoever you choose should be the godly man that you've been praying about since high school. Don't settle for money or opportunity. Be sure you settle based on how he treats you and the amount of unconditional love you have for him. Figure out which of these two guys meets your needs, spiritually, emotionally and mentally, and then be sure that you'll be able to live with their faults. My advice is to not do anything at this point. Ask God to help you make the right choice and then wait on his answer. He will tell you what you need to say when that time comes."

Jess and Denise stared at Sabrina in disbelief.

"What?" Sabrina shouted as the two sat in silence.

"Sabrina," they both said in unison.

"That has to be the sweetest thing you've ever said to me," Denise said rising to hug her friend.

Jess laughed as Sabrina pushed Denise off of her.

"Sit down, girl. We have to maintain composure," she said looking around the restaurant to see who was watching. Running her fingers through her hair she continued, "I'm just saying, wait and see what happens."

Jess bumped shoulders with Sabrina and folded her arms in approval.

"What?" Sabrina asked her.

"I am proud of you, girl."

"Me too." Denise winked at her.

"Ya'll act like I just got baptized or something. I know the Lord, thank you. All I am saying is Gerald ain't out of prison yet and Malcolm is here. I don't know why you have to tell either of them anything until Gerald gets out, that's all I'm saying. I have to go to the restroom. Order me a Cosmo. Ya'll messing up my buzz."

With that, the Brina left the girls and headed toward the ladies' room. The girls watched as she stopped to talk to some guys along the way.

"Sabrina is right, Denise. Only you can decide what you need for happiness. And you have to decide that with God."

"I know. I just don't know if I'm ready for his answer."

TWENTY-TWO

February fourteenth two-thousand seven. Valentine's Day. Gerald could not believe the day was finally here. The day that he would finally be released from hell to start the life that he and Denise had been planning for fifteen years.

Lying in bed he closed his eyes and began to imagine what it would be like waking up next to Denise every day for the rest of his life. His parole hearing was in a few hours and he could hardly wait to hear the words "Mr. Williams, you are free to go."

Those few words, "Mr. Williams, you are free to go" would mean freedom from unruly criminals, prison activities, prison guards, hours without daylight. Freedom! Freedom to be with Denise forever.

Denise would be free too. Free from ever having to come and visit him behind bars. Free from ever having to walk down that long, filthy hall to visit him. Free from sharing their time together in a room full of criminals. Criminals that had done far worse crimes than what he was falsely charged of doing. Those words would free her from having sex-craved men, not worthy of her presence as far as he was concerned, gawk at her ever again.

It provided him no comfort that she was well guarded by prison guards. Prison guards could not protect her from whistles and comments made by prisoners as she walked down the criminally infested hall to visit HIM. The screw-up that forced her into prison life.

Gerald hated that walk more than Denise because he knew what was going through the minds of those men. Most of the guys were serving a minimum of twenty years, and the others were serving life without the possibility of parole. It had been a long time since most of the men at Tree Mountain had been with a woman, let alone a woman as beautiful as Denise. And she was beautiful. The most beautiful woman he had ever known. He fantasized about her often and he could only imagine the twisted images the inmates had concocted in their deranged minds. The thought of them dreaming about her, kissing her, having sex with her, jacking off to her enraged Gerald.

After her last visit a fellow inmate mentioned how full her lips and her hips were. Gerald blew it off at first but then he commented on how round her breasts were. Plump and juicy. Soft like pillows. The inmate egged him on.

"Man, I could suck dem lips all day," he said as he licked his own lips.

Gerald lunged for him over the cafeteria table. He couldn't let that go. That was crossing the line. He already had to live with the fact that some of the most vile men, scum of the earth losers, were fantasizing about his woman, but he wasn't going to let any of them disrespect her.

Turning over, Gerald stared at a picture of Denise hanging on his wall.

"Hey, beautiful," he said smiling as if she could hear him. He swore she smiled back at him. He had the love of one of God's most beautiful creations.

Even though ole boy almost lost his life that day, he wasn't wrong. She was gorgeous. Her best feature was definitely her full lips. They were thick, full, soft, juicy lips just as he described. Natural full lips. No collagen needed. Kryptonite, he would call them because he became weak at the touch. And when she wore red lipstick, shiny red lipstick, he could hardly contain himself. He had to have them. Suck them. Devour them between his.

"Red is my signature color," she would say. And it was, especially on her thick full lips.

Closing his eyes he could see her standing before him. She had the body of Anna Nicole Smith in between trim spa. Full figured. Lots of curves. Plenty to hold on to on a chilly night. He never preferred a skinny woman over a full-figured beauty. He had to have meat on his bones and she carried it well.

To him she was perfect in every way. Perfect height. Perfect shade of caramel. Golden brown skin, as she would say. A flawless complexion. No dark circles, no fine lines, no scratches, no marks. Flawless. Makeup was not needed. Except on those luscious lips of course.

She received compliments everywhere she went from whites, blacks and browns on how smooth and unblemished her skin tone was. They would often ask her what makeup line she used and she would proudly say, "I don't wear makeup." It was fun for him to watch the other women gasp with envy.

Her hair was jet black and on most days she wore it straight with no curls or frills. "Curling irons can damage hair," she would say. So she used them as little as possible.

He thought back to the times he would lie in bed and watch her after a shower. She had a routine of sitting at the vanity every night before lying down, pampering herself with perfumes and lotions. Rose petal fragrances would fill the air as she massaged every inch of her body. Caressing every spot Gerald wanted to kiss. Her thighs, her breasts, her neck. He became aroused at the memory.

He loved Denise, more than she would ever know. She was his world and no one would ever fully understand the torture he was experiencing by not being able to be with her. Especially because he was the reason they were separated. He knew he was not guilty and that he had just spent fifteen years of his life behind bars for a crime he did not commit, but that was nothing compared to the loss he felt by having to leave Denise. She was his life, the best part of his life.

For the most part, Gerald grew up as a well-managed child. Raised by his father who was a well-known pastor at one of the largest black churches in Houston's third ward and a bible-packing grandmother, trouble did not find him often. Collectively, after the death of his mother, they did everything they possibly could to protect him from life on the streets and the penal system.

Gerald was a friend to all and he managed to pick up a few friends along the way that introduced him to things kids in the suburbs never knew existed. But he never allowed them to influence the choices he made. He also knew he would face the wrath of the switch when he got home.

He was known in the hood as Church Boy because he was always the one trying to cool situations down when things got a little heated in a game of basketball or dominoes, and he was always peeping knowledge about something he had learned from his grandmother or father. Most of the kids in the hood appreciated it. Gerald always believed you can't be hard all the time. Everyone has a heart and a conscious and they respected him for always treating them like humans instead of thugs. So to them he was cool peeps to hang out with and they respected his family for always taking care of the hood.

When he got to college he gravitated toward a different type of partygoer. FRAT BOYS. During that time Prairie View was predominately black in attendance and fraternity parties at an all-black college were off the chain. Booze, girls, music, booty shaking and more girls. College life on the campus of PV made it hard for a brother to stay focused on going to class, studying or church, for that matter.

One day some of the frat brothers and some "hunnies," as they were called back then, were hanging out on the steps of the girls' dormitory. For him one girl stood out among the rest. Denise Rush. The moment he saw her, everyone else disappeared.

TWENTY-THREE

One of the things about Denise that instantly set her apart from the rest was her ability to talk. She could really talk. Really have a conversation. Unlike most of the airheads he had met on campus whose main topic of discussion consisted of the latest fashions, music videos and campus gossip about what female was sleeping with what jock on the football team.

Denise could talk about real subjects. The world, goals, dreams, life after college. Topics with substance. She was the type of girl that his father and grandmother told him he needed to be with. She was a Christian. She talked about God a lot. His grandmother would be pleased with her and that was important to him. The moment he met her he knew he had to make her his.

There was one problem. She was interested in his cousin, Keith. Gerald had also been casually seeing a girl who lived in her dormitory, Kathy. And to make the situation worse, Kathy and Denise were neighbors.

He felt pretty sure he could solve his issue. He and Kathy were not committed. They just hooked up every blue, blue, blue moon, when he was feeling lonely; it only happened a couple of times. He definitely didn't see her has a long-term thing and felt it would be pretty easy to break it off. Diverting her attention from Keith would be the problem.

Keith was a straight up playa. Smooth chocolate skin brother. A body built like L.L. Cool J, equipped with the whole licking of the lips, which drove the girls, all girls, absolutely mad. And he just ate it up. He would romance any woman that showed him any interest whether he was interested or not just because he could get them.

Denise asked Gerald to hook her up with Keith. He was crushed but agreed to do the deed. At least that's what he told her. He had no intention of hooking her up with Casanova. He knew what type of guy his cousin was and there was no way he was going to let him scar this beautiful woman for the rest of her life.

So he played it cool. Broke things off with Kathy and pretended to deliver messages to Keith from Denise. She would ask him periodically if he was making any progress but he would usually play it off or tell her he hadn't talked to or seen him in a while to avoid the subject.

He was just biding his time with her, spending time with her every chance he could get. Building on their "friendship." Giving him just the time he needed for her to get to know him better.

He knew it would only be a matter of time and she would eventually give up on Keith. Keith was in her mind. He wanted her heart and he just needed the right moment to show her just how much.

That moment finally arrived at the homecoming game. Prairie View versus TSU. Everyone was pretty wired up after the game because PV won. The only game PV had won all season. In years, really.

Gerald ran into Denise and some of her friends from home after the game. She was walking toward him dressed in a sheer black tube top, leopard miniskirt and six-inch riding boots. She was gorgeous. Sexy. He had never really seen her in that way. Normally she was in warm-ups with a college tee. Typical college student. But standing before him was a woman. A beautiful woman. The moment he saw her he knew. It was time to make her his. He didn't want anyone else to have her.

"Hey, Gerald," she said wrapping her arms around him. "We won! Finally! Can you believe it?"

"Yea, we won," he said in a serious but tender tone. "I think I have won too," he said grabbing her waist.

She stood back a minute detecting the seriousness in his tone.

"What do you mean you won?" she asked.

Grabbing her face with his hands he kissed her forehead and looked as deeply as he could into her eyes. He wanted to kiss her. More than anything he had ever wanted to do in his life.

"I have the most beautiful woman in my arms and I am determined to make her mine."

Denise smiled, even blushed a little before wrapping her arms around him again. At that moment she felt it too.

"What are you doing later?" he whispered in her ear.

"Umm," Denise said nervously, "going to the dance with my sister and best friend from home," she said pointing to Jess and Sabrina who had come down for the game.

"Can we get together?" Gerald asked.

"Well, they'll be in town until tomorrow and I want to spend as much time as I can with them before they leave."

"What about tomorrow night? I want to see you," he pleaded.

She was speechless. Stunned. Consumed with feelings she didn't realize she had.

"Please, I need to see you."

"Okay," she managed to get out.

She had got that Keith wasn't interested in her because he never contacted her and when they ran into each other in passing all she could get out of him was a Blair Underwood smile.

Even still, she had never considered Gerald as an option. He was the guy trying to hook her up with someone else. Friends, as far as she was concerned.

But in that moment, that moment when he kissed her forehead and told her he was determined to make her his, everything changed. She no longer saw him as just a friend. For the first time she saw him as a man. A man who was attracted to and wanted to be with her in every way. And there was no question that she wanted him to.

They agreed to meet at the library the next evening and the rest as they say was history.

Her love for him completely changed his outlook on life. He no longer wanted to party and hang out with the boys. He wanted to be wherever she was, doing whatever she was doing.

He traded in frat parties for studying at the library just to be near her, gave up Sunday dominoes and forty-ounce beers for church and movie night, and whatever time they spent apart was filled with phone conversations and text messages.

On occasion he would still hang out with the guys, usually when Denise was unavailable or had gone home for the weekend. Shooting some hoops, playing some dominoes or just hanging out watching a game.

During their senior year, Denise was making frequent trips to Austin to look for employment. They had decided to move to Austin after graduation because she had several contacts in radio who could hook her up with a job. Gerald was finishing in business and had dreams of starting his own construction company. He knew it would take him a little longer to get on his feet and both decided it would be best if she found a job first so that they would have money coming in while he worked his way up.

One weekend, while Denise was away, Gerald decided to hang out with a couple of his buddies. It was late and almost crunch time for purchasing alcohol so the guys decided to run down to the corner store for more brew before time ran out.

It was no surprise that the clerk immediately went into hater mode. The South still had its share of prejudice and after seeing five black dudes walk in at eleven forty-five at night the clerk was on guard.

Gerald headed straight for the snack aisle while the other guys headed toward the alcohol.

Everyone was already feeling pretty good, and when you get a couple of college kids together with a few beers already under their belts, things tend to get a little loud with the jokes, the *Niggas* and the *Hell Naaaawww's*.

Gerald was looking for his favorite snack, sunflower seeds with sea salt, when the laughter and good times he heard from the opposite side of the store suddenly turned into shouting and cursing.

Dropping his items on the rack he raced to the front of the store to find Terrell at the counter mad as hell. His hands were balled into a fist and he was pacing like a pit bull ready to attack.

TWENTY-FOUR

"What the f--- you mean it's too late to buy beer?" he asked the clerk in a threatening tone. "Man, it's eleven fifty-five. It ain't twelve yet."

"As, far as I'm concerned, it's twelve o'clock," said the clerk bucking up to him.

"What's going on?" Gerald interrupted hoping to calm the situation before things got out of hand. He knew Terrell and knew things could get real ugly real quick.

"This cracker talking bout it's twelve o'clock. Talking bout he ain't selling us no beer. Man, this is bull sh--."

"Terrell, just calm down, man," Gerald said trying to grab his arm and pull him away from the counter to put a little space between him and the clerk.

Terrell's fists were still balled and Gerald knew if the guy said one wrong thing, he wouldn't remember anything else after Terrell got through with him.

"Man, f--- that." Terrell jerked away from Gerald. "We got in here before midnight man. This mother fu--er is trippin."

"Sir, we still have two minutes to purchase the alcohol," Gerald said trying to reason with the clerk. "We don't want any trouble. We just want to buy the beer and leave, sir."

"Well it's twelve o'clock by my watch and you and your little nigger friends can just go home, because you ain't gettin no beer from this store. Not tonight!"

The room was dead silent. No one spoke as each tried to figure out if he really said what they thought he'd just said.

Gerald lowered his head in anticipation of what would come next. Terrell spoke first.

"What the f--- did you just say?"

Gerald looked up and Terrell was standing next to the clerk. In his hand was a black nine millimeter pistol pointed at the guy's temple.

"Terrell! No!" Gerald screamed, running over to try and talk some sense into him.

By now the other guys had run out of the store and Gerald was all Terrell had to keep him from making the biggest mistake he could make in life.

Gerald didn't even know Terrell owned a gun, let alone had it on him. He had to stay behind. He had to be the voice of reason. All the while he was asking himself, what in the hell was he thinking? Terrell was mad as hell and who wouldn't blame him? This white man just called a group of black men niggers. Had he lost his mind? He knew at this point there was nothing he could do or say that would stop Terrell from tearing into the clerk but he had to try. He searched his mind for the right words to calm his friend down and get them both out of the store.

"Say it again, cracker. Say it again," Terrell kept saying.

Gerald said a quick prayer and thought of Denise. She would know what to say and do in this situation. He prayed that she would never be in this situation. He remembered something she would always tell him. "Everything can be handled with good communication."

Terrell was communicating alright, but not in the language and with the words Denise was referring too. The gun he was holding was saying a lot about what he intended to do to the ignorant man behind the counter.

"Come on, man. It's not worth it," Gerald finally managed to get out. "Let's just go, man. Let's just go," he said looking around for cameras. *Please let there be no cameras*, a voice inside him prayed.

"Man, f--- this ass-hole. You gone call me a nigger, pussy, say it again. I dare you. Say it again." Terrell pushed the tip of the gun into the man's temple.

The clerk was beet red. Fear was pouring out of him. "Get the f--- out of my store," he managed to get out.

"Naw, say it again, cracker. You were full of words a little while ago. What up now, pussy?"

"Come on, man. It's not worth it," Gerald pleaded again but Terrell wasn't hearing it. He just kept pushing the gun into the temple of the clerk, staring him down, ready to pull the trigger at the slightest utterance.

"Look at you now, mother fu----. You ain't got nothing to say now do you?"

Gerald finally wedged his way into a small space behind Terrell and the counter. Wrapping his arm around Terrell's broad shoulders he was able to place his hand around the shaft of the gun.

"Terrell! Man, let's go! It ain't worth it! We are in our senior year man and in a few more weeks you'll be graduating. Terrell, man, don't screw that up. You've come too far."

Terrell didn't speak. He just stared at the clerk. You could see the hate and anger in his eyes. If Gerald didn't get to him fast he was going to let loose.

"Yeah, he's ignorant and he's definitely a cowardly MF, but don't let his ignorance ruin the rest of your life. Come on, man. Be smart, man."

Finally Gerald could see the tension leaving Terrell.

"Do the right thing, man. Come on. Let me have the gun," Gerald made another plea.

"My boy just saved your life, mother fu----. You heard me. Better watch who you stepping to, cracker."

"C'mon, man, let's just go," Gerald said still waiting for Terrell to let go of his grip around the trigger.

Terrell finally released the trigger and Gerald jerked the gun away from him placing himself between Terrell and the clerk.

Just when Gerald thought it was all over, the store clerk cried out in pain. Startled, Gerald turned around to find him lying on the ground holding his face with bloodied hands.

"What happened?" Gerald yelled.

"You hit me! That's what happened!" the clerk shouted out.

"What?" Gerald responded confused, searching his mind to try and figure out how the clerk ended up on the ground in a pool of blood. *Had the gun gone off?* Gerald tried to recall in his mind.

"That's what you get, cracker." Terrell stood over the clerk taunting him.

"What the hell happened, man!" Gerald yelled grabbing Terrell.

"Man, I don't know. He just went down. Good for him. Punk bitch."

The events were racing in Gerald's head. The last thing he remembered was snatching the gun. Snatching the gun. That was it. When he snatched the gun from Terrell his arm swung around. Right into the jaw of the clerk, who was still on the ground in a fetal position with blood around him.

Gerald quickly turned to Terrell. "Man, let's get the hell out of here," he said pushing him toward the door.

Terrell quickly yanked the phone cord out of the wall to give them enough time to get out of dodge. "Thanks for the beer, cracker." Terrell got in one last dig, throwing money at the clerk and grabbing the beer.

"I am going to get you, mother f----ers!" the store owner yelled.

The events of that night changed the course of Gerald's life forever.

Denise returned to campus the next day and as hard as he tried to pretend all was well, she knew immediately something was wrong.

When she showed up at his dorm he held on to her as if it would be the last time he would ever hold her again. He knew that had she been in town he would have never been in that situation.

He told her everything.

She wanted him to go to the cops but he wanted to wait and see if anything would come of it. So far cops had not swarmed the campus for them and he didn't see any cameras in the store so with any luck he was hoping it would just all blow over. Besides, he hadn't done anything wrong. There was no shooting. The assault was an accident. If there was a camera it would show that Terrell brought the gun, not him. All he did was try to calm the situation.

After explaining it all to Denise he put on a good front like he wasn't concerned, but he was scared. More scared than he'd ever been in life.

TWENTY-FIVE

Three weeks passed and nothing. There was talk of the incident around campus but no names were mentioned. Gerald thought it would be better not to associate himself with Terrell for a while, spending most of his time in the dorm or with Denise.

A month later, Gerald walked out of the science building to find four police officers standing near the bottom of the stairs. After confirming he was Gerald Williams they took him to the campus police station where city officers were waiting to take him down to the station.

At first Gerald had a hard time grasping what was going on. When he demanded to know why all they would tell him was that they had a few questions to ask him regarding an assault.

Assault, there was no assault, Gerald told them repeatedly.

The store must have had cameras somewhere, which meant bad news for Terrell. He knew there was no way he could help Terrell out of this one. If there were cameras then it was all on film and all Gerald could do was plead with the officers to let him off easy.

The owner provoked them. There was no doubt about that. Terrell could have controlled the situation better, yeah, but there was no assault. The most they could get on him was robbery.

When they arrived at the station, Gerald was taken to a room where two officers questioned him about the incident. They confirmed that there was a tape and he was positively identified.

Gerald went along with the questioning at first, explaining the situation as a matter of fact kind of thing as if he were Terrell's lawyer introducing evidence.

The officers stepped out of the room for a moment and returned with a third man who introduced himself as the lead investigator.

After pleasant conversation the investigator advised Gerald that he had seen the tape and spoken with the officers regarding his responses to their question. He thought he was doing okay until the questions appeared to be more focused on him than Terrell.

"Why were you holding the gun? What were you doing at the store that time of night? What did the owner do or say to initiate the gun being drawn?"

What in the world is going on? Gerald kept asking himself. It was like he had stepped into the movie *Menace II Society* and he was the perp they'd been combing the streets to capture.

They questioned him for over two hours and Gerald soon realized they didn't bring him down to ask him questions about what Terrell had done; they were after him. They were charging him with aggravated assault, not Terrell.

"What the hell is going on here?" Gerald shouted, quickly rising to his feet. "You guys aren't trying to pin this on me. I'm the one that kept things from getting out of control."

"You need to sit down, son. We're only trying to get to the bottom of this."

"Sounds to me like you're playing pin the tail on the donkey and I'll be damned if I play the donkey."

"Son, I am only going to say this once more. Sit down."

The officers explained that he'd been positively associated with the robbery as the person that assaulted the clerk.

"Robbery attempt! Nobody was trying to rob him, man! We just wanted to buy some beer! That's it!"

"So you admit you were there?"

"I told you that earlier. There was no robbery and there was no assault."

In essence, Gerald was telling the truth. The gun hit him on accident and although Terrell did use excessive force, he paid the owner for the beer before he left the store.

Gerald stopped talking.

"I need to make a phone call. Are you charging me with something? I'm not answering any more questions until I speak to a lawyer."

They kept probing but Gerald didn't say any more. Another officer entered the room and whispered something into the ear of the investigator. They both walked to the door and the investigator briefly stuck his head out and continued the conversation.

When he returned to the table he informed Gerald that the store owner had just identified him as the person that hit him with the gun.

"I told you. I hit him with the gun but it was an accident. I was trying to get the gun away. I was trying to help him."

They weren't listening to him. They just told him that the tape they reviewed did not match up with what he was saying and that Terrell had implicated him as being part of the robbery.

"There was no robbery!" Gerald screamed.

Gerald knew they were probing. Terrell wouldn't turn on him. Terrell and Gerald had known each other all their lives. He had always protected Gerald on the streets and he knew that he would do the same now. He was confident of that.

Gerald told them again he was not answering any more questions without a lawyer and they finally allowed him to call his parents. They hired a lawyer and he was released on bail.

Shortly after graduation his trial began and it became clear that the DA was going after Terrell, and Gerald was just collateral damage. Terrell had a long list of offenses and the cops had been trying to find something to pin on him for a while.

Gerald had no priors and his lawyer was confident this would get him off or at minimum probation, but in the end, both were found guilty. Gerald for aggravated assault and Terrell on armed robbery and battery. Both were given twenty years with the possibility of parole in ten.

That was it. Just like that his freedom was taken away from him. Twelve jurors of his so-called peers determined he was guilty as charged. The store owner pointed Gerald out as part of the group of vandals that hit his store and the videotape backed it up as far as they were concerned.

Denise was devastated. When the verdict was read he turned to her. She was sobbing. There was nothing he could do. All he wanted was reach out to her and let her know that things would be okay. But he couldn't. He couldn't console her. He couldn't give her one last kiss. He couldn't even tell her he loved her. He was immediately shackled and carted off for the next decade of his life.

A week after arriving he received a letter from Denise. She told him she believed in him and that she would wait.

Gerald cried at the memory.

"Mr. Williams, they're ready for you," the guard said.

Gerald rose to his feet as the guard opened the cell door. Facing forward as the guard put on the handcuffs and walked him to what he hoped would be a door that would open to the rest of his life with Denise.

TWENTY-SIX

Today's the day. Valentine's Day. The day the love of her life would soon be calling her to say, "Baby, come get me. I AM FREE!"

Denise had taken the day off because it was Friday, February fourteenth and on this day, Valentine's Day, Gerald would be home.

Her day was filled with running here, running there, picking up this and picking up that. She was going to make him a gourmet meal. Pot roast with all the fixings, carrots, peas, potatoes and corn.

Gerald often complained about the "prison slop" they were forced to eat in the mess hall and she wanted him to have a good home-cooked meal when he got home. Apple martini's would be the drink of the evening and strawberries and whipped cream for dessert.

After seasoning the roast with just the right flavors she placed the delicacy in the oven and decided to soak in the tub for a while. It was mid-afternoon and she was expecting his call around three so she wanted to relax a bit because it was going to be a long night.

The sounds of KEM filled the rooms of her home as she soaked in lavender oil and bubbles. Sipping on some of the apple martini she had prepared, she lay in the tub thinking only of Gerald.

She had talked to Malcolm little over the past four weeks. He had called and left messages but after her conversation with the girls, Denise decided it would be best to cool things down.

Her heart belonged to Gerald and her feelings for Malcolm were confusing the situation, so she thought it would be best to just avoid all conversation and contact.

Malcolm on the other hand continued to call and leave messages. Never once asking why she hadn't called. He just kept her up to date with his comings and goings and reminded her that he was thinking of her. It helped that his schedule was so busy with games and practices due to the upcoming playoff season. This gave her a scapegoat, a reason to explain why they hadn't been spending as much time together.

He managed to send her an email asking about her plans for Valentine's Day. She responded simply stating she wasn't sure but would let him know if she was free. She put it as nice as she could of course. Usually she and the girls would hang out and celebrate with dinner and a good movie so if she had to she could use that as an excuse.

After soaking in the tub for about an hour she started to get dressed. Sitting down at the vanity she began to moisturize her body from head to toe. The scent of Moonlight Path filled the room as she massaged her feet and toes. She closed her eyes and imagined Gerald slowly moving his hands across her body, to her thighs and then up to her torso and breasts. A feeling overwhelmed her at the thought of him touching her. Caressing her in a way that only he could.

Once she had completed her full body massage she applied tinted moisturizer from Mary Kay to her face. Makeup was not her thing, except for lipstick, of course, but the product had a moisturizer that she loved. She didn't mind too much the tint of color and needed the protection for her dry skin.

Finishing her hair she searched through two closets to find the perfect red dress for her mate. Gerald loved her in red.

Laying the dress on the bed, she grabbed the red thong she had just purchased from Victoria's Secret and began to slide it up her thighs. Her body moved from side to side as she slid the garment up her legs allowing the back to nestle between the two cheeks of her hips. Turning in the mirror to make sure everything was in the right place she put on the matching red lace bra, which provided just enough cleavage to make any man want more. Gerald would rip it off as soon as they hit the door she was sure.

Pouring another martini, she plopped down on the couch to watch the latest episode of *Dr. Phil* and wait for his call.

Settling down on her couch, still in her bra and thong, she noticed the red light on the phone base indicating she had new voice messages.

The first message was from Malcolm wishing her a Happy Valentine's Day and apologizing for not being able to come to town to celebrate it with her. *That worked out great*, she thought to herself. She was going to tell him about Gerald. She was just waiting for the right opportunity.

There were a couple of messages from Sabrina, frustrated over her latest court appearance with the infamous Stoney Hunter. Things were not going her way in court and she was not happy.

The next few messages were from Mom and her sis about the Mother's Day picnic, which was a whole three months away.

"Blah, blah, blah," Denise muttered back to the machine, waving her hand in circles as if it would make the message play faster.

"Message received Friday, February fourteenth, two-thousand seven, eight a.m." *Beep!* the voice system announced the next message.

"Hey, baby." Denise jumped off the couch and walked over to the machine. It was Gerald.

"Happy Valentine's Day," he continued. "I was hoping you would answer so that I could be the first person to tell you how much I love you today."

"How sweet," she said blowing kisses at the machine. Taking a sip of martini she continued to listen to his profession of love for her as she smiled with delight. She loved hearing his voice. It was very deep, much like a radio DJ late at night playing grown folks' music for grown folks' activities. He could easily change her mood from being angry at him to a smile when he whispered, "I love you," with that deep sexy voice.

"Baby, we've run into another minor complication. It will be another month before I get out, baby. I promise, this will be the last month. Something happened in here that I would rather tell you about in person. Nothing big, but they want to just give it one more month and they promise if there are no other occurrences I will be out. I'm sorry, baby. I know you're disappointed and so am I. There was nothing I wanted more than being able to hold you in my arms and make love to you, especially today. I love you, baby. I love you. Just a little while longer, I promise. Happy Valentine's Day. Come visit me soon."

Beep!

Denise couldn't believe it. She stood still, staring at the answering machine in disbelief. Her body was frozen. Unable to move. Unable to show emotion. Anger began to build inside her.

A two-minute voice message shattered her spirit, shattered her hope and destroyed all remnants of joy. It felt as if he had just slapped her across the face and told her she was not allowed to be happy anymore.

Tears began to fill her eyes with disappointment as she stood, frozen, still staring at the answering machine.

In the distance she could hear messages still playing on the machine but the voices were a blur. The only words she heard were the words of Gerald, *It will be another month, baby.*

The words repeated in her mind over and over. *It will be another month… It will be another month…*

Her skin became warm as her body began to tremble. Trembling with anger, trembling with disappointment, trembling at the thought of more days filled with loneliness.

It will be another month, the voice in her head wouldn't stop echoing.

Her hands began to ache as she stared at the half-full glass of martini crippled by her grip. Letting out a scream of disappointment her arm swung behind her head as if she were a quarterback about to throw a pass to the receiver.

The glass flew across the room, shattering against the front door. Pieces flew across the room in all directions as she yelled out to the emptiness of the room.

"F--- you!" she screamed out as she fell to floor in tears.

TWENTY-SEVEN

Everything was out of focus as Denise began to open her eyes. Trying to focus on what she was seeing she blinked and rubbed them as she tried to recall why she was lying on the ground surrounded by shattered glass. The memory of Gerald's voice message suddenly hit her and she began to notice several items she'd been missing for some time underneath the living room sofa.

A couple of pens, a pair of slippers, the missing half to one of her favorite pairs of red earrings.

Pushing herself off the ground her eyes began to water as she realized Gerald may never get out of prison. Something may always come up and she could be waiting for the entire length of his term before they could begin their lives together.

Still in the red lingerie she had purchased as a gift for Gerald, she grabbed the pair of slippers hiding underneath the couch. The last thing she needed was to end up in the emergency room on top of everything else.

After placing the slippers on her feet she retrieved a robe from the bathroom and splashed some water on her face.

It will be another month, baby was still ringing in her ears as she cleaned up the glass. The house was silent. The sounds of KEM that had serenaded her earlier were replaced with a quiet, eerie loneliness.

Denise was no longer smiling, no longer excited and no longer happy.

A tear rolled down her cheek as she vacuumed up the final pieces of glass that represented the mess the man she loved had left her in.

After placing the vacuum cleaner in the utility closet, she reached into the fridge for her favorite comfort food, cookies-and-cream ice cream, and headed for bed.

Glancing at the clock as she entered her room, she noticed it was only seven thirty. The thought of going to bed at seven thirty depressed her even more.

Taking her ice cream and nearby cover she sat at the bay window looking out into the street at the cars going to and fro. Lovers heading out to celebrate Valentine's Day no doubt.

Valentine's Day, she thought to herself. *Valentine's Day will be the first day of the rest of their lives*, she remembered him saying to her when they last spoke.

"What a joke," she said as she scooped another spoonful of ice cream.

Climbing into bed she started the DVD player.

The movie began just as it had so many other times. Music playing. Ducks swimming through the pond.

She hadn't watched the *Notebook* in months. Here she was again. Alone. No Malcolm. No Gerald.

"I've loved another with all my heart and soul and for me that has always been enough," James Garner said as he narrated the opening lines of the movie.

Denise wasn't really watching the TV, though. She couldn't get Gerald out of her mind. She couldn't get that voicemail out of her head. She was angry, she was disappointed and she was lonely. She was many feelings wrapped into one big emotional mess.

Lying on the bed she watched as the reflection of car lights ran across the ceiling of her bedroom. The phone had rung several times but she didn't have the energy to answer. She would have to explain why she was home alone answering the phone. She didn't understand it herself. How could she explain it to someone else?

Hearing something in the air she lifted her head and looked out toward the hallway. After hearing nothing more she curled into a ball and squeezed a pillow. Staring blankly at the muted TV as Allie and Noah lay in the middle of the street. Early stages of love.

Then she heard it again. *Bump, bump, bump.*

The first thing that popped in her mind was Gerald. Jumping out of bed she slid her feet into her slippers and ran down the hall. Normally she would check the peephole but there was no time to waste.

Swinging the door open with a smile big enough to cover her entire face, she was greeted by a gentleman dressed in a black suit. He removed his hat, which was big enough for the heads of two clowns. He was wearing white gloves and the shiniest black shoes she had ever seen.

"Ms. Rush?" the man asked.

"Who wants to know?" she answered. Getting a little nervous she closed the door slightly and placed her hand on the inside lock. Just in case she needed to slam it shut.

"I have a delivery for a Ms. Rush," he continued.

"I am Ms. Rush," she responded.

"Good evening, ma'am. This is for you," he said, handing her a manila envelope.

"From who?" she asked.

"I suspect the same person who sent you these," he said pointing to the ground just outside the door.

Denise opened the door to find a bouquet of red roses nestled against the bricks of the house.

"Oh my God," she said as she looked around to see if her admirer was nearby.

The man in the drivers knelt down and picked up the bouquet of flowers and handed them to Denise.

"Thank you," she said.

"You're very welcome. I will see you soon," he said walking away from the door.

"Wait, your tip," she said trying to stop him.

"No thank you, ma'am. That's been taken care of," he answered.

As she closed the door she picked up on something he said. "I will see you soon." *What did that mean*, she wondered as she walked to the kitchen to find a vase for the flowers.

The entire house was filled with the fragrance of fresh rose petals. She searched for a card but couldn't find one.

"Umm," she said placing her hands on her hips.

Remembering the manila envelope the man in the suit gave her she ran back into the living room. Too excited to find the letter opener she tore the envelope open with her teeth. Literally shredding the rest with her hands.

Inside was a second envelope with her name written on it. Opening it carefully, so as not to harm the contents, she found two plane tickets along with a letter.

"Denise, please join me for an evening of romance February 14, 2007 @ 9 p.m. By now you have noticed the limousine parked outside of your house. It is waiting to take you to the airport for your flight. He has been instructed to wait as long as it takes for you to say yes."

Denise walked over to the window to find the gentleman that delivered her flowers standing by the longest black limousine she had ever seen.

"Can't wait to see you, Malcolm."

After reading the letter Denise took a look at the tickets. Two round-trip tickets to Paris, France. She couldn't believe it. Her mouth dropped open as she stared at the tickets, shaking her head in disbelief.

Shortly after, the doorbell rang and as promised she opened the door to find the limousine driver with another bouquet. Another dozen red roses.

"This is too much," she said grabbing the vase.

"Ma'am, I have been instructed to deliver a dozen roses every twenty minutes until you come out."

"Oh my God! This is too much," she said again.

Denise didn't know what to do. She closed the door and sat down on the couch. Ecstatic. Unable to fully grasp what was going on.

"Paris! Paris, France," she kept saying over and over.

Reaching for the phone she had to call someone to knock her back into reality.

"Sabrina. No, too much drama. Jess. Jess will be sensible."

She could barely dial the numbers.

TWENTY-EIGHT

"What are you doing calling me?" Jess asked her. She was sure Denise would be wrapped around Gerald for a week.

"Jess, you will never guess what just happened."

"What happened?" Jess asked repeating her sister's tone.

"Malcolm! Oh my God! Malcolm just asked me to go to Paris with him."

"Wait a minute," Jess interrupted. "Malcolm? Paris? Where's Gerald?"

"Gerald didn't get out, and Malcolm just asked me to go to Paris with him."

"What do you mean Gerald didn't get out? Gerald didn't get out?"

"Jess, never mind that! What about Malcolm and Paris? Oh, hold on. The limo driver is at the door."

"Limo driver! Denise, what's going on?"

Denise opened the door to find a third bouquet of roses.

"Oh my God!" she shouted out with excitement as the driver tipped his hat and smiled.

Closing the door, Denise returned to the phone. "Jess, are you still there?"

"Yes! Are you kidding? What in the world is going on over there?"

"Malcolm sent a limo driver here with a bouquet of roses asking me to go to Paris."

"When?"

"Just now!"

"No, sis, when does he want to go to Paris?"

"Tonight! The driver is outside and every twenty minutes he will bring me another dozen roses until I say yes!"

"Shut! Up! Denise, what are you going to do?"

"That's why I called you, sis."

"Well what are you doing calling me? You should be packing to go. It's cool over there so take something to keep warm and make sure you have an umbrella, and a camera."

"Wait a minute. You think I should go? Just like that! Pack my bags and go to Paris. You don't think this is all happening a little too fast?"

"Denise, you need to do what's going to make you happy. You have been spending so much of your life trying to do the right thing for Gerald. It's time you started doing the right thing for you."

Jess was right. Denise had devoted fifteen years to a man who was in prison for most of their relationship. She had spent the last fifteen years missing every opportunity to celebrate and enjoy her own life. She had been in prison just as much as he was and she was fed up with it.

"Denise, you deserve some fun. Go have fun. I'll let Mom and Dad know you're off getting some me-time and I'll take care of Creasy and the house. Just touch base with me at some point during the trip so that I know you're okay."

"Thanks, sis. I love you."

"I love you too! Now go, before there are so many roses in your house you won't be able to get in there yourself."

"Okay, bye!"

"Bye, Denise! Be careful, have fun and make sure that man brings you back safely!"

Denise hung up the phone and ran to her room to change. The robe wrapped around her was still hiding Victoria's Secret so she pulled on a sexy red wrap-around dress and brushed her hair back into a pony tail. After spraying a mist of Vera Wang over her body she threw a few things in a bag and headed to the door.

"Okay, girl, here we go," she said, giving herself a quick pep talk in the living room mirror.

The doorbell rang again.

Taking in a deep breath she opened the door to find the limo driver holding a fourth bouquet of roses.

He couldn't help but notice how beautiful she was. Handing her the bouquet of roses he bowed. "I take it you will be joining Mr. Anderson."

"I have decided to say yes! I would love to go to Paris," she beamed. "Just let me set these inside."

The limo driver smiled.

Placing the vase on the counter she returned to the door and held out her arm to the driver.

"Shall we go?" she asked.

"We shall," the driver responded, wrapping his arm around hers as he escorted her to the car.

When Denise stepped into the limo she found a fifth bouquet of roses lying on the seat. Instead of being neatly arranged in a vase like the others, it was perfectly wrapped in beautiful paper and tissue.

As the car pulled away, Denise placed the roses under her nose and took in a deep breath. Savoring every scent of the beautiful fragrance she read the card, which simply stated "Can't wait to see you. Malcolm."

TWENTY-NINE

Butterflies multiplied by the dozens in her stomach as the limo neared the airport terminal. Sounds of Kim Waters filled the cabin space as her mind raced with a million thoughts and fears.

As excited as she was about spending time in Paris with Malcolm, she couldn't help but think about Gerald.

Memories of disappointment emerged as she recalled his voice message. *It will be another month, baby.* Out of everything he said, those were the words that pierced through her heart. *It will be another month, baby.*

A small part of her felt guilty about accepting Malcolm's invitation but the fact that Gerald had failed her again infuriated her and for the first time in their relationship her frustration was far greater than her love for him.

People were moving to and fro at pick-up and drop-off locations along the terminal drive, filing in and out of cars, unloading baggage, loading baggage. Sneaking in quick hugs and kisses. Some saying hello. Some saying goodbye.

Denise sat anxiously as the driver passed several airline terminals. She wasn't really sure what airline she was flying. She wasn't really sure about much of anything other than the fact that she was going to Paris. That she was sure of.

As they slowly approached the last terminal, Continental Airlines, Denise began to gather her things together to jump out of the car without much delay; however, the driver didn't stop.

"Okay, what's going on?" she asked herself.

Clearing her throat she knocked on the window separating her from the driver.

"Excuse me, but which airline will I be flying?" she asked.

"Mr. Anderson has a small private jet waiting for you, ma'am."

"Oh my God! A private jet! Shut! Up!"

"Yes, ma'am. We will be there shortly." He chuckled at her excitement.

Denise sat back in her seat and clasped her hands together as if she were a little girl about to get a cookie out of the cookie jar.

Just a few hours ago she was lying on the floor in the middle of broken glass, broken promises and broken dreams with a very broken heart and now, she was on her way to Paris to meet Malcolm, on a private jet to boot.

The car pulled slowly around to the back of the airport passing several commercial aircrafts along the way. Denise could see a smaller aircraft in the near distance.

Soon enough, the limo stopped in front of the stairs leading up to the plane's entry door and the driver exited the limo. As he stood talking to someone near the stairs she peered through her window at the flashing lights from the aircraft twinkling in the night as several men worked diligently to prepare the plane for flight

The driver walked over to the passenger door and opened it, holding out his hand to assist her out of the car.

Denise sat frozen.

"Ms. Rush," he said.

Taking a deep breath she peeked outside. "Yes?" she asked as if she didn't know what he wanted.

She suddenly became overwhelmed by it all. Second thoughts began to creep as she listened to the hum of the plane's motor.

"Ms. Rush," the driver said still holding out his hand.

"Umm, hmm. Yes," she said clearing her throat.

"Paris is waiting, ma'am," he said.

Taking another deep breath she willed her hand to move and placed it in his as he helped her out of the car.

Standing frozen like a wide-eyed little girl seeing Cinderella for the first time at Disneyland, she looked up the stairs before her. They seemed to have no ending. Two female stewardesses stood smiling and waving down at her.

"It's okay," the driver said. "They won't bite."

Denise smiled at the driver and reached in her purse to tip him.

"It's okay, ma'am—"

"It's been taken care of, right," she interrupted, giving him a wink. The driver nodded in agreement.

"Well then, I will just give you this," she said, kissing him on his right and left cheek. "Thank you," she said giving him a hug.

One of the stewardesses had made it to ground level to escort her to the aircraft.

"Right this way, Ms. Rush."

Denise followed holding on to the rail as if it was her lifeline to reality. Her head was spinning so fast she was afraid she might fall off the cloud she was on if she let go. When they reached the entryway she turned to find the driver had already gone.

"There's no turning back now," she said to herself.

Suddenly the captain appeared from the cockpit.

"Hello, Ms. Rush. I'm Jonathan Harper, your flight captain."

"Nice to meet you, Mr. Harper," she said reaching out to shake his hand.

"Welcome aboard the Tiffany."

"These two beautiful ladies will be your flight attendants attending to anything you may need to make your flight more comfortable."

"Hi! I'm Monica and this is Marilyn," the petite woman said shaking her hand.

"Nice to meet you both," Denise responded nodding at both ladies.

"We'll be departing within the next fifteen to twenty minutes," the captain continued.

"How long is the flight?" Denise interrupted.

"About thirteen hours with the time change, ma'am," he responded.

Shut! Up! What in the world am I going to do for thirteen hours? she asked herself.

"Right this way," one of the attendants directed her.

Denise followed her into the main cabin where she was greeted by candles, more roses and gifts spread throughout the interior. Hershey's Kisses and rose petals were laid out on the cabin floor and on a table at the end of a black leather sofa were several brochures providing descriptions of various tourist spots and excursions in Paris.

THIRTY

Denise excitedly picked a few of the Kisses off the ground and plopped down on the couch grabbing the brochures. After scanning a few of the choices, she leaned over the couch to stare out the window.

The sky was clear and full of stars and she could see planes coming and going in the distance. It was the perfect night for a flight. The winds were calm and the weather was beautiful. At least in this part of the world.

Unlike most people she knew, Denise loved to fly. Her favorite part? Takeoff. There was something about the speed of it all. Starting from zero miles per hour and building to a speed beyond imagination gave her an adrenaline rush.

She could see men below preparing to direct the plane to its runway and in the distance she could see a black limo approaching. Denise assumed it was probably some rich person on their way to another private jet. The limo passed out of her view and she settled back into the couch to continue scanning brochures.

A few minutes later the captain's voice came over the loud speaker. "We've been cleared for takeoff. At this time we need all passengers to fasten their seatbelts."

"All passengers," she said to herself. "It's just me. Maybe he means the two flight attendants."

Denise moved over to one of the chairs located near the attendants' door.

After securing her seat belt, she began to wonder what she was going to say to Malcolm when she saw him. They hadn't exactly had a lot of conversation over the last few weeks and she knew he would have a lot of questions as to why. Questions she wasn't ready to answer.

After several minutes the plane had still not moved and she was beginning to wonder what was holding them up. *Paris was waiting* as the driver so eloquently put it.

Trying to keep her mind from freaking out, she picked up the bouquet of roses from the nearby table and closed her eyes. Allowing the sweet smell of what was now her sixth bouquet from Malcolm to calm her nerves.

Suddenly she heard a voice from the cockpit area that did not sound like the captain.

"I believe you are one rose short, ma'am," the voice whispered.

Denise recognized the voice instantly. "Malcolm," she whispered.

She opened her eyes to find him standing in the entry of the cabin dressed in a black tuxedo. He was holding a single red rose.

"I believe you only have eleven roses and you need this one to complete the dozen."

Denise quickly released her seatbelt and ran to him. She leaped into his arms and he lifted her into the air. She was crying and sobbing on his shoulder as he turned her around in circles.

She didn't know why she was crying; she was just crying. Crying because he looked so beautiful. Crying because of all he had done for her. Crying because she was happy to see him. Crying because she loved him. Or maybe she was crying because in that moment she knew it was the end of her relationship with Gerald.

"Why are you crying, sweetie?" he asked rubbing her back. "This was supposed to make you smile."

"Oh, Malcolm, it did and I haven't been able to stop smiling since that limo driver pulled up at my house. I can't believe you did all this for me. What are you doing here? I thought we were going to meet in Paris?"

"It's Valentine's Day and what better way to celebrate our first than Paris."

Denise couldn't bear to look up. She kept her head down looking at the floor. Crying. Tears were flowing uncontrollably and she couldn't stop them. She was feeling every emotion imaginable and most of all guilt was eating her alive. She had been ignoring him for several weeks and here he was giving her a Valentine's Day that most women could only dream of.

Malcolm grabbed tissue off the nearby table and lifted her chin. Gently wiping the tears away he kissed her forehead.

"Look at me," he whispered.

Denise began to tremble.

"Denise, look at me," he said again.

She opened her eyes and stared into his as he kissed her lips. His lips moved softly against hers, then more urgently. She opened her mouth and urged a deeper kiss, their tongues caressing.

Warmth swept through her body. She wanted him to take her right there in that moment. Take her, mind, body and soul. Every part of her wanted to feel him inside of her. Making love to her as she had never been made loved to before.

She pulled back before the feeling overcame her and she would be unable and unwilling to stop it.

Handing her the rose he walked her into the cabin. "Let's get buckled in for takeoff, sweetie."

"Okay," she said still sobbing. Malcolm walked Denise over to the couch and buckled her in before securing himself next to her. He reached over to the nearby phone and advised the pilot they were ready for takeoff.

Denise just stared at him tissue paper shredded in her hands as he wrapped his arms around her. She buried her head in his chest as the airplane raced down the runway.

THIRTY-ONE

Startled by the captain's voice, Denise lifted her head from Malcolm's lap.

"Where are we?" she asked rubbing her eyes.

"Paris," Malcolm answered.

"How long have I been sleep?"

"Most of the flight, sweetie. You were pretty exhausted, huh?"

"I guess so," she said yawning. "What have you been doing?"

"Watching you sleep," he said brushing hair out of her eyes. "Do you know how beautiful you are, Denise?"

"Umm, no. Don't think I got that memo," she said rising from her seat to look out the window.

Malcolm walked up behind her and wrapped his arms around her waist.

"Well you are," he whispered in her ear. "Flawless."

Denise turned to him and he lowered his face to hers. For a moment they stood in silence. Staring deeply into each other's eyes, into each other's soul as he caressed her cheek with the palm of his hand.

His touch was soft. Loving. Sensual.

She took his hand and gently kissed the palm and placed it back on her cheek, closing her eyes as he pulled her into him.

She could feel him. Caressing her lips with lips. Gently nibbling with each touch before deepening the kiss and making love to her mouth with his tongue. They kissed with a passion that sent chills through every part of her body.

She was experiencing a feeling that she had never her experienced with any man. Not even Gerald. A feeling she never wanted to end. The warmth of his body sent juices flowing through her body and her soul moaning with pleasure.

When they arrived in Paris a limousine was waiting to take them to the Hotel Plaza Athénée. Malcolm had reserved the Terrace Eiffel Suite at one of the most famous hotels in all of Paris. It was located smack dab in the middle of the city, right off the infamous Montaigne Avenue.

As soon as Denise stepped out of the car and saw the hotel she was reminded of an episode on *Sex and the City*.

Sex and the City was her all-time favorite TV show. She had seen every episode two and three times over, and the episode in question was when Carrie went to Paris with her Russian boyfriend.

She recalled that when Carrie stepped out onto the balcony of their room there was a magnificent view of the Eiffel Tower. Denise smiled at the thought.

"Hello and welcome to the Hotel Plaza Athénée," the attendant greeted them. "I am Felipe and I will be escorting you to the front desk. Raul will bring in your luggage while we get you checked in."

Denise and Malcolm followed the man into the hotel as he led them to the front desk.

From the minute they stepped out of the limo there were attendants waiting on them hand and foot. Felipe stayed with them until they were checked in and another attendant escorted them to the elevator and stayed with them until they reached their hotel suite.

When they arrived at their room, Denise was floored. The entire room was surrounded by windows. Windows overlooking the city of Paris. It was the most gorgeous sight she had ever seen in her life. Every window offered a view of the Eiffel Tower. There it was lying in front of the clear blue sky as if it were a perfectly crafted piece of fine art. It was breathtaking.

Denise squealed and ran out on the terrace as Carrie did in the episode she'd recalled earlier. Malcolm tipped the attendant generously and joined her on the terrace.

It brought him great pleasure to see her so excited. She was jumping up and down and clapping her hands like a little child about to get some ice cream. Pointing at the tower as if she was telling Malcolm that was the flavor she wanted.

Malcolm locked his arms around her waist and they stood still for the first time since they arrived at the hotel. They stood still and admired one of the world's most magnificent structures.

After a few minutes and a few kisses, Malcolm left Denise on the balcony while he retreated into the suite to shower and change. He was still wearing a tuxedo and he was anxious to get comfortable and relax a little before they headed out for the first item on the agenda. Shopping.

Denise sat down in a balcony chair to breathe in the air and reflect on all that had occurred over the last twenty-four hours.

The dozens of roses, the private jet, the beautiful hotel, the Eiffel Tower, it was all so surreal. Paris was always her dream trip but never in her wildest dream would she have believed she would actually go and she certainly never could have imagined being there with Malcolm.

Standing up she leaned against the balcony rail to look down at the avenue, which was full of activity.

People were walking to and fro. Some taking pictures while others strolled along hand-in-hand admiring the beauty of it all. But for the most part everyone appeared to be doing Denise's favorite thing. Shopping!

She had only thrown a handful of clothes in her suitcase because she didn't want to keep the limo driver waiting. Besides that she didn't want to wear clothes from Highland Mall in old "Paree." That wouldn't do. Totally unacceptable. She wanted to live and dress like the French even if it was short-lived and put her budget in complete bankruptcy.

Malcolm had finished showering and changing, and Denise ran in to freshen up a bit before they headed out for the afternoon. Malcolm didn't mind spending their first few hours hitting the stores. He'd promised her she would have time to do so and besides he was kind of happy to be getting it out of the way so they could spend the rest of their trip engulfed in the romance he had planned for her.

By the time they finished hitting every store and boutique on the avenue it was nearly dark. Barely able to walk, they entered the hotel lobby.

Denise had a firm grip on three shopping bags in each hand and Malcolm carried an additional five. As they waited for the elevator he glanced over at Denise who was humming the tune softly playing through the hotel Muzac system.

Looking down at the bags they were both holding he turned his sights back to her. She smiled childishly and shrugged her shoulders giving a little chuckle.

"Oh you're going to play Ms. Innocent, I see," he said, as they both let out a quiet laugh.

They strolled down the hall as if they were teenagers walking through the halls of Bastrop High School, giggling and laughing at the smallest things. Discovering love for the first time.

When they reached their room, Malcolm slid the room key into the door and looked over at her.

She was standing close to him. Her breast was resting comfortably against his arm and he caught his breath.

Glancing down at his arm she smiled coyly.

He kissed her. Just a sweet peck and then he looked into her eyes without saying a word.

"What is it?" she asked.

"Nothing," he replied.

She giggled. He kissed her again. Longer this time and more intense.

"We aren't going to have any room to put all these bags," he said coming up for air.

"I am sure I can find somewhere."

"You'll have to buy another suitcase to take them home."

She sighed. "Then I guess I'll just have to buy another suitcase to take them home. And what better place to buy a suitcase than Paris. Wouldn't you agree?"

He smiled and kissed her again.

"Are we going to go in or just stand out here in the hall and give each other sweet kisses and giggle the rest of the evening?" she asked.

"We definitely have to go in so that I can give you those sweet kisses in other places," he said kissing her deeply and passionately again.

"Well then! Open the door, Mr. Anderson."

THIRTY-TWO

Turning her back to the door he leaned in to whisper in her ear, "I have a surprise for you." He covered her eyes with his hand.

Denise could smell the scent of his cologne. It was Drakkar. Her favorite. Taking in a deep breath she savored the scent.

"Don't peek," he said leading her through the suite, his hands still covering her eyes.

She had no clue what was going on but she knew she was going to love whatever it was.

"Wait right here, *mi amore*. Don't move and don't peek," were the instructions he gave her.

In the very near distance she heard the opening of a door as the scent of lavender filled the room.

She felt Malcolm's touch as he took her hand, led her through the doorway and carefully sat her down in a chair.

"Okay, I want you to count to ten and then open your eyes."

"Malcolm, what are you up to?"

"Count to ten and then open your eyes. Promise!"

"Okay, I promise."

The next thing she heard was the closing of the door.

"Malcolm," she called out.

"Count to ten," he shouted through the door.

As promised she counted to ten and slowly lifted her eyelids to find she was sitting in the master bathroom.

"Oh my God," she said covering her mouth.

The room was glowing with light from candles placed throughout the room. Fresh rose petals were spread beautifully across the floor and the tub was filled with bubbly water and lavender oil.

Sitting neatly wrapped on the sink was a gift box. Denise lifted the card which read, "Denise. Thank you for coming to Paris with me. I have had such a wonderful time already. There is no one else in the world that I would want to be here with. Please relax and enjoy the bath. Take your time and savor every moment. Don't rush. When you finish you will find a little something in the garment bag hanging on the door to go along with the little something in this box. I hope you are happy. I will be waiting for you. Malcolm."

Smiling, Denise placed the note back on the sink and quickly undressed. Glancing over at the towel cabinet near the door she noticed a CD player. Pushing play, the sounds of Paris filled the room. The whole set up was very *Breakfast at Tiffany's* and Denise was loving every minute of it.

Stepping into the tub she grabbed the bath pillow located on a ledge above the tub and, after hitting the Jacuzzi button, placed a mask over her eyes and sank into the water.

Bubbles swiftly moved across her body as she drifted to sleep thinking only of Paris and Malcolm Anderson.

About an hour later a sudden chill shot through her body. She was still soaking in the tub. The temperature of the water had gone cold and most of the bubbles were gone.

Unplugging the drain she ran warm water for a little bit to warm up the chill that replaced the warm bubbly feeling she'd felt earlier.

Rubbing her eyes she focused in on the bright digits illuminating from the CD player.

"Eight o'clock!" she shouted. She had been soaking in the tub for over an hour. *Oh my God. Malcolm must be so disgusted with me.*

Hurriedly she jumped out of the tub and scrambled for a towel and possibly a robe before suddenly remembering the garment bag Malcolm had left for her.

Reaching for the bag she laid it on the table near the vanity and began to apply moisturizer to her skin. Her hands and feet looked like the skin of prunes, or dried raisins, so she needed plenty moisturizer to smooth it all out.

She liked that the bathroom was big enough to hold the vanity. She also liked the king-sized bed in the master bedroom.

She still couldn't believe she was in Paris, in one of the most extravagant hotels on earth and in the best suite they had to offer. The bathroom housed a whirlpool bathtub, his-and-her showers, a couch, a chair and a full-sized vanity. Not to mention a toilet, a bidet and three sinks. Three! She wondered who could ever afford something this luxurious.

"Apparently Malcolm," she said aloud, "and Oprah."

Malcolm had thought of everything. All of her favorite scents were placed in a straw basket located on the vanity table. White Diamonds, Passions, Vera Wang and Irresistible, just to name a few. Removing each perfume sample from the basket she sprayed each in the air before deciding on White Diamonds for the occasion.

Grabbing the gift box from the corner of the table she began to unravel the bow, which was inscribed with the words *Open me please*. She noticed a gold plate attached to the top of the box that read *Tiffany's*. That alone made her almost afraid to open it; however, after taking a deep breath she decided she was up for the task.

Prying the box open with two fingers she peeked in briefly as if she were afraid something would jump out at her. In the darkness of the box she saw something shine as if it was winking at her. Opening the box all the way she found a beautifully crafted diamond necklace.

Carefully lifting the piece out of the box she held the diamond cut chain against her skin. Three diamonds lay next to her chestnut skin as she stood in the mirror admiring its beauty. She was mesmerized. She couldn't believe such a beautiful piece existed.

The middle diamond was slightly larger than the others attached on the left and right and all three were encased in gold.

If she had to guess it was at least four carats. No that was just the middle. The two smaller ones had to be at least two carats and if you threw in the matching earrings she was walking around with ten carat's easily.

THIRTY-THREE

After applying makeup, she opened the garment bag to find the most beautiful red dress she had ever seen. A very sleek and very elegant red dress. Sure to accentuate every full-figured curve on her body.

As she slid the dress off the hanger she couldn't help but notice the label read Versace.

After looking more closely she realized it didn't only say Versace, it said, "Versace Exclusive. Created and made for Denise Rush."

Her mouth flew open forming a perfect circle of disbelief.

Carefully she slid the dress over her head and the material fell over her skin. Just the touch of her dress made her feel sexy as her breasts nestled into the cups of the gown and the skirt glided over her hips finally settling near her ankles.

The dress was designed with a double-V neckline. One stretching out to her shoulders forming a spaghetti strap, which connected the two sides of the dress just below the shoulder blade, and the other settling into her breasts revealing the perfect amount of cleavage, guaranteed to awaken the sexual desire of any man with eyes.

As she turned to see every angle of the dress in the mirror she couldn't help but wonder when the fairytale was going to end.

Part of her felt like she was sliding further and further down a rabbit hole and if she continued to allow herself to fall without trying to save herself she would never be able to get back to reality.

The other part was throwing all caution to the wind. For once she wanted to go the opposite way of right and do what made her feel good. Take care of her needs.

Here was a man who was doing everything he possibly could to show her how much he love and adored her. For the first time someone was taking care of her.

For most of her life it had always been the other way around and she was tired of always focusing on everyone else while neglecting her own desires, ignoring what she wanted and needed to be fulfilled.

Grabbing the shoebox near the door she recognized the business name as one of the boutiques located on the avenue near the hotel.

Carefully removing the bow from the box she found a pair of red Manolo Blahnik sling backs, which perfectly matched the dress. Malcolm had thought of everything.

Sliding the shoes on her feet and strapping them in, she gave herself one more glance. Finally she was ready.

Ready for what? she had to ask herself. *Ready to put Gerald in her past? Ready to move forward and see where things were going with Malcolm? Ready to give herself to him completely?*

Taking in a deep breath she turned off the lights and opened the door. The master bedroom was illuminated by candles and she could hear the sound of Maxwell coming in from the living room of the suite.

She found Malcolm standing in the entryway of the balcony holding a red rose. He was staring out into the Paris sky, gorgeously dressed in a tuxedo.

"Malcolm," she whispered.

Her turned to her and smiled.

"I hope that smile means you're happy to see me," she said.

"Indeed I am," he replied.

He walked over to her and handed her the rose before kissing her hand and bowing gracefully in front of her.

"Thank you," she said.

Wrapping her arm in his he walked her out to the balcony where a table was beautifully set for two.

"For you, madam," he said pulling out her chair.

"Thank you," she responded taking her seat.

Denise sat taking in the ambiance as Malcolm poured wine in their glasses.

Candles were set in various places on the balcony in glass casings and there was a nice breeze in the air. It was a tantalizing and intoxicating type of breeze. The kind of breeze that gave a woman chill bumps that awakened every sensual hormone present throughout her body.

Hormones Denise wanted to stay asleep.

In a coma.

Malcolm waited on Denise hand and foot throughout the evening. Preparing her plate just the way she liked it, keeping her wine glass full. Whatever she needed all she had to do was say the word.

They dined on roast, potatoes, vegetables and the sweetest wine Denise had ever tasted. Imported from Germany.

Denise savored every moment.

"You're so beautiful," Malcolm said, complimenting her again. Denise smiled and dropped her head down.

"Don't do that," he said reaching over to lift her chin.

"Do what?" she asked as her eyes met his.

"Hold your head down. I want to see your beautiful eyes."

Denise smiled again and looked out over the balcony.

"Malcolm, you have really outdone yourself. I don't deserve any of this."

"Don't do that either. You deserve the world, Denise."

She laughed.

"Why are you laughing?"

"I apologize for taking so long in the tub."

"Don't apologize. It was for you. I wanted you to relax. I'm glad you enjoyed it."

"Malcolm I have enjoyed everything. This dress… what can I say, it's beautiful! Gorgeous! How did you get Versace to make *me* a dress?" she asked as if it was an impossible task.

"We went shopping once and I paid attention. I already knew red was your favorite color, so it wasn't hard to go from there."

"And the jewelry, how long can I keep it?"

"It's yours, baby," he said laughing.

"Shut up! It is? Wow, this is too much. When did you have time to plan all this."

"It's been in the works for a while. I just wanted to make this Valentine's Day special for you."

"Malcolm, it is. The best ever! I can't stop smiling. I'm going to have TMJ from smiling so much."

"Smiling keeps you healthy," he said taking her hand.

Malcolm stood up and guided her to a corner of the balcony closest to the Eiffel Tower.

Maxwell's *Whenever, Wherever, Whatever* began playing in the distance.

"May I have this dance?" he asked.

"It would be my pleasure," she answered.

Placing her hand in his he wrapped his arm around her waist and she rested her head on his chest.

"Take my heart and my love… Take of me all that you want… and if there's a thing that you need, I'd give you the breath that I breathe…" Maxwell's words spoke to Denise as the two swayed together.

"Take my heart and my love," Malcolm sung along with the music, staring into her eyes as he recited the words of the song.

As she stared back at him his love for her grew even deeper. Every part of him was completely in love with the woman before him. She was his first love and no love he had ever known could match the love he had always had for her.

He had loved her his entire life and it consumed every part of his being and finally he had her in his arms. He would stop breathing if he had to let her go.

"I love you, Denise. I will do whatever it takes to make you feel safe. If you allow me, I will protect you at all costs and you will be loved with my entire heart and soul."

"Oh, Malcolm," she whispered.

He kissed her softly.

Glancing up at the sky she watched the stars twinkle above them. The moon shone down on them like a spotlight.

The night was clear.

She looked up at Malcolm who was smiling down at her.

"Did I say thank you?"

"Yes, but there's no need. It has all been my pleasure. I would do it all over again to see you smile."

She laid her head on his chest again. For a while neither spoke a word. Their bodies moved as one as they swayed to the music.

Denise looked up at Malcolm again. "Thank you for coming into my life."

"Thank you for allowing me," he responded.

And they kissed.

THIRTY-FOUR

Several weeks had passed since Paris although Denise could remember it like it happened yesterday.

After returning from fantasy land she walked into pure chaos at the station. Everyone and everything was in full swing preparing for church association set to begin in a few days. Final planning meetings were underway and Denise spent most of her time traveling between the district church and the station.

Guest speakers and the guest artist would soon be in town and her schedule would be filled with one interview after another.

Memories of her time with Malcolm kept her going.

After leaving Paris, Denise accompanied Malcolm to Florida for a game in which he scored forty-five points. Best game he ever played. He was sure it was because she was there.

They spent the remainder of their time at Disney World and Universal Studios during the day and spent their nights on moonlit boat rides with margaritas under the stars.

When the whirlwind ended and reality set in, he was back to playoff games and she was inundated with work.

"Thank God it's Friday," she told a co-worker on her way out the door.

Looking forward to Friday night happy hour with the girls, she jumped in and out of the shower and headed out the door without even sitting down to rest.

She really hadn't spoken to the girls since returning to town and they were dying to know details about her trip.

She couldn't wait to tell them everything.

"Well hell's bells, look what the cat drug in," Jess kidded her.

"Hi, sis," Denise responded hugging her sister.

"Hi, babe!"

"Wassup, Bri?"

"Don't be Bri'ing me. I am still upset that you didn't tell me you were running off with Mr. Man."

"It was short notice, Sabrina. I literally didn't even have time to pack. One minute I was having the worst Valentine's Day in the history of Valentine's Day and then in an instant I was being whisked away to Paris."

"So, how was it?" Jess asked eager to hear the details.

"Words can't explain," she answered, handing Jess the digital camera.

"You already know what I want to know," Sabrina said pointing her finger at Denise. "Did we bump and grind?" she asked moving her torso back and forth.

"Sabrina! That's none of your business," Jess scolded her.

"Jess, please you know you want to know too. Come on, Denise. Fess up. Did he tap that ass or what?"

"First of all, I have a right to ask because she is my sister. Out of obligation I have a right to know."

"Well," Sabrina prodded further.

Denise laughed at the both of them.

"Well for your information," she teased, tapping her fingers on the table. "No! He did not tap my ass."

"Ahh, damn!" Sabrina cried out in disgust.

"Good for you, sis! It's always better to wait."

"The girl has been waiting for fifteen years. How much longer can she wait?" Jess looked over at Sabrina. "Did you forget I have been waiting all my life?"

"No I haven't forgotten but that's only because you have no clue what you're missing. Denise on the other hand knows what it feels like to have that ass tapped."

"Okay, guys, I'm still sitting here. Can I talk about my own life for a minute without the commentary?"

They all laughed.

"We came close the first night in Paris, but he was a real gentleman. He would only take it as far as I would let him and I did everything I could to restrain myself."

She told them about the city and how romantic it was and how romantic Malcolm made it for her. Even Sabrina had to admit that was the ultimate dream for any woman. "If you like that sort of thing," she added. Denise went on and on about her trip through three cosmos and appetizers.

"Girl, it was just too much fun. Magical," she said nudging Sabrina.

"It must have been magical. Did you forget about the jailbird?" Sabrina nudged her back.

"Sabrina! Why you gotta go and ruin the moment?" Jess scolded her again.

"Well it's the truth. Before Paris it was Gerald this and Gerald that. You haven't mentioned Gerald since you sat down. And what the hell happened? Why didn't he get out of prison? What was his excuse this time? What are you going to do about him?"

"There's nothing to do about him. He's still in prison. At this point I have to face reality. Gerald could be looking at serving his entire sentence. I've been disappointed over and over again. From the minute he got his self into this situation. I am tired of disappointment. I want happiness and right now happiness is being with Malcolm."

"What happened, sis? Why didn't he get out this time?"

"I don't know. He said something happened and they needed to review his case a little further. At this point it doesn't really matter. After spending time with Malcolm in Paris I realized I can't keep putting my life on hold in hopes that he may get out. I can't say I don't love him. Gerald has always and always will be my first great love. I haven't totally committed myself to Malcolm either. I am just saying I am going to explore a relationship with him and see where it goes."

"That's all good, Denise, but you do know that Malcolm is a man."

"Uh, I think I am aware of that, Sabrina, yes."

"I'm just sayin you can't hold the brother off forever. Eventually he is going to want to tap that ass. What are you going to do then?"

"Sabrina, you don't know that," Jess said, "I—"

"Yes we all know you're still a virgin, Jess," Sabrina interrupted, "but we're not talking about you."

"Yes I am," Jess continued, "and Lawrence is fine with that. He doesn't pressure me to do anything I don't want to."

"Hell he's probably a virgin too, so it works well for the both of you." Sabrina rolled her eyes. "But we're not talking about you. We are talking about Denise."

"That's enough, Sabrina," Denise said, interrupting the both of them.

"All I am saying is Malcolm is no virgin and with the women that will be throwing themselves at him, you better not wait too long to give it up, girl."

"Malcolm and I are just fine and when and if it ever gets to that point it will be my decision as to who I let tap and what I let them tap and if I decide not to it will be something he will have to decide if he can live with."

"And if he decides he can't?" Sabrina probed.

"Then that will be his decision and we will deal with that when it happens."

Even though Sabrina was getting on her nerves, Denise had to admit she had a point. Eventually she would have to tell Malcolm why she kept pushing him away and she did have every intention of telling him. Eventually.

THIRTY-FIVE

Music night at the association was in the full swing of things when Denise arrived at the church.

Cars were piling into the parking lot of St. Johns Tabernacle as eager members of the Baptist organization hurried into the church to find the best seat in the house for the evening's anticipated performances.

The Monday night event proved year after year to be the most popular night of the week-long gathering of Baptist Christians, which included seminars, prayers, sermons music, music and more music.

Tonight's event included performances from the district's combined choir made up of choir members from various churches. Members from youth choirs, men's choirs, women's choirs and mixed choirs participated in the event to sing praises unto the Lord.

There were also guest appearances scheduled, courtesy of Power 105.9 of course. Yolanda Adams, Kirk Franklin, Israel Houghton and several Austin city officials were on hand for the event.

Second in anticipation to musical night was Sunday's brotherhood night, which closed out the event each year.

Brotherhood night was especially near and dear to the single ladies.

Over one thousand black men dressed in black tuxedos would soon enter the sanctuary marching to a catchy gospel tune. It was an event that brought single women from all over the Central Texas area to the tabernacle.

Of course most of the men were not single, but the women were hopeful.

With the help of police officers on hand to direct traffic, Denise was finally able to locate a good spot near the cafeteria on the west side of the church.

Dashing in through one of the side doors she found Sabrina and Jess near the front entrance waiting on her arrival; the girls found seats near the front of the stage.

Denise dashed into the meeting rooms to talk shop with her producers and after giving the order of service a quick once over with the MC she greeted the evening's special guest and returned to her seat for the show.

"You guys would not believe how crowded it is out there," she commented. "I think every year this thing gets bigger and bigger."

"You have some big name artists in here," Sabrina responded. "Kirk Franklin! You couldn't have gotten a bigger gospel singer to fill this place up."

"Where did Jess go?"

"She's over there with the very fine Pastor Eason. Talk about a sexy chocolate brother."

"Sabrina, that man is married."

"I know that, Denise! I was just making note that he is one fine! Sexy! Chocolate! Brother. Um. Um. Um. Ought to be a crime."

Sabrina felt a tap on her shoulder.

"Hello, counselor."

It was Stoney Hunter.

"Counsel," she responded coldly.

"Nice to see you here. Out of the office, I mean."

Sabrina faked a smile.

"This is Katherine," he continued, pointing to the blonde woman standing next to him.

Sabrina and Denise leaned over simultaneously to find a very frail white woman smiling back at them.

"Nice to meet you," she said extending her hand to Sabrina.

"Likewise," Sabrina answered not accepting the invitation.

"Hello. I'm Denise," Denise said, reaching over Sabrina to grab the lady's hand.

"So you are the woman that has baby up all night planning strategies?" Katherine said to Sabrina.

"Do I now? Glad to know I have him scraping for ways to try and win his case. I on the other hand am having no problem getting to sleep," Sabrina said coyly.

"Simmer down, counselor," Stoney interrupted, noticing her sarcasm.

The blonde continued talking a mile a minute doing her best at an attempt to fit in among a sea of black women.

Standing a tad bit taller than he with platinum locks she had that irritating white cheerleader tone in her voice that Sabrina despised.

Like yea! Oh my God!

Stoney had not uttered a word. He actually looked a little irritated each time she spoke.

"Why are they still standing here?" Sabrina muttered to herself.

"Yes, baby and I belong to New Hope Baptist Church off of Spring Street," she was telling Denise. "Baby and I, blah, blah, blah…" she continued.

Sabrina glanced at up at Stoney again. She could tell he was nervous and apparently so was the cheerleader who was digging her nails into his arm as tightly as she could in an attempt to make sure everyone knew they were together.

"Well it was nice meeting you, Katherine," Denise said trying to wrap up the conversation. She could tell Sabrina was about to pounce any minute.

"Likewise," she said responding to Denise.

"Sabrina."

"Yes," Sabrina answered sarcastically.

"It was nice meeting you finally. Good luck in court," the blonde said with a smirk as they walked away.

"Oh hell naw! No she didn't," Sabrina said grabbing the pew in front of her to stand.

Denise wrapped an arm around her to keep her in place. She knew her friend and her friend was about ten seconds from going off on Stoney and his lady friend. Luckily the program was starting and people were hurrying back to their seats, blocking her path to doing a complete fatality right there in the center aisle of the sanctuary.

As anticipated, the program exceeded expectations. The evening was spirit-filled and kept most of the members on their feet for lots of praising, dancing and worshipping the Lord.

After the program the girls decided to grab a cup of coffee at the corner coffee bar to unwind a bit before heading home.

After the usual conversation topics and a couple of espressos the girls parted for the evening and on the way home Denise detoured to Wal-Mart to pick up a few things before arriving home to several voice messages.

"You have twenty new messages," the machine announced. Too tired to listen to them she pushed stop and poured herself a glass of wine.

After flipping through the channels several times she found a good movie and settled in to doze off to sleep.

THIRTY-SIX

The week went by pretty fast and Denise couldn't wait for brotherhood night to come and go. As much as she enjoyed association week she couldn't wait for it to be over.

Between work and church there was not much time for anything else in life including Malcolm, who was still bogged down with playoff games. Luckily he was able to get a break to attend the event and she was looking forward to spending some time with him.

Denise had finally reached a point where she was able to admit to herself she had fallen in love with him.

Her every thought and action took Malcolm into consideration. He had become part of her heart; he was always on her mind. He was everything she'd ever wanted in a man. He satisfied her spiritually, emotionally and mentally, and she was proud of the fact that they still had not had sex. Both agreed that sex would only complicate the relationship and they decided to hold off until they were sure where they were headed.

To replace the urge and temptations they spent most of their time hanging out in public places or sitting out on the deck having hour-long conversations. They discussed everything from the latest *Idol* contestant to get the boot to Scripture.

They prayed together and often held their own private bible study, over the phone or at his place when he was in town. On Sundays when he was free he would fly into town to attend church with her.

Spiritual satisfaction was important to Denise. She strongly believed if a man knew and understood his role as a Christian then he would know how to treat his brother or sister in Christ, and having that knowledge would mean he would know how to treat the partner God blessed him with.

The thing she liked most about Malcolm was that he understood that a relationship was more than fifty-fifty. He understood that a person has to give more than fifty percent of themselves to the person they loved if they wanted a successful relationship.

Malcolm satisfied ninety percent and more.

Emotionally he was there for her in ways that no man had ever been. He was a real gentleman. If there was anything she needed he readily took care of it for her. Whether it was fixing the car, taking out the trash, picking up bread, dropping off dry cleaning or simply opening the car door, all she had to do was mention it and he was there, willing to do it for her.

He was very affectionate and attentive. Always wanting to hold her hand, kiss her forehead, wrap his arms around her, stare into her eyes. Always telling her how beautiful she was.

There were no games and no guessing with Malcolm. How could a woman not fall in love with him?

She felt his love for her and he did everything he could to make sure she never felt insecure about where she stood with him. She adored him and he showed her every day that he adored her.

As much as she had grown to love and care for Malcolm, a piece of her still belonged to Gerald. Not a day went by that he didn't cross her mind. She wondered if he was okay, wondered if he had got word on when he was getting out. He had left several voicemails but she deleted them before listening to them. She didn't want to hear any more excuses. All she ever wanted to hear was "I am free," but that never happened.

She didn't want to have to face the questions and the disappointment in his voice when he wanted to know why she hadn't been available to him. Why she hadn't come to see him. Why she hadn't returned any of his calls. Why she hadn't written him.

She wasn't ready to explain and she wasn't ready to deal with the confrontation.

The letters she received were neatly tucked away in a box, unopened. She was ready to move on and the very sound of his voice would make her want to drop everything, including the relationship she was building with Malcolm, and run to him.

She still loved him. But she could no longer put her life on hold for broken promises and dreams. She had waited long enough for those dreams to come true only to be disappointed over and over again.

Malcolm was here and he was giving her everything her heart had desired with Gerald. Malcolm was her future and he was ready to love on her. And she wanted him to.

As men lined up along the sidewalk at church, women nestled into their carefully chosen church pew for the event. Mothers, sisters, wives, daughters and girlfriends were all present to support their man. Of course there were plenty of single women on hand, chomping at the bit and ecstatic to see over one thousand black men in one place at one time.

The girls rushed pass the men lined up along the sidewalk outside the church. Denise had to literally drag Sabrina along.

"Welcome. Welcome. Welcome," the MC announced. "Tonight! My people, I said TONIGHT! Is brotherhood night! It's brotherhood night ya'll! Tonight is the night that we celebrate black men in the ministry. Tonight is the night where we join together as black men. United as one! To praise His name! And if you haven't seen them, ladies, they look good ya'll. Did you see them? Don't they look good? Wives! Be proud of your men tonight. Fathers, be proud of your daughters and, mothers, be proud of your sons. Now, for my single ladies in the house, do we have any single ladies in the house tonight?"

There was laughter and clapping across the church.

"To my single ladies tonight! Check the ring finger first please. Check! The ring! Finger!" He pointed to his hand as laughter ensued.

"In a few moments the program will begin so if you all would please make your way to your seats and clear the aisle for the event we've been waiting for all week. Thank you all for coming. Let's have a joyful time in the house of the Lord, amen."

"Amen," the congregation responded.

"Girl, did you see all the brothers out there?" Sabrina asked, fanning her face.

"Sabrina," Jess started in, "remember the reason—"

"I know what the reason is, J. I don't need you to tell me what the reason is."

"Sabrina, stop. Can we just have a good time tonight, guys?" Denise asked. "No bickering please."

The girls hurried to find seats as the music began to play.

"Ladies and gentlemen! Rise to your feet and join me in welcoming, with a thunderous roar of applause, the men of the St. John Regular Baptist Association." The congregation began to clap and cheer as the sound of trumpets blared out from the choir stand.

The music of *Israel and New Breed* filled the sanctuary as people rose to their feet applauding.

The church doors swung open and thirty white doves were released into the air outside and the first church sign emerged through the entryway.

"Mount Rose Baptist Church of Bastrop, Texas. Reverend R.D. Smith Pastor," the MC announced.

About twenty men entered the church shouting, "A church in touch with the ALLLLLLLL Mighty!"

THIRTY-SEVEN

Following them were many others with church signs and banners, chanting for their church and pastor. One after another men poured into the sanctuary as women stood by cheering them on.

"Mount Olivet Baptist Church. Reverend Carson Pastor," the man announced.

"Oh that's Malcolm's church!" Denise screeched as she scrambled for her camera.

Fifty men piled into the church representing Mount Olivet. They were well represented as camera flashes brightened the way for the men walking into the church.

Denise had recently purchased a top-of-the-line Nikon, which captured every second and movement of the man she'd grown to love.

As he neared their eyes locked, and he smiled and winked in her direction. In that moment, her love deepened even more. She felt him in the bottom of her heart and soul. In that moment she knew he was the person that God had intended her to be with all along. She blew him a kiss as he marched by.

As they marched in most of the men were seated in the center aisle of the church; others took their place in the choir stand to form the male chorus.

Sitting in the tenor section was Malcolm Anderson.

She could hear his voice above everyone else's as the men began to sing their opening song. The men led a congregational hymn and from there the order of service continued as written on the program. However a Baptist service could always be counted on to deviate from the program.

Pastor Carlson, who was on the program to introduce the speaker of the hour, had to let everybody in the church know that sitting in the walls of the church was a real-life Detroit Pistons basketball player.

"Put your hands together and welcome our brother home," he instructed the congregation.

"Malcolm Anderson!"

There was a round of applause as everyone rose to their feet with smiles and cheers. Malcolm stood behind the podium and humbly received the welcome from the crowd.

He had never been a person who bragged or boasted about what he had or what he'd accomplished, and Denise could tell he was embarrassed by all the attention. Nonetheless he politely thanked everyone for their support and prayers, and after he finished speaking he received another round of applause.

As he began to walk back to his seat he turned one last time to face the congregation and give one last wave to his adoring fans. Focusing his eyes on Denise he blew her a kiss before sitting.

Her heart smiled.

The program continued as Reverend Smith, the speaker of the hour, delivered a powerful message about leaving a mark on the world. His words stressed the importance of ensuring people remembered you not by what you accomplished but by how you treated, loved and helped others.

About an hour later the sermon ended and many began to gather their things in preparation for the typical quick exit after the offering. Sabrina and Jess were among the guests making their escape.

Denise, however, stayed for the remainder of the service. Malcolm had planned a late dinner for the two of them and she had to make sure everything was wrapped up as far as the job was concerned.

The service ended and Denise made her way to the conference room to say final thank yous and goodbyes to those who had participated, on behalf of the station.

After checking one last time to ensure there was nothing more she needed to close out before leaving she headed back into the sanctuary to find Malcolm surrounded by twenty or more single women, signing autographs and taking pictures.

He looked up to see her standing at the end of the aisle and began to walk away from the crowd. She motioned for him to continue what he was doing. She wouldn't dare break the hearts of so many women desperate for just a touch of his skin.

She sat down and thumbed through the program as she reflected on the events of the day. Out of the corner of her eye, she saw Malcolm bend down, allowing a little girl to kiss him on the cheek.

How sweet, she thought as he signed his last autograph for her and walked toward her.

"You have to be the sweetest man I know, Malcolm Anderson."

"You think so?"

"I know firsthand."

"Shall we go?" he asked holding out his arm for her.

"We shall," she said accepting the invitation as she locked her arm in his.

§

"Malcolm, you missed your turn, sweetie," she said pointing to the road leading to Carrabba's, her favorite restaurant next to Pappadeaux's.

"I know we said we were going to Carrabba's but I wanted to take you somewhere else. Is that okay, baby?"

"Sure," Denise responded gleefully.

He continued driving toward the hill country as they discussed events that occurred during the week of services. She made sure to compliment him on how handsome he looked in his tuxedo. Anything he wore made him irresistible but there was something about a sixteen hundred dollar Versace. Malcolm sported a classic three-button black suit with dual vents on the back custom fit for every inch of his body. It was chic and sophisticated and he looked good.

She couldn't get mad at those females for wanting him because she wanted him too. She smiled at the thought and the satisfaction of knowing he was hers and all hers.

The car approached a steep hill and Denise grabbed hold of Malcolm's arm to brace herself for the incline.

"Be careful, sweetie," she said nervously.

He looked at her and smiled. "Of course I will," he said rubbing her hand. "I'm carrying very precious cargo."

She smiled at him and closed her eyes. From the vibrations of the car she could tell they were near the top of the hill. She let out a sigh of relief as the car slowly came to a stop. Malcolm looked over at her and laughed. Her eyes were still shut tight and her nails dug snugly into his suit.

"Dang, it's a good thing I have something covering my skin. If not you would be drawing blood right now," he said laughing again. "Open your eyes, baby," he whispered as he leaned over and kissed her forehead. Denise opened one eye and looked at him.

"What are we doing, Malcolm?"

"Look," he said pointing toward the front of the car. Denise slowly turned her head following the direction of his arm.

They were on top of what had to be the highest point in Austin and before them were beautiful glass houses overlooking the lake. Dozens of them glimmering in the night. Shining high above the water. Each attached to a covered pier's house boat or luxury yacht.

"Oh my God, Malcolm. It's beautiful."

"Yeah, it is, isn't it?"

"Breathtaking," she continued taking a deep breath.

"So are you," he said staring at her.

She turned to look at him.

"Breathtaking," he whispered as he placed his hand behind her head and leaned in to kiss her. She moaned with pleasure as he savored her lips, expressing his love with each stroke.

She had quickly become his everything. Everything he had ever wanted in a woman. Malcolm had always been very selective in choosing the women he dated. They had to dress, act and think a certain way or he had no conversation for them. Even the few that he chose to date never measured up to the imaginary woman he knew he wanted to be with.

In that moment, here with Denise, overlooking the water and the houses, he suddenly realized why those relationships had all ended. They ended because the imaginary woman he'd been searching for was Denise. And she was not imaginary. She was as real as real could be. And she was in his arms. Denise was the one. She had always been the one.

THIRTY-EIGHT

At Denise's urging, Malcolm started the car and they began rolling down the hill. Denise had closed her eyes again grabbing hold of his arm even tighter as her stomach dropped during the fall. Only this time she wasn't nervous or frightened. After what he had just shown her she was all smiles and at peace.

They rode through several neighborhoods admiring the designs of the homes. A few of the homes were so beautiful they parked the car in front of them discussing what they liked and what they would change.

After turning a few more blocks Malcolm pulled into the circular driveway of a house that appeared to have been recently built. Posted in the yard was a sign that read sold, and a sign near the front doors that read open house.

Malcolm parked and opened his door to get out.

"Malcolm, what are you doing, we can't go in there," she said looking around to see if anyone was watching.

"Baby, it says it says open house, besides, no one can see us we are way off the road. Come on."

"No, Malcolm," she whispered pulling at his arm.

Grabbing her hand he kissed the back of it and got out of the car. She watched as he jogged around to her side and opened the door. She stepped out of the car.

"Wow," she said stunned by the beauty of the home.

She clung to him as they walked up the sidewalk leading to the home's double doors. They reminded her of the doors from the Jolly Green Giant story. Oak doors. At least eight feet in height. They were so tall it was if the top off the door disappeared into the night.

"King Kong could fit through these doors without having to knock them down," Malcolm laughed.

Denise ran her fingers over the oak as far as she could reach, admiring the craftiness of the design. The doors' trim was elegantly designed in gold with fourteen panes of glass snugly held in place.

Six of the panes were arranged just above the doors in the shape of a rainbow and four large, beautifully designed panes took up most of the doors' surface.

A wooden bar ran across the width of both doors creating a U-shape design across both panels. It kind of reminded her of the Longhorn mascot, Bevo. It definitely had that Texas look and feel.

"This is beautiful, Malcolm," she said running her hands along the gold trim.

The door handles formed a circle of marble brown and the color matched the oak wood doors perfectly.

Denise peeked in through the glass door. "It's pitch black in there. Can't see nothing."

"So let's go in," Malcolm said reaching for the handle.

"Wait, Malcolm, are you sure about this?" she asked grabbing his hand. "There might be an alarm," she whispered.

"Look, sweetie," he said pointing to the sign near the door. "Open house! There's no electricity obviously so there can't be an alarm. Besides, I have a flashlight. Come on, let's take a look." He pulled the door open.

Malcolm turned on the flashlight and grabbed her hand as they stepped inside. Denise followed closely behind.

Her eyes widened as they entered the foyer. There were large vaulted ceilings, beautiful hanging chandeliers and two spiral staircases leading all the way to the second and third floors. It was beautiful. A mansion. The interior design was something she'd only seen in movies. Movies like *Scarface*.

They walked around the first floor of the home observing and commenting on every nook and cranny.

The kitchen had two of everything: two stoves, two refrigerators, two microwaves and two dishwashers, each located on opposite sides of the very large room. The floor, the countertop, the island were all marbled. Her whole house could fit in the kitchen alone.

The rails and banisters on the spiral staircase were made of crystal glass trimmed in gold.

"Can you believe this, Malcolm?" she asked in complete awe.

The second level housed the bedroom suites. Five bedroom suites, to be exact, with a bathroom in each.

The master bedroom was the size of the home's foyer and living room put together, which was a pretty good size considering the living room could hold about three separate living room sets.

It was equipped with his-and-her walk-in closets for clothes and separate his-and-her closets for shoes.

"Heaven," she muttered at the sight.

The entire room was surrounded by windows and Town Lake could be seen from every angle.

Denise peered out of the window in awe of the view below. Along the lake there were water fountains spread about one hundred feet apart and every ten seconds water would shoot out of the center spout into the air. Each time the water shot up, it was illuminated by colored lights below that would change. Red, green, blue, purple.

There was a full moon and the light shining down glistened on the water as a gentle wind softly pushed the water northward.

Down below Denise could see a yacht perched underneath the pier at the back of the property. From what she could tell it looked very fancy.

"Look, Malcolm," she said excitedly. "A boat!"

Denise loved boating. She loved water. Loved being out on the water. There was something beautiful about water. Peaceful.

Squinting her eyes to read the writing on the back all she could make out was a D. The boat cover was blocking the rest from view.

"D," she said out loud.

She assumed it was probably named after the wife of whoever owned the home. "D! Malcolm, this house has to be owned by Donald Trump. The back of that boat starts with a D. It has to be him. Who else could afford this?" she asked throwing her hands in the air.

Malcolm enjoyed watching the excitement in her eyes. Her pupils were as big as the stars shining in the night.

"Shine the light over here, baby," she whispered.

Malcolm shone the light in the direction of the master bathroom.

Mirrors surrounded them as they walked down the hall and entered to find a large Jacuzzi bathtub sitting smack dab in the middle of the room. It was large enough to seat eight people at least. Two separate shower stalls were located diagonally from one another on opposite sides of the room. Of course it came equipped with marble flooring and wall tile.

They continued their exploration up the staircase to the third floor, which was a loft area designed for two home offices, a game room and what appeared to be a sixth bed and bath.

"Unbelievable," she whispered.

Malcolm walked up behind her and placed his arms around her waist.

"Well I see you're impressed."

"Beyond imagination."

They stood for a moment looking out the window of the loft at the other homes glistening in the near distance.

Denise was captivated by the beauty of it all but Malcolm was captivated by her scent. Her very presence.

As Malcolm nibbled her ear softly, she moaned with pleasure.

Grabbing hold of his arms she wrapped them around her tighter as he began caressing her neck with lips.

"Hmm…" Malcolm said stopping and moving away slightly. He knew if he kept going he would want to take her right there in the loft.

THIRTY-NINE

"Let's check out the yacht," he whispered in her ear.

Before Denise had a chance to answer, he was pulling her arm and leading toward the stairs.

"Malcolm, we better go. Before we get caught."

"Baby, who's going to catch us? The rats from the field over there? Come on."

"Look there's an elevator," she said pointing to the doors just outside the master bathroom.

"No electricity, remember," he said guiding her down the stairs carefully.

As they approached the yacht, Denise became more and more nervous. She was sure they were breaking a law or something. Malcolm assured her that all would be well and convinced her that it wouldn't hurt to just take a look.

"Malcolm, no," she said as he jumped into the boat.

"Denise, it's okay. Do you trust me?"

"Yes I trust you but this is just wrong. We shouldn't be on these people's property."

"Come on," he said holding out his hand. She placed her hand in his and he led her up the stairs of the vessel to the upstairs deck. Denise sat down on the closest bench she could find afraid to move or touch anything.

"Here, hold this for a minute, baby," he said handing her the flashlight as he walked to the cabin door of the yacht.

"Malcolm, I can't believe we're doing this. What are you doing?" she asked as he jiggled the handle.

Denise stood and pointed the flashlight toward the grounds of the home to see if there was anyone standing in the shadows. When she turned her focus back to the cabin door there was no one there. Malcolm was gone.

"Malcolm," she whispered. "Malcolm! Oh my God. Malcolm!"

Afraid he had fallen over she leaned over the side of the boat.

"Malcolm," she called out. "Oh my God. Okay, okay, okay, get a grip. You didn't hear any water splash, so he couldn't have gone over the side. He must have gone into the cabin," she said trying to calm herself down. "Malcolm," she said again, hoping he would come out.

Slowly she walked to the door and grabbed the handle.

"I can't believe I'm doing this. Malcolm," she called again. Taking a deep breath she pushed the handle down as quietly as she could and cracked the door open. Just enough to peek in.

"Malcolm!" she whispered into the room. Still there was no answer.

Opening the door a little wider she could see light at the bottom of a stairwell leading into the cabin space.

"Malcolm! This isn't funny," she whispered, praying he would answer her. Malcolm!"

Opening the door all the way she slid in through the entrance and closed the door quietly behind her. Gripping the flashlight, she bent over to try and peek below to see if she could see him moving around, but the overhead was too low for her to get even a glimpse.

Taking a deep breath she walked down the stairs holding on to the railing for dear life. As she neared the bottom she could smell jasmine. The sweet scent of jasmine filled the cabin space.

Malcolm's hand appeared and suddenly she was swung around against the wall panel and he was kissing her, ravishing her lips.

The moment his lips touched hers she forgot all about how scared she was or where she was. She was safe. She was in his arms and that was all that mattered.

Music began to play and she pulled away to see where it was coming from. Peeking over his shoulder, two young men appeared from a room in the cabin.

Waiters.

Each had a napkin neatly hanging around their wrist as they stood near a small table with dinner set for two.

"Malcolm! What in the world is this?"

"This, is all for you," he answered gesturing to the room.

She was in disbelief.

"But, how? When? Whose boat is this?"

Malcolm smiled and nodded at one of the gentlemen, who began pouring the wine. The other man removed covers from the dinner trays.

Denise marveled at how beautiful the cabin was decorated. There was a mixture of candles and Christmas lights throughout.

Malcolm tipped the men as they exited the cabin.

"Baby," he said holding out his hand. "My lady, your dinner awaits."

Taking hold of her hand he kissed the back of it and then briefly moved to her lips before seating her at the table.

"You continue to amaze and surprise me, Mr. Anderson," she said, taking out her napkin.

"I hope in a good way," he responded as he placed his chair next to hers.

"In ways you could never imagine." She smiled at him. "The time we've spent together over the last few months has given me so much joy. More joy than I deserve—"

"Ahh, baby," he interrupted. "You deserve this and so much more."

"You're too sweet," she said. "This is too much. When did you plan all of this? Whose boat is this?"

"I've been planning this for weeks and this is my boat."

"And the house?"

"Yes, it's also mine."

"Oh my God! Malcolm, it's beautiful. It's all so beautiful. You've done so well for yourself and I'm so proud of you. Did you ever think you would be here in this place, at this point in your life?"

"I don't know. It's all a little surreal for me at times. I never imagined I would be playing ball, let alone for the Detroit Pistons and I never thought I would be able to afford things some people will only be able to dream of having. I can tell you this," he said holding on to her hand. "I have always believed, in the deepest part of my heart, that one day you would be a part of my life."

Her eyes began to tear.

"Malcolm! I love you."

She couldn't believe she said it. *I love you.* She'd been trying to fight those words every since she ran into Malcolm Anderson at the basketball game. Her tongue could no longer fight words she felt so deeply in her heart.

She made a decision in her heart to no longer second guess herself or her feelings for him. She loved him and she wanted to tell the world.

"I do, Malcolm. I love you. You make me feel special, beautiful, appreciated and important. All my life I've been giving, giving, giving. Taking care of everyone else's needs. Making decisions in my life based on how happy it would make someone else. It's like I've been standing in this maze, unsure of how to get out. Which way to turn. Which road to walk down. And then you guided me through it, away from years of loneliness and confusion. You put a smile on my face and convinced my heart it was okay to love. Your love makes me happy. Your love excites me. Your love makes me confident that I can do and accomplish anything. I look forward to each day because you're a part of it."

"Denise, I feel the same way. I tried not to push you. I know you've been hesitant and unsure."

"Never about you, Malcolm. I have never been unsure about who you are and what you mean to me. I have just been unable to express how I feel until now."

"And now?" he asked.

"And now, I know exactly what I want and you have already given it to me. You are a kind, gentle and sensitive man. I've been wanting to tell you how I feel for some time. I was just afraid. Afraid of letting my heart open up to someone."

"I know, Denise. I knew in your own time you would discover your feelings for me. I wasn't going to rush or push you because I wanted you to be sure of what you were feeling. I couldn't make you love me. I just hoped in time that you would."

FORTY

"You have been patient and I don't deserve any of this," Denise said.

"How many times do I have to tell you that you deserve this and way more? I knew by your actions that you cared for me. A lot of times we see what we want to see and hear what we want to hear. I didn't want to make the mistake of assuming your heart was with me when it was really with someone else."

Denise looked away. Her heart had been with someone else. Part of it still was.

"But today, baby, you told me how you feel," he said pulling on her chin and kissing her nose. "It doesn't matter how long it's taken you. Maybe it was the ambiance of the night or maybe it was the boat, the music or the house. Whatever it was, I don't care. I'm just glad you're able to say the words. Today I no longer have to guess what you're feeling because I heard the words roll off of your beautiful full lips and they never sounded sweeter to my ears."

"Oh, Malcolm!"

Denise got up from her seat and sat in his lap.

"I love you, baby," Malcolm said, "and all I want in life is to be able to take care of you and show you how much I love you."

Denise was crying. Gerald may still hold a piece of her heart but Malcolm was the person who was here and now. She may not love him the way she loved Gerald, but she did love him.

"Let's go out on the deck," he said.

Denise and Malcolm climbed the stairs leading to the deck. Denise walked over to the railing and they had a laugh about how she thought he'd fallen in.

Embracing each other they stared out into the night. It was clear and the wind had picked up, gently pushing the water as the full moon shone bright in the sky, lighting up the night like a spotlight on the world.

Laying her head against Malcolm's chest, she closed her eyes. He wrapped his arms tighter around her as they swayed to the music drifting from the cabin.

"Denise, there's nothing I wouldn't do for you. You are the first thing on my mind when I wake up in the morning and the last thing on my mind when I lay down to sleep."

He lifted her chin gently and directed her eyes to meet his.

"I love you. More than you will ever know. I can't breathe without you because you are my air."

"Oh, Malcolm," she said.

She could hardly breathe herself at the moment.

"I thank God every day," he continued, "for allowing us to run into each other that day at the game. I believe he brought us together at a time that was right for both of us. He allowed us to mature as individuals and discover our relationship with Him so we could find one another. I believe it was His divine plan all along. Denise…"

"Yes?"

"Thank you for allowing me to come into your life."

Tears were streaming down her face as he leaned in and softly kissed her forehead.

"I have something to show you," he said as he turned her around to face the house. "So what do you think?" he asked, wrapping his arms around her waist.

They leaned against the rail and admired the home he had just purchased.

"It's beautiful, Malcolm."

"Will you help me decorate?" he asked.

"Of course I will," she assured him.

The light from the moon shone upon the grounds and in the distance Denise could see something hanging from the siding of the home. It was some sort of banner.

"What's that, Malcolm?" she asked grabbing the flashlight. She walked closer to the far edge of the boat to make out the words.

"Malcolm, what is that?" she asked leaning over the railing focusing her eyes on the object. It read, "Denise Make this House a Home! Marry Me!"

Whipping around in disbelief she found Malcolm on bended knee holding a little black box in the palm of his hand.

"Oh my God," she said with excitement.

"Denise, my heart can't be without you. I can't be without you. You have become part of my soul. I need you in my life because you feed and nurture my soul for survival. Will you marry me?"

Denise was in shock. Her mind was racing and she couldn't move. She couldn't move. She couldn't speak. Every emotion imaginable was running through her and she was unable to control any of them.

She was happy. She was sad. Happy because this wonderful man had just proposed to her in the most romantic way possible. He was offering her everything a woman could ever want in life. And she loved him. Sad because she knew accepting his proposal really meant the end of her and Gerald, and she couldn't help but think of what that would do to him. Part of her still held out hope for the two of them. Saying yes to Malcolm meant an end to the hope she'd had for basically her whole adult life.

Reaching for the black box she trembled. All she could do was stare at it. Fearful of what was inside. What it represented.

"Open it," he whispered. "It won't bite."

She smiled at him. Taking a deep breath she slowly released the clip holding the box together and pulled back the lid.

"Malcolm! It's gorgeous!"

The black velvet box revealed a five-carat marquise cut elongated diamond ring. The ring was set in twenty-four-carat gold and the massive diamond sat perched on top sparkling in the night.

Removing the ring from the box, Malcolm asked her again. "Denise, marry me," he said holding up the ring, still on his knee. "I love you. You make me happy and I want to make you happy for the rest of your life. Marry me!"

Grabbing hold of her hand he gently slid the ring onto her ring finger.

"It's on your finger now. You have to say yes," he laughed.

"Malcolm. Oh my God. I can't believe this is happening."

"Marry me," he said again.

Denise couldn't speak.

"Baby!"

Denise looked at the ring and traced the design with her finger.

"Well! You know," she finally responded. Really up until that point she hadn't been able to breathe. "If I say yes it means I will have to divorce Brian McKnight first. And let me assure you, he will not be a happy camper."

"Brian McKnight will come up missing if that's what it takes for you to say yes."

She belted out a laugh.

"I love you, Denise. Marry me!"

"Malcolm," she said grabbing his hand. "I will marry you."

"Yes?" he asked excitedly.

"Yes," she confirmed.

Malcolm picked her up and twirled her around in the air. She held on to him with tears of joy flowing down her face.

"Wait, I have one more thing to show you," he said.

After exiting the boat Malcolm removed the covering from the back of the yacht to reveal the writing Denise had caught a glimpse of from the loft window.

It read "Denise."

FORTY-ONE

Malcolm and Denise strolled around the home one last time, only this stroll had a different feeling. A feeling of love, security, the future.

This time as she walked through the darkness she imagined how she was going to decorate the home. The home that she would share with Malcolm. Her husband.

The house was even more beautiful knowing that one day she would be living there with a wonderful man.

On the way home they discussed possible wedding dates. Denise was hesitant on setting anything within the next few months and asked Malcolm if they could push the date out for late fall to give her more time to plan. But he convinced her that that it would be better to be married before pre-season games so they could have more time to enjoy being newlyweds. Denise agreed and the date was set for late summer.

They arrived at Denise's home a little after one a.m. and Malcolm walked Denise to the door.

"Now," he said holding her against the door as he wrapped his arms around her back, "you aren't going to change your mind are you?"

"Not a chance," she responded, kissing him sweetly.

"And you're going to tell the beggar it's over, right?"

"The beggar?"

"Brian McKnight."

Denise laughed out loud.

"It will be hard for him to accept, but I think I can make him understand."

"I love you, Denise. Thank you for coming into my life."

"Thank you for allowing me in," she responded.

After kissing passionately for several minutes they were interrupted by Creasy scratching at the door.

Malcolm waited until she'd entered her home and locked the doors before leaving her for the evening. After waving goodbye through the window she led Creasy to the back door to do his business.

As soon as she closed the back door the doorbell rang.

"Malcolm what did you forget?" she asked.

The doorbell rang again.

"I'm coming!" she yelled.

Locking the back door she ran into the living room and turned off the alarm.

"I said yes I will—" she said as she opened the door.

"You will what?"

"Gerald!"

"Hey, baby," he said softly.

"Oh my God! Hold on. Let me find the key."

Rummaging through the living room in search of her keys she began to panic. "Hold on! They're right here somewhere," she called out. "Hold on let me look in the back," she said running down the hall.

She couldn't think. Her mind was racing and her heart was pounding in her chest. *Had he seen her with Malcolm? What was he doing out? When did he get out?* A million questions invaded the space in her mind as she tried to remember where she left the keys.

"Baby," she heard him calling through the screen.

"Just a minute," she called back running to the back door to grab the keys still hanging in the lock.

"Found them," she called out as if she had just located the keys to a brand new seven hundred series BMW.

Fluffing out her hair in the entry mirror and wiping away the sweat that had formed from the adrenaline rush on her nose and forehead, she took a deep breath and calmly unlocked the door.

Gerald was smiling at her.

Taking another deep breath she spoke. "Oh my God! Is it really you?"

"Yes it is really me," he answered.

"Well come in," she said motioning for him to enter into the home that was supposed to have been theirs.

Denise gave him a polite hug as he walked through the door. She made a quick perimeter check up and down the street before closing the door behind them. She knew Malcolm had gone but he was known for popping back up for one last kiss. She prayed he had no plans to come back by for the evening. It was late and he would always call before coming so she wasn't really worried about him popping up, but she knew he would be calling soon to tell her goodnight.

She turned around to find Gerald looking at the fish tank.

"Wow, baby, you weren't kidding," he said. "These fish are huge."

"Yeah they've been around for a while now."

"So give me another hug, baby," he said turning back to her with his arms out. "You don't know how long I've waited to hold you like this. Here. Outside of the prison walls."

She smiled nervously and placed her arms around his neck. She was being careful not to get to close, but to her surprise, he made no effort to pull her closer.

"Gerald, have a seat. Do you want anything to drink or eat?"

"No I'm fine," he said taking a seat in the armchair next to the couch.

Denise was again taken by surprise that he didn't want to sit near her on the couch. He always wanted to be right up under her.

"Gerald, how long have you been out?"

"For several weeks now."

"Several weeks! Why didn't you call me?"

"Well. Honestly I wasn't sure how you would respond to my getting out. You haven't exactly been returning any of my phone calls or letters, and I wasn't sure what I would be coming home to."

"So what have you been up to?" Denise asked trying to change the subject. She wasn't ready to start explaining what was going on.

"For the most part I've just been trying to get acclimated to the free world again. Finding a place to stay. A job."

"Did you find a place?"

"Yea, and a job. I'm going to be working at a barber shop on Twelfth Street."

"That's great, Gerald."

"Yea, it's just temporary though. I plan on opening a full-service salon. I'm working with the bank to get backing for it."

"Wow, you have been busy."

"Yea. So what have you been up to, Ms. Lady?"

"Oh you know, the usual. Working. Paying bills. Hanging out with the girls."

"I missed you."

"It's good to see you, Gerald," she said patting his leg as if they were old friends. She wasn't really sure how to respond to him. She was at a loss for words so she let him do most of the talking.

"So where's our son?" he asked.

"Huh?" Denise responded, caught off guard. "Oh Creasy? He's outside. Let me go get him." She was glad of the opportunity to remove herself from the awkwardness of it all. When she let Creasy in he ran straight to the person who would have been his father.

She watched as Gerald played with Creasy, who couldn't have been happier. He was a hyper puppy and loved the attention.

As she watched the two of them she couldn't help but notice a change in her former lover. He seemed to have an inner peace she hadn't seen before. He was calm, more mature, seemingly content with life. During their conversation he never mentioned their relationship or pressured her into explaining why she had dropped off the face of the earth. He didn't even talk about what happened during his last days in the prison. Denise wasn't sure what to make of any of it.

"Well I guess I better let you go," he said standing up.

"Okay," Denise said uncomfortably. "It was nice of you to stop by," she said opening the door, unsure of what to say or do next.

"I apologize for it being so late. I had been putting it off for so long and when I saw you at association, I knew I had to talk to you," Gerald said.

"You were at association?" she asked surprised.

"Yea, but we'll talk about it more tomorrow," he interrupted.

"Tomorrow?"

"Tomorrow," he affirmed and kissed her cheek before leaving.

FORTY-TWO

"What!" Sabrina shouted across the table.

Denise had called an emergency lunch meeting with the girls to update them on the events of the past night. They were ecstatic about the marriage proposal and the ring; however, the news of Gerald trumped everything.

"Jailbird finally got out of the nest," Sabrina laughed uncontrollably.

"What did you do, sis?" Jess asked concerned.

"There wasn't much I could do. Malcolm had just left and two seconds later Gerald shows up at my door. I was speechless. Didn't know what to do or say. I tried to be as pleasant as possible without allowing myself to fall into his arms."

"Did you want to fall into his arms?" Sabrina asked coyly.

"A small part of me did, but mostly I was just nervous as heck. I didn't know how to act."

"So wasssup? What happened on Valentine's Day?" Sabrina asked. "What was his excuse for letting you down yet again?"

"He didn't even mention it. But guess where he did show up?"

"Where," Sabrina and Jess asked in unison.

"Association!"

"What!"

"Yep, said he was there."

"So what the hell has he been doing for the last two weeks? Following you around town?" Sabrina asked hitting her fist against the table as if she was interrogating a witness.

"God, I hope not," Jess said in a concerned tone.

"He had to be. How else would he know you would be at association and it's kind of funny he happened to show up right after you just got home. Negro probably been sitting outside your house every night."

"I don't think so," Denise responded, unsure herself.

"So did he tell you what his intentions were?" Jess asked.

"Nope! We talked like we were old friends catching up."

"That must have been difficult," Jess responded. "After all the two of you have been through and shared together. It must have been hard to sit there and pretend there was nothing between you. No emotions. No love."

"It was hard," Denise said, putting her head down. Her eyes were beginning to water and Jess handed her a napkin.

"I was sitting there. Next to this man who I have loved most of my life. Unable to touch him. Unable to kiss him. We hugged each other like you would hug a married deacon in the church. After he left I couldn't get to sleep. I tossed and turned all night. Malcolm called to let me know he made it home and I pretended like I'd been asleep since he left. So then I felt bad about that. Deceiving him. The man who had just proposed to me."

"Ah, sis, this is supposed to be a happy time for you."

"You're right. A happy time with Malcolm. Why did Gerald have to come back now?"

"What are you going to do?" Sabrina asked.

"I'm going to marry Malcolm. I accepted his proposal and I'm going to marry him."

"And what of the jailbird?"

"Well, I will just have to explain to GERALD," Denise said, emphasizing his name in Sabrina's direction, "that I have moved on. I love Malcolm and he's my future. I wish Gerald well but our time has passed and he'll just have to accept that."

"Oh I'm quite sure he knows you moved on. If you were wearing the Titanic when he got there, he knows that ship has sailed," Sabrina said grabbing hold of Denise's ring finger.

"Oh no!" Denise cried in a panic. "The ring! I had the ring on when he was there. Malcolm had just given it to me and I know I didn't take it off. There was no time. Oh my God. Do you think he saw it?"

"Of course he saw it, girl. How could he miss it? Takes up your whole damn hand."

"Well, sis, he would have seen it at some point, and you said he was at the association so I'm sure he saw the two of you together."

"Yea, but I should have taken it off. Oh it must have made him feel horrible. It must have been like a slap in the face."

"Are the two of you going to see each other again?" Jess asked.

"We didn't make any definite plans, but before he left he said we would talk today."

"Girl, you better meet that man in a public place. You know he been locked up for a while now. No sex! He may go into a fit of rage on you. Hmm. Now that I think of it that might not be a bad thing."

"Shut up, Bri. Gerald would never take advantage of me. I just have to explain to him the situation and let him know I've moved on. My future is with Gerald."

The girls gasped.

"I mean Malcolm! That's where I belong now. With Malcolm," she declared before taking a deep breath.

§

After returning to her office Denise asked her assistant to hold all her calls. After the drama of last night's events the last thing she wanted was a lot of people buzzing in her ear about what did or didn't go well at association.

She was going to spend her day alone in her office in peace. She needed to get caught up on everything she had put on the back burner because of that glorious event.

After sending out a few emails and making a few phone calls she nibbled on the sandwich she had delivered to her office for lunch and stared out the window.

She had one of the best views of Lake Travis from her office window. Just beyond the lake you could see the downtown skyline.

As she sat quietly listening to her docked IPOD, she propped her feet up on the windowsill and thought of Gerald.

"Where are you?" she whispered as she looked out toward the city.

"Denise," her assistant said softly, interrupting her thoughts, "here are your messages and I just wanted to remind you I'll be leaving for the day."

"Oh! Okay, that's fine. Thanks, Sam. Have a good evening."

"You too, boss!"

Denise thumbed through her messages.

"Meeting, meeting, canceled meeting, blah, blah, blah," she said reading each one out loud, uninterested, until she got to the last post-it note.

Denise meet me at Mount Bonnell, six P.M., Gerald!

"Oh my God," she said grabbing the phone.

"Hello?" Jess answered.

"Sis, he wants me to meet him."

"Who?"

"Gerald!"

"Okay, so meet him."

"I can't meet him!"

"So why are you calling me?"

"So you can tell me what to do, sis!"

Jess laughed out loud.

"Denise, what did he say?"

"He wants me to meet him at Mount Bonnell at six."

"Did he say why?"

"No. The message just said meet him there. How does he even know about Mount Bonnell. Gerald is not from Austin. What does he know about Mount Bonnell?"

"Denise, does it really matter? The point is are you going to meet him?"

"I don't know what I'm going to do."

"Well you guys need to talk, Denise. It doesn't mean you don't love Malcolm but you have to bring closure to your relationship with Gerald so you can have a future with Malcolm. I gotta go, sis, but call me later and let me know what happened."

"What do you mean what happened."

"At the meeting with Gerald."

"I didn't say I was going."

"Bye, sis."

After hanging up the phone Denise sat quietly in a state of total confusion. She knew what Jess said was right. She and Gerald needed to talk. He had to have seen the ring, and he had to have seen her with Malcolm at the church. There were a ton of questions she had for him and she was sure he had a ton of questions for her. She owed it to him to meet him. She at least owed him an explanation and she definitely needed closure.

FORTY-THREE

Standing at the bottom of what seem like never-ending stairs, Denise stared toward the top of Mount Bonnell.

Gerald was up there. Waiting for her. Waiting for explanations. Maybe even waiting to rekindle their relationship.

As she slowly began her climb, she thought about what she would say to him. How she would tell him that she got tired of waiting and that she decided to move on. Not only was she moving on but she was engaged to another man.

Holding tightly to the rail, as she continued her ascension, she prayed to God to give her the strength to do what she had to do and that Gerald would be able to understand.

The climb up to the top of the Mount was no joke and she was no Jackie Joyner-Kersee. When she finally reached the last step, she stood still for a minute to catch her breath before looking around for Gerald, happy to see he was nowhere in immediate sight because she could barely breathe and sweating like a pig from the climb.

After finally catching her breath she walked toward the path to see if she could locate him.

Maybe he changed his mind, she thought just before she heard her name.

"Denise!"

Spinning around she saw Gerald running toward her. He was dressed in a jogging suit, which clung to every curve of his muscular body. Her body couldn't help reacting to the sight of the man she had loved for so long.

"Whew, get a grip girl," she said under her breath.

"Hey," he greeted her grabbing a towel from a bag sitting on the bench nearby.

"I hope you don't expect me to join you," she teased as she watched him wipe the sweat off his gorgeous body. Every move he made excited her.

"Naw! You're too beautiful to sweat," he said wiping hair away from her face. "I'm just finishing my run. I come out here every day and run the trails. I thought it would be a good place for us to meet. To talk. Plus the view overlooking the lake is amazing."

"Yes it is," she said looking out over the water. "How did you find out about the Mount?"

"The internet of course. I was looking for trails and came across it."

"Oh!" She was unsure of what else to say or what direction the conversation should go next.

"Walk with me," he said grabbing her hand. "You want some water?"

"No I'm fine thanks."

"So I know you must have a lot of questions, Denise."

"That's funny. I thought maybe you would be the one with all the questions."

"First, I want to explain to you what happened. Why I didn't get out on Valentine's Day like we'd hoped."

"Gerald, really, there's no need."

"No, I think I should explain."

"Honestly, knowing doesn't change things. It is what it is and we are where we are. I know that you know I've moved on."

"Yeah, I kind of noticed the rock on your hand the other night."

"I'm sorry you had to find out like that."

"It was pretty painful I must admit. I didn't show it because I'm a man," he said fist pumping his chest. "But on the inside, I was crushed."

He guided her toward a bench and they sat down. Denise could feel the conversation heading in a direction she wasn't ready to tackle just yet so she quickly changed the subject and talked about different aspects of the Mount.

"You seem to know a lot about this place."

"Yea when we were younger, the girls and I used to come up here and hang out. That was before they built all the trails and made it a tourist spot."

"There's still so much of the city I haven't seen. I always imagined you driving me around once we got here. After college, I mean. You would show me places where you hung out and places that were important to you, teach me how to get here and go there. Since I've been here I really haven't done a whole lot. For the most part I've just been trying to get on my feet."

"Gerald, why did you come here? I mean to Austin. You and I haven't spoken in what seems like months. Did you think you would just come here and we would pick up where we left off?"

"Honestly, I don't know. I mean I hoped you were still available. I knew you were fed up with the situation and I couldn't blame you. I guess I thought if I came and got myself established that I could win your heart back. Your trust back."

"You never lost my trust, Gerald. I've never doubted your love for me. I just reached a point where I wanted and needed more than you were able to give me."

"Are you happy?"

Denise didn't respond.

"Denise, are you happy?" he asked again. Grabbing her chin, he gently pulled her face toward his so their eyes would meet.

"Malcolm treats me very well. I never want for anything. How could I not be happy?"

"You haven't answered my question, baby."

Hearing that word roll off his tongue sent chills thorough her body. *Baby.* Until he said the word she didn't realize how much she missed hearing him call her that. At that moment she wanted him to grab her and kiss her harder than they'd ever kissed before.

"Gerald, let's not go down that road," she said standing up to avoid having to answer the question.

"So when's the wedding?" he asked.

"Gerald!" She didn't want to answer that question either.

"I understand; it's none of my business. Besides it's starting to get late and I know you have to go to work tomorrow."

"Yes I do."

"Denise I know you've moved on. I only want to ask one thing of you and I hope you will say yes."

"What is it?" she asked, afraid to hear the question.

"Spend one night with me."

FORTY-FOUR

Denise made all the arrangements. The limo would pick her up at seven and then swing by to grab Gerald around eight.

She had made dinner reservations at the Driskill, one of the most upscale restaurants in Austin. Afterwards they would ride around Austin for a few hours to see the city.

That was it nothing more. No night cap, no reminiscing about the past and no sleeping over. Just two old pals catching up.

Malcolm had a playoff game out of town so Denise figured it was the perfect opportunity to give Gerald his one last wish and move on with the rest of her life.

As the limo pulled up to the apartment complex where her ex resided, she began to get nervous. She had no idea how the evening would turn out but she was very clear on how she didn't want it to end up. Seeing Gerald after all this time stirred up memories and emotions she thought had been buried since she made the decision to pursue a relationship with Malcolm.

She never expected him to get out of jail as soon as he did and she figured the longer he was in there, the better able she would be to move on. Besides that, she would have never imagined him moving to Austin when he did get out. He was from Houston. The distance alone would have kept her safe emotionally.

When the limo turned the corner Denise could see Gerald standing out front.

The limo driver pulled onto the curb and jumped out to open the door for him.

"Hey, you," Gerald said jumping in and taking a seat next to her.

"Hello, Gerald. You look mighty spiffy this evening."

Denise was being politically correct. What she really wanted to say was, *Damn! You are fine. Gorgeous as ever and your cologne is waking every hormone in my body.*

"Well, you look gorgeous yourself, my lady."

Denise gave him an uneasy glance and Gerald picked up on it.

"I know you're not my lady anymore. But you were once and it doesn't change the fact that you look gorgeous," he said gently touching her cheek.

"Thanks." She smiled at him.

"So where are we headed?" he asked.

"Downtown."

"And what's up with the limo big baller?"

"Well I thought that since we were going to ride around and look at the city, it would be easier for me to point things out without having to concentrate on the road. Is it too much?"

"Hell, no! This is the bomb. I feel like P. Diddy."

They arrived at the restaurant and Denise felt a little more comfortable once they were around other people. Spending time alone with Gerald was not the best idea and the scent of his cologne was making her and her body very nostalgic.

The evening moved along pretty smoothly. Denise was not feeling the pressure of reliving the past and for the most part the conversation was focused on funny memories of college.

After dinner, they laughed over a cup of coffee and talked about their jobs and his immediate plans for the future. Neither one of them mentioned her pending marriage and Denise did everything she could to avoid the subject.

After coffee they retreated back to the limo and rode all around downtown and through the hills.

Austin wasn't known for beautiful high-rise buildings but the music capital of the world had a lot to offer as far as downtown night life. It was no New York but there were enough people walking up and down the street, club hopping and hanging out at local bars to give anyone visiting the impression that the city definitely had it going on.

They rode around for about an hour before the limo took them to Town Lake where she had planned an excursion on a private boat.

"Denise, I'm having such a good time," Gerald said turning to her as they crossed under a bridge that was famous for providing a home to millions of bats.

"Good, Gerald. I wanted you to enjoy yourself."

"I am. When I asked you to give me one night I never expected this."

Well what did you expect? she wondered.

"I told you I was going to show you Austin," she said aloud.

"And you have. I'm speechless. The limo, the dinner, the boat ride. You better be careful. I just might get the impression you're trying to seduce me."

They both laughed.

"Denise, I'm sorry I put your life through so many ups and downs—"

"Gerald—" she interrupted him. She had been avoiding the conversation all night and still wasn't ready to face all the memories.

"No let me finish," he pleaded with her. "I wanted things to turn out so differently for us. I spent those fifteen years in prison thinking of nothing but you. You were my strength, and thoughts of you and our life together gave me the energy I needed to survive that place. But when you stopped writing and you stopped accepting my calls I knew I had borrowed all the patience from you I was allowed. Even though my gut was telling me you'd moved on, I'll admit part of me was very angry about it at first, but my heart was understanding. You had every right to move on. I don't know why you waited so long. But even still, I always thought I would be able to win you back once I got out. I certainly didn't think you'd be engaged to another man."

Denise placed her hand over her engagement ring.

"Don't hide it. It is what it is. But I want you to know this. If that guy ever lays a hand on you, mistreats you, sleeps around on you, neglects you, curses at you or even breathes the wrong way. I will be there and he will regret every harm he has ever caused you."

"Gerald," she said looking away.

"Denise," he said turning her back to face him.

"I don't care who you are with or how long you are with them. You are my soul mate. I will never love anyone the way I love you."

"Oh, Gerald."

They were sitting so close. Denise could feel the heat radiating from his body and it was taking control of hers.

"No amount of time or space will ever change the way I feel about you. And I believe that no man will ever change the way you feel about me."

Her heart was melting at every word out of his mouth. The closeness of his body, the smell of his cologne and the way he was looking into her eyes was convincing her that his words were true. He wanted her and she was wanting him.

"I love you, Denise. I have always loved you and I will always love you. Our hearts were brought together the minute we kissed on that football field that night. You can't see it right now but they are still connected." He placed her hand on his chest. "I love you."

"Gerald, don't," she said in between breaths.

"Denise. I love you," he said again cradling the back of her head gently with his hands.

"Gerald. Please, stop," she whispered softly, not wanting to say the words.

"Denise," he said again pulling her face closer to his. "I love you." He placed his lips on hers and they kissed. Fiercely. Passionately. Their bodies pressed against one another as he wrapped his arms around her neck.

There was a force present beyond her control that responded to his every touch. She couldn't stop it even if she wanted to. And she didn't want to.

FORTY-FIVE

Denise woke up the next morning feeling horrible.

"What have I done?" she kept asking herself over and over as she lay in bed, disgusted with herself for being so weak.

Images of her night together with Gerald flooded her mind.

Things should have never gone that far. Things were out of control. I just got too caught up in the memories and the lake and he was looking so sexy and smelling so good, she said to herself.

"I am so weak!" she cried out.

She decided not to go to work figuring people would see it all over her face. Her betrayal of Malcolm. She was ashamed.

The phone rang nonstop throughout the day. Most of the calls were from Gerald. He left voice messages that she erased before even listening to them. She couldn't talk to him. She didn't want to talk to anyone, but especially not him. She couldn't even bear to hear his voice.

How stupid was she to think that they could go out on a romantic night and things wouldn't end up the way they did. It took everything in her to walk away from his apartment door when her body was crying out, *Take me now!*

After spending most of the day in her robe out on her deck reading self-help books to try and refocus her mind spiritually, she decided to venture out for Starbucks.

After quickly showering and brushing her hair, she placed Creasy in his castle for a nap and headed out the door.

Only, she couldn't escape him. There he was. Gerald. Leaning against his car in front of her house.

"Gerald, what are you doing here?"

"Denise, we need to talk and you wouldn't answer the phone."

"So you came over here to stalk me?"

"Baby, I'm not stalking you. I just needed to see you."

"Don't call me baby, and there is nothing to talk about. I'm engaged, Gerald. Malcolm and I are going to be married next month."

"Last night should have changed all that."

"Last night never happened. We didn't do anything. Last night was us getting carried away and getting caught up with the past."

"Last night was not the past. It is the present and you kissed me like a woman who is in love with a man right now, today. Last night was about what we still feel for each other and Denise I know you still love me."

"I'm not going to do this with you, Gerald."

"Do what? Admit you still love me."

Denise turned to go back into the house.

"Denise, wait," he said pushing her hand away from the lock. "Babe… Denise, we shared something last night. You know it and I know it and if my neighbor hadn't interrupted us we would have shared something more. I know you still love me and I still love you. Don't you think we deserve a chance? A chance to make up for all the years we were apart?"

"We were apart because you were sent to prison. That's why we were apart. I stood by you. I waited for you. I put my life on hold because of your circumstances. Over and over again. I was disappointed but I stood by you and I stood by us."

"I know you did. But if you marry him, all those years of waiting will be for nothing. I'm here, with you, right now. I'm sorry about the time we missed while I was away, but I'm not going anywhere, I promise. We deserve this chance. I know you still love me. All you have to do is say the words. Look at me, baby."

Denise couldn't look at him. If she looked at him she would reveal everything inside of her.

"Denise, say the words," he said grabbing her hands.

She put her head down. Everything in her wanted to say those words. Everything in her wanted to grab him and kiss him and pull him into her bed and show him that she still loved him.

Her cell phone rang in her purse.

"Denise, don't answer it. Please. Come back to me," Gerald pleaded.

Denise looked down at her phone. It was Malcolm. Seeing his name flashing in big bold letters brought everything back into perspective. It was a reminder that that Malcolm was her future.

"Denise. I love you baby. Please come back to me. Give us one more chance. Please."

Denise took a deep breath and looked into his eyes.

"I am engaged to be married next month, Gerald. I love Malcolm. What we had is over. Please don't call or come by again. Let me move on with my life and leave me alone."

With that she placed her key in the lock, went into her house and closed the door.

"You are my life," she heard Gerald speak through the door. The pain she heard in his voice made her fall to the ground in tears.

The next sound she heard was the closing of his car door but she never heard him drive away.

Peeking out the window she watched him. Sitting in his car. Hands clenched around the steering wheel. Staring out into the distance. For five minutes he just sat there. Unable to move. He just sat there until he finally gathered enough strength and courage to start the car. As he drove off and turned the corner, disappearing from her sight, her heart sank.

"Good bye, Gerald," she whispered.

Closing the curtain she curled up on the couch and fell asleep. She never made it to Starbucks.

FORTY-SIX

"Today's the day, girl," Sabrina said running into the hotel suite master bedroom. "It's your birthday! It's your birthday!" she continued turning around in circles and doing the prop. An old eighties dance move.

"Sabrina, it is not my birthday," Denise moaned placing a pillow over her head.

"Let's go, sis," Jess said entering the room. "Rise and shine. Today is the day that you marry the man of your dreams."

That made Denise smile. She rolled over and looked at her engagement ring.

"I's getting married ya'll," she said with laughter, repeating the words made famous by Oprah Winfrey.

"Yes you are so. Get up out of that bed and let's get you ready to start your future, honey," Jess said coming out of the bathroom with a robe.

The day was filled with hair appointments, nail appointments, pedicures and hair waxing, in between running errands to pick up this and that, things needed to complete her day.

Denise had planned her dream wedding. Six bridesmaids, which consisted of her administrative assistant, a couple of cousins and of course two maids of honor, Sabrina and Jess.

Malcolm's groomsmen included several NBA players and a couple of childhood friends. One of which was the best man.

Her colors were lavender and white. Purple and white roses were tied strategically on palm trees throughout the lakeside lawn of the resort and onto the backs of lavender chair covers that overlooked Town Lake.

Denise had always wanted to have a traditional church wedding but when she took a tour of the famous Horseshoe Bay Resort in Marble Falls, Texas, she knew that was where she wanted to be married.

She and Malcolm would be exchanging their vows in front of all of their family and friends with the sun setting behind them over beautiful lake waters, lit jumping water fountains and palm trees.

After they said their "I do's," the married couple and their guests would move to the beautiful Palmero Lago Pavilion, decorated in her wedding colors with live purple and white flower arrangements on each table.

After the reception Malcolm had arranged a driver for their yacht, which would sail them away from their friends and family to begin the rest of their lives as Mr. and Mrs. Malcolm Anderson.

The girls had spent the night at the resort, partying and living it up. Mostly they hung out at the bar sipping cosmos and looking at old pictures of much younger times.

Horseshoe was like a mini-vacation itself. It came equipped with a spa, a fitness center, sandy beaches, the pool, boat rides, fine dining and luscious suites.

She and Malcolm could have had their honeymoon right there and she would have been happy. In fact they booked the honeymoon suite for the evening. But for the actual honeymoon, they opted for a different resort.

The day after the wedding they would be flying off into the sunset to the Sandals Resort on the beautiful island of Jamaica.

Denise couldn't wait to get there. She had been to Jamaica briefly on a cruise once but didn't get to enjoy the full experience of the island because they had to get back on the boat. She had always vowed to go back to see the rest of what Jamaica had to offer.

"Denise!" Jess screamed. "Hurry up! The wedding is going to start in about an hour and we don't even have your makeup on!"

"This dress is not the easiest thing to get into, you know."

"Do you need some help?"

"No I just about got it," she said zipping it up as far as she could, her arms twisted in the back like a pretzel.

Denise stared at herself in the mirror. This was the day she had dreamed about ever since she was a little girl. Ever since she got her first Barbie and Ken doll. Ever since she saw Cinderella marrying her prince. Ever since she saw Victor Newman marry Nikki Reed for the first time on *The Young and the Restless*, and ever since she saw Allie run into Noah's arms at the end of *The Notebook*.

She knew all her life that one day she would marry that man. The man who would love her and protect her for the rest of her life.

But as happy as she was seeing herself in the mirror in her gorgeous white gown, knowing what was waiting for her just outside on that beautifully manicured lawn, she couldn't help but think of Gerald.

"Denise! Come on!" Sabrina called out impatiently.

"Okay, ready or not, here I come," she said opening the door slowly.

As she entered the living room of the suite, Jess and Sabrina gasped for air.

"Oh, sis," said Jess crying. "You're beautiful."

Denise smiled. She smiled the happiest smile any bride could ever smile.

"Oh my God," her sister said running over to hug her. "Malcolm will be blown away. I am so happy for you, sis. I love you. Your life begins today and you have so many wonderful things to look forward to."

Denise hugged her sister with joy and looked over at Sabrina.

"Sabrina! Are you… Are you crying over there, girl?" Denise asked.

"No!" Sabrina said turning toward the door.

"Yes! You! Are!" Jess said running to her. "I knew you had a soft spot," she said poking her in the shoulder.

Sabrina couldn't help but laugh.

"Denise. You do look beautiful. Absolutely gorgeous. Any man would be blessed to have you as a wife."

"Ah, Sabrina! That has to be the nicest thing you have said… well… to anyone!"

They all burst out in laughter.

"But I'm glad you said it to me," Denise finished, hugging her friend.

Jess guided Denise toward the chair in front of the vanity as Sabrina covered her in towels.

"Oh my God, where's the fan?" Denise called out. She was very hot by nature and had to have a constant flow of air circulating or her little nose would bead up with sweat quicker than you could say the word.

She had insisted that the resort lower the temperature in the ballroom to fifty-five degrees. She didn't want to be sweaty, hot and uncomfortable all night especially in her gown. She had also requested they put two large commercial fans in separate corners of the ballroom away from the guests just to make sure there was a constant circulation of air.

"Okay, sweetie. That's it," Jess said, throwing up her hands about twenty minutes later as if she had just put the last touch of paint on a piece of art. "You ready to go meet your destiny?"

"More than you could possibly imagine. I need the two of you to go and scope things out and make sure everyone is where they're supposed to be. Namely my future husband. How much time do we have?"

"Okay, girl, you got about thirty minutes," Sabrina said looking down at her watch.

Sabrina and Jess left the room and Denise walked over to the full-length mirror. She couldn't believe the day had finally come.

Walking over to the window she looked out over the courtyard toward her final destination. The altar.

Down there, among the beautiful palm trees and beautiful ponds, was Malcolm. Waiting to marry her. No one could have ever told her that she would be looking out of that window, wearing the most beautiful wedding gown ever created, about to marry Malcolm Anderson.

She could see her reflection in the mirror. Her dress was exquisite. It was another Versace exclusive. Malcolm pulled in another favor and Denise worked directly with the talented designer to create a one-of-a-kind one-piece strapless corset wedding gown.

The corset top was simple, beautifully decorating the neckline and perfectly sculpting the frame of her body into the skirt, which was somewhat of a couturier style, caught up with diamond-shaped pearl motifs throughout.

For the something new, Jess had given her a silver necklace with a single dangling pearl, which hung in the perfect spot just above her cleavage. Sabrina could be counted on to provide the blue undergarments. From Victoria's Secret of course.

Malcolm's grandmother provided the borrowed accessory. A pearl bracelet that matched her necklace perfectly. It had been in the family for years and worn in many weddings. It was lovely. Ivory pearls and clear diamond-shaped crystals provided just the right amount of elegance to accent her beautiful designer dress.

Perched on top of her carefully wrapped hair was a beautiful diamond tiara, which provided the attachment for her veil.

As she stood admiring herself her thoughts were disturbed by a knock at the door.

"Come in," she said, still staring out at the people below.
"Wow!" She heard seconds later from behind her.
"Gerald!" she said spinning around.

FORTY-SEVEN

"There is not a word in the dictionary that properly describes your beauty," he said in awe.

"Gerald, you can't be here. Please! I can't deal with this right now."

"Don't worry. I'm not here to ruin your day. Although you and I both know that it should be me standing out there on that lawn waiting for you."

"Gerald, please. You have to leave now."

"I will leave. But not before I've said what I have to say. I need to explain to you why I didn't get out that last time, on Valentine's Day."

"None of that matters now, Gerald. I'm marrying Malcolm. It's over."

"It may not matter to you but it matters to me. Denise I only came here to explain to you why I didn't get out that day. You need to know what kept me from you. Please sit down and hear me out," he said guiding her toward the vanity chair.

Kneeling down in front of her he held her hands in her lap. His head was hung low and his eyes were filled with tears.

"Gerald." She whispered his name. As nervous as she was about having him there, she had always wanted to know why he didn't show up on that day.

"That last day you came to visit me something happened. I guess some of the other inmates saw you leaving and one of them made some disrespecting comments about you. Guys had made comments about you before but this one guy, he just wouldn't leave it alone. He just kept going on and on and on telling me his disgusting fantasies. Describing your body, licking his lips, holding his crotch. He wouldn't shut up and I snapped. I had to let him know he wasn't going to disrespect you like that. You are my jewel and I had to let that punk know I wasn't going to be no fool. So I lunged at him and the rest was history. The parole board understood the circumstances but decided to give me a few more weeks as punishment and as an example to the rest of the lockups. I wanted to tell you and explain but you wouldn't take my calls. I'm sorry, Denise. I'm so sorry that I screwed things up for us." He began to sob, laying his head in her lap.

"Gerald," she said trying to get up. "I told you, none of that matters now. We can't change the past."

Denise got up and walked over to the window.

"I know we can't, Denise, and I didn't tell you what happened in the hope that it would change your mind. I just didn't want you to go through the rest of your life wondering why I didn't come through in the end. I know I'm a screw-up and you deserved better than what I gave you."

"Gerald, I've never thought you were a screw-up. Ever. I have loved you all my life, but sometimes our plans are not God's and we are where we are."

"You're right," he said walking over to her. He stared at her for a moment.

"Gerald, you have to go now," she pleaded.

"Denise. You are absolutely breathtaking. I am leaving. But I want you to know that I wish you all the best in the world because you deserve it. No matter where you are or what you're doing, I need you to know that I will always love you. It doesn't matter to me that you've slept with him. It doesn't matter to me that you're going to go down there and confess your love in front of all those people for him. It doesn't matter that you will be wearing his ring. None of that matters to me. Because I know, that deep down inside your heart, our love is still alive and no ring and no amount of money will ever change the way you feel about me and the way I feel about you. I will always love you."

"Gerald—" she started but he placed a finger on her lips before leaning in to kiss them softly.

"He better make you happy or, trust me, he will answer to me," he whispered in her ear in a protective tone before leaving the room.

Tears began to flow down her face. Thoughts of Gerald and all of the plans they had made flooded her mind. Pictures of the two of them flashed through her mind as if she was watching a fast-moving reel of their life. Special moments they shared, places they had gone, places where they'd eaten, goals they had planned and the night on Town Lake, all consumed her thoughts and she realized he was right. She was still in love with him.

What are you doing? she asked herself.

Looking in the mirror she saw images of herself and Gerald at the altar. Confessing all that they had promised to each other over the years. She saw them walking down the aisle after being pronounced man and wife. She saw them walking into that beautiful ballroom hand in hand, drinking champagne, eating cake and having their first dance. Gerald had always been her future. How could she just throw that away?

Running to the door she swung it open to find that Gerald standing there. It was as if he knew she would follow him.

"Gerald," she said crying, "I never slept with Malcolm," she confessed.

"I know you didn't. You couldn't. You still love me."

He kissed her.

"I never slept with Malcolm," she said again and again. Crying and embracing him as they kissed more passionately than they had ever kissed before.

§

"Why is that girl always late?" Sabrina asked, impatiently looking at her watch.

"She said she would be a little late," Jess said defending her sister.

"A little late is five or ten minutes. It's been thirty minutes."

"There she is," Jess said pointing to the door.

"Hey, guys! Sorry I'm late. I couldn't get out of that meeting."

"No problem, sis," Jess said nudging Sabrina.

"So have you guys ordered drinks?"

"Yea and drank a couple waiting on you," Sabrina said rolling her eyes.

"Why you gotta have an attitude all the time, Sabrina? What's the matter? Stoney ain't hittin it right no more?"

"Ohhhh, that's a low blow, sis, low blow. Wayyyy below the belt."

"Stoney is hitting it just fine, thank you very much."

"I still want to know how that came about," Denise stated matter-of-factly.

"Yeah me too," Sabrina said questioning herself. "I woke up the next morning like, what the hell?"

As the girls burst out in laughter the waiter brought over a round of drinks.

"I can only stay for a little bit, girls. You know tonight is our anniversary," Denise said with joy.

"Can you believe it, sis? It's been one whole year."

"Yea I know. That day was so crazy."

"What are you guys up to tonight?"

"Dinner and a movie. That will give you guys enough time to get to the house and do what I asked you to do," Denise said winking at them both. "Sabrina, did you go by Cindie's and pick up some fun stuff for us?"

"You know I did. Found some stuff for me and Stoney too. You know how we like to play soap opera."

"Please, no details!" Jess held her hands in front of her eyes.

"Do you ever regret it?" Sabrina asked Denise.

"Regret what?"

"Your choice."

"No. A part of me will always wonder what I may have given up, but in my heart I know that I made the only choice that made sense."

"You are happy?" Jess asked her.

"Very happy," Denise responded. "Oh there he is. I'll see you guys when we get back, okay?"

Denise jumped up from the table and ran to the car parked out in front of the bar. Jumping in the passenger seat, she reached across the console, gently grabbed his necked and pulled his lips to hers, kissing him passionately before he could get a word out.

"Umm," he said, enjoying the taste of her.

"Hey, baby," she said after they finally broke for air.

"Hello, Mrs. Malcom Anderson."

ABOUT THE AUTHOR

Cheryl Lee is a native of Bastrop, Texas, where she lives with her son Nicholas. She has a BA in Health Administration and is currently working on an EMBA at Prairie View A&M University. She has worked in the Communication industry for more than 25 years, is engaged in her community serving as a Commissioner on the Bastrop Planning and Zoning Committee, and advocating for social justice and worker rights through membership with grass roots organizations.

In her free time she loves to go to the movies, binge watch her favorite TV series, and travel.

Her passion for writing developed from her love of music and poetry. Growing up, she could often be found in her room writing down the words of love songs and poems. To her, the words were more than just a verse, they told a story. Those stores and life experiences compelled her to write a love story that every person reading her book can relate to.

CPSIA information can be obtained
at www.ICGtesting.com
Printed in the USA
LVHW090800100721
692094LV00026B/330/J